Dear Reader,

These two novels had their origin in an exhibit at the Museum of Science in Miami, Florida, featuring a predatory three-toed wolf. I started thinking "What if...?" and ended up with two amazing books that featured wolves—both the animal and the human kind!

I wrote these novels when I was just learning how important it is to the reader to know not just what the characters are doing, but how they feel about what they're doing. This was also the moment I realized how much I enjoy telling "the rest of the story."

After I finished *Never Tease a Wolf,* I started immediately on a second novel, *A Wolf in Sheep's Clothing,* to find out what happened to the two compelling secondary characters whose story was only hinted at in the first book.

It's my pleasure to offer these two novels to you again in a format that allows you to "read on" when you come to the end of the first book...and want to know more.

Happy reading,

Joan Johnston

JOAN JOHNSTON

Big Sky Country

MIRA®

MIRA®

BIG SKY COUNTRY
Copyright © 2004 by MIRA Books.

ISBN 0-7783-2245-9

The publisher acknowledges the copyright holder
of the individual works as follows:

NEVER TEASE A WOLF
Copyright © 1991 by Joan Mertens Johnston.

A WOLF IN SHEEP'S CLOTHING
Copyright © 1991 by Joan Mertens Johnston.

www.MIRABooks.com

Printed in U.S.A.

CONTENTS

NEVER TEASE A WOLF   9

A WOLF IN SHEEP'S CLOTHING   155

NEVER TEASE A WOLF

ACKNOWLEDGMENTS

The facts about wolves at the opening of each chapter are taken from the book *The Wolf: The Ecology and Behavior of an Endangered Species* by L. David Mech, and are reprinted by permission of the author.

I want to thank Ed Bangs, a wildlife biologist with the U.S. Fish and Wildlife Service in Helena, Montana, who provided me with information about the Northern Rocky Mountain Wolf Recovery Plan, and who kindly took me through the steps for relocating a wolf under the plan.

And I especially want to thank my friend Richard Wheeler, who spent a week in mid-May driving me through snowstorms in and around Big Timber, Montana, so I could get a good look at the Boulder River Valley and the hot springs at Chico. Your help was invaluable, Dick!

1

*Wolves demonstrate aggressive behavior
when meeting strange wolves.*

Abigail Dayton saw a light on in the upper story of the old-fashioned wood-frame ranch house, so she knew there had to be someone there. But no one was answering her knock. She had an appointment to meet Luke Granger at 6:00 a.m. It was 5:55. He might be in one of the outbuildings, tending to his sheep, but she was betting he was still inside nursing a cup of hot coffee—something she could dearly use. April mornings could be quite frigid in the foothills of the Absaroka Mountains.

She tried the doorknob. Not surprisingly for this rural area of southwestern Montana, the door was unlocked. Abigail shoved the heavy oak door open and took a hesitant step inside.

"Hello? Agent Dayton, Fish and Wildlife Service. Anybody home?"

She heard the rattle of pans and a virulent curse and followed the noise toward the back of the house, where golden light streamed from an open doorway.

There was nothing remotely feminine about the living room she passed through, which contained a mounted twelve-point elk head over the fieldstone fireplace and huge pieces of wood-and-rawhide furniture centered on a Navajo rug. The picture windows overlooking the snow-capped Absarokas were bare of frilly curtains—or any kind of curtains, for that matter.

Abigail carefully stepped over several farm and ranch journals, a plaid Western shirt with pearl snaps and a crumpled beer can that littered the hardwood floor.

She stopped abruptly in the doorway to what turned out to be the kitchen, not believing the fascinating picture she beheld.

On the worn linoleum floor sat a broad-shouldered, long-legged man with three lambs in his lap. He was trying desperately to balance three bottles of formula in three eagerly sucking mouths. Dark lashes lay against his sun-browned cheeks, and shaggy black hair fell across his forehead nearly to his thick black brows.

A stubble of dark beard shadowed his face, which was thin, almost gaunt, with cheekbones that appeared even higher because of the sunken hollows beneath them. His mouth was wide, but his lips were thin, almost severe. She wouldn't have called him handsome. Striking, maybe.

However, it wasn't his face that drew her attention, but his hands. They were large and work-worn, with a sprinkle of black hair across the knuckles. Powerful hands, performing a delicate task with utmost gentleness.

His low voice modulated from silky to harsh and back again as he alternately crooned to the lambs and swore at them. But his touch stayed slow and easy. Those were hands that would know how to caress a woman.

Abigail was startled by the direction of her thoughts. She'd been alone since her husband Sam's accidental death three years before. The rancher's tenderness with the lambs reminded her how much she missed having a man hold her in his arms. She repressed the feelings of loss and pain, forcing herself to focus on the reason she had come here.

"You look like you could use another hand," she said.

The rancher's head jerked up at the sound of her voice, and his fierce gray eyes narrowed as he stared at her. "Who the hell are you? What are you doing here?"

Abigail bristled. "I'm Agent Dayton, Fish and Wildlife. *You* called *me*—or rather, the Service. I have an appointment with you this morning."

He raised a questioning brow. "They sent a woman?"

"You have a problem with that?" she asked, tensing for a fight.

"Nope. Especially since I won't be needing your services after all. So you can take yourself right back where you came from, Agent Dayton."

Abigail didn't like the rancher's tone of voice and wasn't about to accept his abrupt dismissal. "What happened to the wolf you sighted—the one you called about—that I'm here to catch and relocate before it kills any of your sheep?"

"You're too late."

"Too late?"

"Why do you think I'm sitting here with these three bum lambs? Damned renegade killed two of my sheep yesterday. I phoned your office to cancel our appointment late yesterday afternoon."

Abigail groaned. She'd left the office in Helena at noon yesterday and spent the night at a bed-and-breakfast in Big Timber, a tiny town halfway between Bozeman and Billings, so she could be here in the Boulder River Valley on time this morning.

"I've got a call in to Animal Damage Control to handle the problem," he said. "Now get out."

Abigail's mouth thinned into a bitter line. Animal Damage Control, a division of the U.S. Department of Agriculture, could—and would—use "lethal measures" to dispose of any wolf that killed livestock. Fish and Wildlife was fighting a losing battle with its recovery program, devoted to saving the gray wolf, which was an endangered species. It was especially difficult when most wolf habitat bordered on sheep and cattle ranges. She could understand the rancher's concerns, but she was angered by the quickness with which "relocation" had been abandoned in favor of "elimination."

She made a decision then and there to change Luke Granger's mind. There was no reason why she shouldn't have a chance to catch and relocate that wolf. With the sophisticated radio-tracking collars the Service was using now, she could keep an eye on the renegade, and if it ever threatened Granger's sheep again, she would put the animal down herself.

Abigail squared her shoulders and lifted her chin, preparing to do battle.

"Look," she said. "You're going to get reimbursed by that private environmental organization, the Defenders of Wildlife, for the two sheep you lost—assuming it doesn't turn out to be a coyote that killed them. In that case, of course, you're responsible for the loss. But—"

"I know wolf sign when I see it," the rancher interrupted. "This renegade has a three-toed right forefoot. Probably lost the fourth toe in a trap. And big. I've got plenty of wolf sign, all right. Tracks and bite marks and scat."

"Maybe there are extenuating circumstances. Maybe—"

"Maybe you should get your cute little butt out of here."

Abigail felt her cheeks heating with a combination of anger and embarrassment as his eyes roamed up her jean-clad legs toward her derriere. She rued the fact that her sheepskin-lined denim jacket ended at her waist.

His eyes deepened to a smoky gray and focused on her primmed mouth as he drawled, "Or maybe you'd like to hang around and—"

"Now, you look here, Mr. Granger. I—"

"Luke. You know, I'm kinda partial to green-eyed gals. 'Specially ones with pretty blond hair like yours. How long is it, anyway? Can't tell the way you have it all hitched up on top of your head like that."

"We are not discussing—"

Suddenly he wasn't on the floor anymore, he was standing up across from her. The lambs began bleating frantically. Abigail knew exactly how they felt.

Luke Granger took a step toward her. Abigail was determined to hold her ground, but he was a head taller than she and standing so close to him was disconcerting. She could feel his body heat, almost see the muscles rippling under the plaid wool shirt stretched across his broad chest. His jeans fit like a second skin, leaving little—and there was nothing little about him—to the imagination.

His moist breath fanned her face, causing goose bumps to rise on her arms. Abigail took a step backward—and tripped over one of the lambs.

"Whoa, there," the rancher said as he reached out to catch her. "Can't have you bruising that cute little—"

"Don't say it!" Abigail hissed.

The rancher tightened his hold to keep them both from falling, pulling her breasts up flush with his chest and her belly into the V created by his spread legs, thus capturing her hands at her sides.

Abigail felt a surge of desire so strong it frightened her. She stared with awe at the rugged face of the man who had her trapped in his arms. A suffocating fear surfaced, surprising her because she had no idea of its source. She only knew she had to get free. *Now.*

"Listen, Mr. Granger, I don't know what you think you're doing, but—"

His hand snagged the clip holding her hair on top of her head and released it. Honey-blond waves swirled down around her shoulders. He sifted his fingers through the silky mass. ''Beautiful,'' he murmured.

Abigail shivered with pleasure. ''Let me go, Mr. Granger,'' she said in a calm, rational, but disgracefully breathless, voice.

Luke knew he ought to let her go. But it wasn't that simple. He'd only taken her in his arms to keep her from falling on her fanny. But once she was there, her lithe figure aligned with his, he hadn't been able to resist the urge to release that clip in her hair.

He hadn't expected the fierce rush of heat between them, hadn't expected his body to tauten with need. He wanted her in a way he hadn't wanted a woman in a long time. He wanted to feel her naked beneath him, wanted to feel their heated bodies—

''Mr. Granger, I...'' Abigail's voice faded as she recognized the raw heat in the rancher's eyes. It was both thrilling and terrifying. Her breath came in panting gasps and her pulse speeded. She saw the question in his eyes. It would take only one word from her to unleash that fierce desire. But she couldn't make herself say it.

Luke swore softly and fluently under his breath. The look in her eyes, her pulse and her trembling body all signaled that she shared his feelings. She hadn't said no, but she wasn't saying yes, either. He'd never taken anything from a woman she didn't willingly offer, and he wasn't about to start now. Nevertheless, when she shifted slightly in his arms, instead of releasing her, he tightened his grasp.

''I'd like to leave now,'' she said.

''I gave you a chance to leave,'' he said in a harsh voice. ''You chose to stay.''

Abigail wasn't prone to panic. But things were getting decidedly out of hand. She was an expert at setting traps, but this was the first time in recent history she could remember getting caught in one. And the trapped feeling was only getting worse. She knew she couldn't let this go any further. Well, there were not-so-civilized ways to handle Neanderthals like Luke Granger.

"I am an agent for the United States government, here on official business. You lay one hand on me—" Abigail gasped as his hand lifted her chin and slowly angled her face up toward his "—and I will…"

Her wide green eyes met his lambent gaze. His mouth lowered. Abigail gasped when Luke's lips met hers with a brief touch, a halting taste.

"You taste sweet, woman," he said in a husky voice.

Abigail stiffened, to keep from melting in his arms. "I'm warning you—"

Luke's mouth came searching again. His touch, his taste, combined to seduce her. Abigail tensed as she felt the heat pooling in her belly. But along with the thrill, the fear returned. She had to stop him. She lifted her booted foot, aiming for his instep.

But a strong hand grasped her thigh and held it tight, thwarting her intention.

Startled, Abigail looked up into a pair of rueful eyes.

"That would have hurt," he said.

"That was the general idea," she retorted.

He didn't let go of her thigh right away, just held it nestled against his own, letting the heat build between them.

Finally she said, "You can—" Her voice cracked. She cleared her throat and repeated, "You can let me go now."

Slowly, ever so slowly, Luke let her thigh slide down his leg to the floor, his eyes never leaving hers, so he saw the renewed flare of desire she couldn't hide. And her surprise and confusion at what had happened between them.

What had happened, anyway? he wondered. It had started out innocently—he had reached out to keep her from falling—but somewhere along the line, other needs had taken precedence. He had no explanation for his behavior. But here he stood, fully and painfully aroused by an agent for the Fish and Wildlife Service! It was hard to say which of them was more upset by the encounter.

It was time he called a halt to this thing—whatever it was—that had flared between them.

Luke looked hard at the woman standing across from him, trying to discern what it was about her that had attracted him. He was baffled. There was something about her green eyes, maybe it was the way they slanted at the corners, that reminded him of a sleek feline animal.

A lot of women he knew reminded him of cats, soft and clingy and inclined to purr when you rubbed them in the right places. But once they got their claws into a man, they never let go.

He noted that Agent Dayton—he knew her by no other name—also had flawless peach skin that rose over wide cheekbones, a no-nonsense nose, and a chin that had been upraised in challenge since the moment he'd laid eyes on her.

Her lips were extraordinary. Full and lusciously pink, they virtually disappeared into a thin line when she was angry. Right now they were pursed. Pouty. Kissable. He couldn't regret kissing her, but he wasn't pleased that he'd succumbed so totally to her allure.

"You'll be needing this," he said at last, retrieving her hair clip from his shirt pocket where he had tucked it and handing it to her. "You'd better get going if you're going."

She stuck the clip in her front jeans pocket without trying to fix her hair. "If I can have just a moment of your time—"

"I thought you were in a hurry to leave?"

"I have a favor to ask first."

"You sure have a funny way of asking for favors, Agent

Dayton.'' He walked over to pick up a bottle that one of the lambs had nudged into a corner. "If I hadn't stopped you in time, I'd be limping on a bruised instep right now."

She avoided his accusing look, staring instead at the pitifully bleating lambs.

"I think we're going to need a little more peace and quiet to talk," Luke said. "Grab a bottle."

She dropped to her knees, collared a lamb and offered it a bottle. Luke followed suit with the other two lambs, and when all three lambs were once again sucking greedily, he prompted, "I'm listening."

"I want you to let me capture the wolf that attacked your sheep, instead of sending for Animal Damage Control."

"No."

"Why not?"

"I can't afford to lose any more sheep," Luke said.

"That's a poor argument. The Defenders of Wildlife will reimburse you for any sheep you lose to a wolf."

"*If* I can prove it was a wolf did the killing. But you know, and I know, Agent Dayton, that I may not find some of those wolf-slaughtered sheep for a while. And when I do, there may not be enough of the carcass left to know what killed them. Then I'm out the price of a spring wool shearing, or a lamb sold for slaughter in the fall."

He saw from the look on her face that she wasn't ready to concede defeat.

"Doesn't it bother you to be responsible for the death of an animal that's an endangered species?" she asked.

His brow furrowed before he said, "That's not the point."

"That's precisely the point," she argued. "Unless individuals like you are willing to help, we haven't got a prayer of recovering wolves in Montana."

"Maybe the wolf's day is done. Maybe they ought to be extinct."

"You can't believe that!" she said in a shocked voice.

One of Luke's lambs had emptied its bottle and wandered off to the pallet in the corner of the kitchen that had become the lambs' bed. Luke used his free hand to scratch the shadow of whiskers under his chin. "Wolves are a menace to stock."

"If you're going to use that rationale for letting the wolf become extinct, you might as well exterminate every other animal that becomes inconvenient to have around," she said, green eyes flashing.

Luke flushed. "What about survival of the fittest?"

"What about it?" she challenged. "Surely you aren't going to suggest that wolves are endangered because they haven't evolved to survive in their environment. All wolves really need to survive nowadays are hides impervious to bullets and stomachs that can handle poison."

Luke had opened his mouth to retort when they were interrupted by the entrance of a wiry little man wearing jeans, a quilted vest, plaid shirt, cowboy boots and a baseball cap fringed by wisps of gray hair.

"Didn't know you had company, Luke. I'll just take myself back outside—"

"Wait a minute, Shorty." Luke carefully lifted the slumbering lamb out of his lap and settled it on the pallet in the corner of the kitchen next to the other one. "The lady isn't 'company.' This is Agent Dayton from Fish and Wildlife."

Shorty chortled. "Well, can you beat that? They got females doing purty near everything these days."

As soon as Luke lifted the lamb out of his visitor's lap, she scrambled to her feet and held out her hand to the old man.

"Hi. Abigail Dayton."

Shorty stared at her hand for a moment. Then he took off his cap with his left hand, exposing a bald head, and dragged his right palm across his jeans to wipe it off before extending it to her. "Shorty Benton. Pleased to meet you, ma'am."

"Please call me Abigail."

Luke's mouth curved in a wry grin. "She's had me calling her Agent Dayton all morning. What's your secret, Shorty?"

"I mind my manners," Shorty said. "Which is more than I can usually say for you. You offered this young lady any coffee yet?"

Luke sheepishly shook his head no.

"Well, that's your problem, see," Shorty said as he headed for the stove. "Can't hardly 'spect someone to be civil this hour of the morning if she ain't been offered a cup of coffee. You want some coffee, Miss Abigail?"

"I'd love a cup."

Before Luke could count to five, he and Abigail were seated across from each other at a quaint wooden kitchen table with a mug of hot, black coffee in front of each of them, and Shorty was cooking up some eggs and bacon on the ancient gas stove.

"Shorty's sort of a fixture around here," Luke said.

"Are you two family?" Abigail asked.

"Near enough," Shorty said. "I've diapered that boy's bottom."

The warm, husky sound of Abigail Dayton's laughter sent a shiver of pleasure rolling down Luke's spine.

"'Spect Luke told you that wolf he sighted done killed some sheep," Shorty said as he expertly flipped a fried egg.

"He told me. I've been trying to convince him to let me capture the wolf anyway," Abigail said.

"S'pose he weren't too hot on the idea. Luke can be a right stubborn cuss."

Luke shifted in his chair, trying to find a more comfortable position without disturbing the lamb that had left the comfort of the pallet and settled its head on his thigh.

"Maybe I haven't been using the right arguments. What would you suggest?" Abigail focused her gaze on Shorty, and Luke watched the old man turn to mush at the pleading look in her big green eyes.

"How 'bout it, Luke?" Shorty asked. "You gonna give the lady a chance to catch that wolf?"

"Stay out of this, Shorty," Luke warned.

Shorty watched the hairs come up on Luke's neck. It was plain as a wart on your nose that Luke didn't want to spend no time with Abigail Dayton. But Shorty had seen the sparks flying when he'd found the two of them sitting on the floor together.

Luke might not want to be attracted to the lady, but he was. Which was a surprise in itself, because Abigail weren't Luke's type. Oh, he liked blondes, all right. But they usually had a might more curvy bodies and went in for a lot of face paint and fancy clothes. And they all knew the score. Miss Abigail was likely a babe in the woods by comparison. To Shorty's way of thinking, she was exactly what Luke needed.

In the ten years since his divorce, Luke hadn't spent more than a month or two with a woman before she was out of his life. Shorty grimaced. That boy wasn't going to let any woman get too close. Not after the examples set by his mama and his ex-wife.

No, if Luke had his way, Miss Abigail and her pleading green eyes would be out the front door before the sun was fully up. Shorty had to make sure that didn't happen.

"I 'spect, Luke, you better take Miss Abigail up on her offer."

"Why is that?" Luke asked cautiously.

"'Cause I just recalled them sheep was killed by coyotes.

Yep. Coyotes. And when some official comes nosing around asking questions, so's to fill in all them claim forms, that's what I'm gonna say.''

''You old piece of wolf bait! You say that and I'm going to have to eat the loss on those sheep. You wouldn't dare!''

Shorty served two perfect, over-easy eggs onto Luke's plate and added a half dozen strips of bacon. He grinned, exposing tobacco-stained teeth, and said, ''Try me.''

Luke fumed silently while he made short work of his breakfast. Shorty would do it, too. But he wasn't about to let that old reprobate manipulate him into doing something he didn't want to do. Unfortunately he wasn't immune to Abigail Dayton's pleading eyes either. The woman's arguments were getting to him. Not that he intended to let her know that. Once you let a woman get the upper hand, it was all over but the crying. He wasn't about to let Abigail Dayton find out she had any influence whatsoever on his decisions.

But maybe he'd been a bit hasty calling Animal Damage Control. If Agent Dayton was good at her job, it wouldn't take them long to trap that renegade wolf.

He sneaked a peek at her face, surprised to find a look of anxiety and hopeful expectation. It would take a real bastard to disappoint a face like that. Luke might be a lot of unsavory things, but a bastard wasn't one of them. Although, knowing his mama, it was mere luck that he wasn't.

''All right,'' he said quietly.

''Does that mean you're going to let me catch the wolf?'' Abigail said, her eyes full of hope.

''I'll give you three days.''

''Ten.''

''All right, a week,'' he conceded.

Her jaw jutted, and she shook her head. ''Ten days.''

Any other woman would have compromised, Luke

thought. He was being damned generous to let her trap the wolf in the first place. But he could see she wasn't going to back down. Hell, if she couldn't do it in a week, he could. It wouldn't be any skin off his nose to give her what she wanted. "Ten days," he agreed.

From the smile that lit her face you'd have thought he'd said the wolf could just help itself to all the sheep it wanted, and he wouldn't complain.

"You won't be sorry," she said. "I'm good at what I do. It may take me more than a week, but—"

"I'll make sure it doesn't," he said. "Because I'm going with you."

Her emerald eyes flashed with irritation that she quickly concealed. "I appreciate your offer to help, Mr. Granger. But I work alone."

"Not on my land, you don't," he said in a hard voice.

Luke watched her lips thin into an angry line, while a flush turned her cheeks from peach to rose.

"Of course I can't stop you from coming along," she said in a carefully controlled voice. "But don't you have other things you need to do?"

"No need to worry about that," Shorty piped up. "I can handle things around here while Luke's busy with you."

Luke watched as Abigail Dayton shot a disapproving glance at Shorty that sent him scurrying for the door.

"I got some things need finished 'fore the day's done," the old man said.

When she turned her gaze back on Luke, he smiled like a wolf with a juicy lamb in its teeth. "Either I go with you, or you don't go. Make up your mind which it's going to be."

Her hands curled like she was itching to get at his throat. She quickly stuffed them into the back pockets of her jeans and said in a terse voice, "Get your coat, Mr. Granger. The daylight's wasting."

2

Individual wolves can differ greatly.

"As long as you're coming along with me, you might as well make yourself useful," Abigail said as she settled into the worn leather seat of her battered pickup. "Where did the wolf depredations occur? That's the best place to pick up the trail. Oh, and the passenger door—"

Luke was already settling in on the other side of the bench seat by the time Abigail finished "—is hard to get open." Obviously not so for a man used to working with his hands. Abigail realized suddenly that the hands she'd seen being so gentle with the lambs must also be quite strong.

"Head for the East Boulder road," Luke said, gesturing out the open window in the direction he wanted her to take. "I lease land up in the mountains from the government. My sheep graze there once it warms up."

Abigail shivered as the brisk wind turned her cheeks red. "This is warmed up?"

"May is only a few days off. It's been warmer this year than usual—an early spring. Maybe I'm taking a chance thinking there won't be any more snow, but there's already grass on the mountains, so I'm willing to risk it."

It was easy to see how Sweet Grass County, which encompassed the Boulder River Valley, had gotten its name. The valley was covered with a carpet of rich, bright green, most of which was feed that had been planted by sheepmen, Abigail conceded. But she could imagine it mantled with knee-deep grass, as it must have been when the first mountain men had come here. The Boulder River, its banks lined with towering cottonwoods, sparkled on a meandering course down the center of the valley, which eased into mountainsides covered by darker green juniper and jack pines.

Abigail turned off the narrow two-lane highway onto a dirt-and-gravel road that followed the east tributary of the Boulder River up into the mountains. Mule deer and elk abounded. It was unfortunate the wolf hadn't stayed with its primary prey instead of feeding on Luke Granger's sheep.

Wolves generally ran in packs, and it was important to separate a wolf that had started hunting stock because it was likely to encourage other pack members to the same behavior.

Luke had labeled this wolf a renegade—meaning it hunted alone. "Are you sure this is a solitary wolf?" Abigail said. "Not part of a breeding pair? Or a pack, maybe?"

"None of the sheepmen I know have sighted any wolves this spring," he said. "Or found any wolf sign. The three-toed monster I saw might have been half of a breeding pair. I have no way of knowing that. If so, the female would be denned up with her pups this time of year."

"If you had her mate killed, the pups would go hungry," Abigail pointed out.

The male wolf making a kill would swallow as much as he could and return to the den. When the pups licked the wolf's mouth and nose, it would regurgitate food for the pups to eat. Thus, no father, no food.

"I'm not running a wolf farm here," Luke said. "I raise sheep."

Abigail kept her mouth shut, despite the urge to argue, and spent the rest of the drive up into the mountains in silence. She took advantage of the time to enjoy the beauty of the sun and open sky, and the colorful wildflowers—

Dodge willow, columbine and purple crazyweed—gracing the mountainsides.

"Stop up there, where you see the break in the forest," Luke said. "There's a trail."

Abigail pulled the pickup off to the side of the road.

"We'll have to hike from here," Luke said.

Abigail could tell from the way he looked askance at her, that he expected a protest. But she was wearing sturdy walking boots and had her gear packed so she could carry it on her back all day if necessary. On more than one occasion, she had.

"You need any help with that?" he asked when she hefted her pack onto her shoulders.

Abigail smiled and said, "I'm fine. Lead on."

Luke caught himself staring at the beauty of her smile and jerked his head away. She didn't fool him. When a woman smiled, he'd learned to beware. She usually wanted something. Sometimes his money. Sometimes his body. But there wasn't an unselfish bone in a one of them, at least, not that he'd seen.

He took off into the forest at a rate intended to tire her in a hurry, so she would see this wasn't going to work. But half an hour later, when he reached the site where the wolf had killed his sheep, she was right behind him. And she wasn't even breathing hard.

"Here they are," he said gruffly as he pulled a tarp off two dead sheep. "I did what I could to preserve the evidence until somebody could confirm what I found."

Abigail slipped the pack off her back onto the ground and knelt beside the remains of two white Rambouillet sheep. The impression of a three-toed wolf paw had dried in the earth beside the larger of the two ewes. The paw print alone wasn't proof of a wolf kill. A coyote could have made the kill, and a wolf might have come along and feasted on the carrion.

She turned to the other sheep and found the proof she needed. There was only one wound on the sheep. To be certain, she measured, but the diameter of the bite was too big to be that of a coyote.

"This was done by a wolf, all right," she admitted with a sigh. "How did you find the carcasses?"

"I was out riding and flushed a bunch of ravens and magpies. When I came to take a look, this is what I found."

Abigail began asking all the questions necessary to confirm that Luke Granger was entitled to reparation for the loss of his sheep. The form she filled out would be forwarded to the environmental group so they could determine whether, and how much, to pay the rancher.

"Any livestock carcasses around that might be considered attractants?"

Luke stuck his hands into his back pockets, stretching the fabric tight enough that Abigail suddenly found the ground at her feet very interesting. "I bury my dead lambs, Agent Dayton. I don't leave them in a stack behind the barn to attract wolves."

"Then you're the exception to the rule," Abigail replied tartly, her head snapping up and her eyes seeking out the rancher's face.

The muscles in his jaw were working, and Abigail was sure he wanted to say more. But he didn't.

Abigail ran a hand through her hair and looked around to see if she could find which way the wolf had traveled. "What kind of terrain will we find in that direction?" she asked at last.

"More of the same. There's a creek that runs down the mountain about a mile off."

From long practice, Abigail had learned that she had more

luck catching a wolf if she set her traps in places where the wolf was likely to go: a crossroad between two deer trails; any place near water where there were wolf tracks; a moose or elk feeding spot; and, of course, the site of the kill.

"I need to locate some spots for my traps. You ready to do some more walking?"

"I'm at your command," Luke responded with a tip of his Stetson. He opened his mouth to offer again to help her with the pack, but she already had it on her back and was heading off through the forest. He shrugged and followed her. Miss Abigail Dayton was a grown woman. If she wanted help, he was sure she would ask for it.

Abigail had a great deal of stamina, and she was in excellent physical shape, but the pack was heavy, and the mountain terrain was grueling. But she would choke before she asked Luke Granger to share the load. He'd made it clear he didn't think a woman could handle the job. Well, she would show him!

At first she was glad Luke wasn't the talkative type. One of the best parts of her job was spending time like this, quiet time outdoors, where working was a joy. After a while, her curiosity got the better of her. She wanted to know more about Luke Granger. It was obvious he wasn't going to volunteer any information about himself.

So as she pulled on her gloves and spread a ground cloth at the first of the sites she had found to put a steel-jawed leg-hold trap, she asked, "How long have you been in the sheep ranching business?"

He gave her a sidelong glance, but finally answered, "All my life. This place was my father's and my grandfather's and his father's before him. How long have you been tracking wolves?"

"Two years." Abigail finished carefully winding a ten-foot-long drag chain that was attached to the trap into the hole she had dug. ''Before that I was a park ranger stationed in northwestern Montana with my—'' Abigail set the opened trap on top of the chain and covered it with a piece of waxed paper, careful not to get any human scent on anything.

''With your what?'' he prodded.

''My husband.''

Luke drew in a harsh breath at that surprising bit of information. ''You're married.''

''A widow.''

Her eyes met his, and there was such a wealth of suffering and sadness there that he wanted to take her into his arms. There were other feelings that kept him from doing it— inexplicable feelings of jealousy for a man she still mourned and the knowledge that only a fool would ask for the kind of pain that inevitably came along with caring for a woman.

''What happened to your husband?''

''Grizzly attack.''

That was unusual enough that Luke knew he must have heard about it at the time. Then he remembered. ''I read about that—three years ago. Some hikers were lost in the forest at Glacier National Park, and the park ranger went in after them. The hikers were toting a grizzly cub they'd found. The ranger caught up to them about the same time as the cub's mother. He saved their lives—and lost his own. Am I right?''

She nodded. Tears had welled in her eyes, and she brushed them away with her sleeve and continued sifting dirt over the waxed paper to conceal the trap, blending in some pine needles to make the spot look more natural.

''He must have been quite a man,'' Luke said quietly.

''He was,'' Abigail replied. ''Sam and I were childhood sweethearts. We went all through high school and college together. I married him my senior year after my—''

Luke waited for her to finish her sentence, and realized that it must be another case of something else hurtful in her past. "After what?" he asked gently.

She looked up again, and he saw more of the anguish he'd found before. "After my parents were killed in a plane crash. My father was the pilot, and my mother was with him because they always went everywhere together. He was heading down to Colorado to look at some bulls—I was raised on a cattle ranch near Bozeman—and something went wrong. They never did find out what caused the crash. Mom and Dad were killed instantly." Or at least, that was what Abigail had made herself believe. She couldn't bear the thought of her parents suffering—like she knew Sam had. "They died as much in love, after twenty-two years together, as they were the day they married."

Abigail estimated about sixteen inches forward from the trap and put down a few drops of a gland lure called Widow Maker. If everything worked as it should, when the wolf stepped forward to sniff at the lure, his foreleg would land in the trap.

Once the wolf started running, the ten-foot chain would follow, and the curved hook at the end of the chain would catch on a bit of brush or a dead log and stop him. Without a firm hold to pull against, the wolf wouldn't be able to tear off its foot trying to escape the trap.

When she checked the traps she would be able to locate the wolf by following the trail left by the dragging chain. She would use a tranquilizer dart, then cage the wolf for relocation. The steel jaws of the trap were still slightly separated when closed and would leave minor puncture wounds that healed in a matter of days.

It wasn't a perfect system, but it was the best they'd been able to devise.

Abigail was brought from her reverie by the sound of Luke's voice.

"That must have been traumatic for you. To lose your parents. And then your husband."

"As you can see, I survived." *Barely.* It had been awful, at age twenty-one, to lose her parents. It had been catastrophic, at a mere twenty-three, to lose her husband. Sam had been more than her lover; he had been her best friend. It had been terrifying to be ripped from a warm, loving cocoon and thrust out into the cold, cruel world to make her way alone.

At first, she'd wanted to die herself. Once the initial shock and horror of Sam's death had passed, she hadn't been able to find the courage to stop living. Instead, she'd donned the necessary protective layers to defend herself, and she'd survived. But nothing about the past three years had been easy.

Abigail stood and carefully removed the ground cloth she'd used so there would be no human scent near the trap. "One down, three to go."

Once she'd collected everything in her pack, she set out again.

Despite the feeling that he was making a big mistake not to leave Agent Dayton to her business—at which she was quite good and extremely efficient—and get back to his own, Luke came up off his haunches and followed her.

When he'd caught up to her, and they were walking side by side, he asked, "Do you have any children?" Luke didn't know why he'd asked the question, it had just popped out.

She ducked a juniper branch, then said, "No. Sam and I wanted to wait and spend some time just enjoying each other. We thought we had plenty of time."

Her wan smile touched something inside Luke that he'd thought was encased in solid stone. It sure was a good thing she wasn't his type. Because he was pretty certain no man was ever going to measure up to a heroic figure like Sam Dayton.

"What about you?" Abigail asked. "Have you ever been married?"

"Once," Luke replied curtly. "That was enough."

"How long ago was that?"

"I've been divorced for ten years. And I don't want to talk about it."

Abigail clucked her tongue. "Must have been quite a woman to put such a lasting burr under your saddle."

"She was a two-timing bitch, with one hand on my wallet and the other hand on my—"

"Your what?" Abigail prompted.

"My privates," he said, using the least offensive word he could find. He smiled sardonically when even that word caused Abigail to flinch. He dropped a little behind her so he could watch the interesting way her hips moved under the weight of her pack.

"So you've sworn off women as a result?" she asked.

"Sworn off marrying them, anyway," he said.

"All women aren't like you describe your wife."

"Could have fooled me."

"I find it very sad that you've condemned yourself to living alone the rest of your life because of one bad experience."

"If you're so hot on marriage, why haven't you remarried?"

She smiled at him over her shoulder, and he felt his chest constrict.

"That's simple," she said, focusing her attention back on the trail in front of her. "I haven't found a man I could love as much as I loved Sam Dayton."

"And never will," Luke muttered under his breath.

Abigail stopped in her tracks and turned to confront him. "What did you say?"

"You obviously heard me the first time."

"I heard you. I just didn't believe what I heard. If I found a man I could love as much as Sam, I'd be married like *that!*" She snapped her fingers. "I loved being married. I loved being in love. I *want* to be married and have children and enjoy the comfort and companionship of—"

"That kind of happily-ever-after only happens in fairy tales," Luke interrupted harshly. "You're remembering the good stuff, and forgetting all the bad, because of how he died. You—"

"How *dare* you say I didn't have a good marriage! Sam loved me. And I loved him. We—"

"Probably never had an argument in your lives," Luke said.

"We didn't!"

Luke snorted in disbelief.

"Or maybe we did," Abigail conceded, shoving her hair away from her face in irritation. "But they were honest arguments where we addressed our differences and settled them. We didn't let them fester and become big problems. We were friends. Can't you understand that?"

Luke shook his head. "No, I can't. My mother and father... Hell, you don't want to hear the sordid story of my childhood."

Abigail put a hand on his arm to keep him from walking away. "I do. I do want to hear."

Luke felt something shift inside as he met her sympathetic gaze. Against his better judgment, he found himself telling her about his mother. "She never loved her husband. Or her son. She only loved herself."

And other men. And my father's money.

"I used to wonder why my father ever married her. Until

I fell in love for the first time myself. Then I understood how it happened. Because, God help me, I'd chosen to love a woman who was no better than my mother.

"My parents never divorced," Luke continued in a bitter voice. "They lived together in misery for twenty-five long years. They went to an anniversary party a neighbor held for them, but they never made it home over some icy mountain roads. I heard later that my mother had made an embarrassing scene at the party, saying she didn't know why she'd stayed with him all those years. She didn't know what they were celebrating. She felt like she'd spent twenty-five years in hell."

Luke's bleak eyes met Abigail's horrified gaze. "I still don't know if it was an accident, or whether my father drove over the edge of that snowy mountain on purpose."

Her grip tightened on Luke's arm in an attempt to offer some support, but he shrugged it off.

"Anyhow, I came to my senses after I'd been married for a while and saw that my wife was just as unhappy and unsatisfied as my mother had been. I made up my mind I wasn't going to spend the next twenty-five years being miserable and maybe end up driving us both over a cliff. So I divorced her. And I haven't had the least inclination since to set myself up to endure a fiasco like that again."

"I'm so sorry," Abigail said.

Luke's gray eyes blazed with anger. "I don't want or need your pity!"

"It's not pity, exactly," Abigail said as she turned away and knelt to set another trap. "It's just that, once you've been loved by someone as I've been loved, totally and without reservation, you want everyone else to experience the same thing."

"I've learned my lesson," Luke said. "I'm not going to make the same mistake twice."

"Not even if you found a woman who loved you?" Abigail said in a soft voice. "I mean *really* loved you?"

"How can you tell the real thing when you see it?" Luke questioned with a cynical twist of his mouth. "I don't believe I've ever seen the genuine article. Are you sure it even exists?"

"Oh, it exists all right."

Looking at her radiant face, Luke had to believe she was telling the truth—at least as she saw it. "So do you think you're ever going to find another man to love who's as perfect as Sam Dayton?"

"I honestly don't know," Abigail admitted.

"Are you even going to try?" Luke asked, an edge in his voice.

Abigail frowned at him. "Not that it's any of your business, but yes, of course I'd like to find someone who can love me, and who I can love—"

"As much as Sam," he interrupted.

"Yes. That much."

She shoved everything back in her pack and marched off to find a third trap site, not bothering to wait for him.

Over the past three years, every man she'd met had inevitably been compared to Sam—and fallen short. She always found something to fault in any man who threatened to engage her emotions. He was too tall. Or too short. Or too smart. Or not smart enough. His touch was too soft. Or too hard. It was like the three bears and their porridge. There was never a man who was "just right."

Have you forgotten how you felt in Luke Granger's arms?

That was an aberration.

Are you sure?

No, I'm not sure.

Don't you think you should check into the matter?

That could be dangerous.

Or perfectly wonderful.

All right. All right. I'll check it out. Maybe. If an opportunity presents itself. Which I doubt will happen.

Make it happen.

Luke followed closely on Abigail's heels and quickly caught up to her. "I don't believe in all this idealistic love stuff you're spouting," he said.

"That isn't surprising, considering your history," Abigail said. "But people *need* other people. I—"

"I don't *need* anyone," Luke contradicted. "I've managed fine by myself for the past ten years."

Abigail cocked a disbelieving brow. "Really?" She dropped to her knees at the third trap site. "What about your biological need for—" Abigail knew she shouldn't bring up the subject. But he was the one who'd started this conversation. She was going to finish it. "For sex," she finished.

For a moment Luke was speechless. He started to say he didn't *need* sex. The truth was, he'd been without a woman for longer than he wanted to admit. Long enough to know he needed one now. Long enough that he was finding it hard to be around Abigail Dayton without wanting her. So maybe she had a point.

"All right," he said. "Maybe I do need sex. But I don't have to love a woman to satisfy my sexual needs. And she doesn't have to love me to enjoy the act, either." *Put that in your pipe and smoke it, Agent Dayton.*

Abigail stopped what she was doing to stare at Luke in dismay. "Oh, you're wrong," she said. "So very wrong."

"About which part am I wrong?" he asked, sticking his hands into his back pockets to keep them from reaching out for her.

"About what a woman feels in a man's arms. There is always more than just sex involved," Abigail protested. "A woman's feelings are never disconnected from...from the physical sensations that naturally occur when—''

Abigail found herself mesmerized by Luke's heavy-lidded gaze. When he knelt beside her, she had enough presence of mind to say, ''Stay on the ground cloth. I don't want to get any human scent near the trap.''

He obliged her, but there wasn't much room on the four-by-four-foot square of canvas, and when he had settled, no more than an inch separated their bodies. He reached across her to move a pine branch out of the way, and his forearm brushed against her thigh.

Abigail stiffened as the intimate contact sent a frisson of feeling through her frame. She ignored him, hoping he wouldn't notice her reaction to his touch.

A moment later he reached for another piece of debris, and their shoulders met. She held her breath until a small space once again separated them.

In a matter of minutes the sexual tension was unbearable. What made it worse was that Abigail couldn't ask Luke to stop without admitting that what he was doing was arousing her. But enough was enough.

''What, exactly, is it that you hoped to prove by this demonstration, Mr. Granger?'' she demanded at last.

He glanced down at what was now plain evidence of how even these slight touches had affected him, then looked up and met her gaze. ''That I don't have to love you to want you,'' he said.

Abigail quivered with unwanted desire.

''And you don't have to love me to want me,'' he added, staring at the flush that had risen at her throat.

Abigail wasn't sure how to respond. To say she felt no physical response to him would be an outright lie. On the other hand, Luke might think her feelings weren't involved in her reaction to him, but she knew herself too well to believe otherwise.

However, she had no intention of letting this go any further. It was too dangerous a course of action even to consider. Abigail didn't let her thoughts ponder on why it was dangerous or exactly what was at risk. She only knew she couldn't let this...seduction...continue. Under the circumstances, there was only one thing to do.

"No," Abigail said.

Luke searched her face to discern her feelings. Her cheeks were flushed, but her features were carefully controlled, revealing nothing. "No?"

Abigail swallowed hard and said, "No."

Luke hurt with wanting her. But she'd made her feelings crystal clear. "Have it your way, Abby," he said in a voice harsh with controlled need. "But don't lie to me—or to yourself—anymore. You're no different from any other woman. You can want a man without loving him—or even liking him very much." He stood abruptly and stalked over to lean back against the pine, not bothering to hide the evidence of his desire.

Abigail opened her mouth to try and explain that he was wrong, that her feelings were engaged, and snapped it shut again. If he knew the truth she would be vulnerable to him. She turned back to the task at hand and quickly finished setting the third trap.

"One more to go," Abigail said when she was done. "We can head back toward my pickup. The fourth trap goes near the dead sheep. The wolf may come back to feed on the carcasses."

They didn't speak again until the last trap was set, and Abigail had dropped her pack in the back of the pickup.

"What's next?" Luke asked.

"I need to talk with all the neighboring ranchers, to see if any of them have sighted the wolf or lost any stock."

"Do you need me for that?"

Abigail wished to heaven she could say no. The truth was, it would be easier if she had someone local along. People were always more willing to talk to a familiar face than to a stranger. She settled for admitting, "It would help to have you along."

He swore under his breath. "Let's get some lunch at my place. Then, I'll take you around."

Abigail turned the truck around and headed back down into the Boulder River Valley. Somehow the drive back seemed much longer than the drive out.

Well, did you find out what you wanted to know?

Yes.

So what do you think?

I think I'm in serious trouble.

3

Certain postures and gestures express the
inner state of the wolf; other wolves,
upon seeing this behavior, may respond in
characteristic ways, depending on their feelings.

Luke spent the drive back down the mountain thinking. Maybe Abigail Dayton's mind had been saying no, but her body had been saying yes. So where did that leave him? He glanced at her from the corner of his eye. Her straight blond hair was blowing wildly around her face, which was set in serene lines. You would never have known to look at her that the woman was soft to the touch, or that she had a backbone like iron.

Damn it, he couldn't help admiring her. She was doing a man's job, and doing it well. Yet there was an obvious feminine side to her that hadn't been lost to her masculine pursuits. His brow furrowed. Still, he couldn't understand why he was attracted to her.

She came about shoulder-high on him—about the right height for her body to meet his in all the right places. But there wasn't even a handful of bosom on her, and she didn't have hips worth mentioning. It had to be those green, cat's eyes and that flawless skin that had captured his imagination. He wanted to see those eyes glazed with passion, and to know if her skin was as soft, smooth and peach-colored all over as it was on her face and neck.

He refused to consider the possibility that anything else

about the woman—her character, her sense of humor, her sympathy and willingness to listen—had sparked his interest in her.

Miss Abigail Dayton would be around for at least a week. That was plenty of time to seduce her—and prove his point. Love wasn't necessary for a man and woman to have satisfying, not to mention downright enjoyable, sex. He had no doubt that by the time that renegade wolf had been caged, he'd have her in his arms and in his bed. It was a moment he was looking forward to with relish.

Shorty had lunch ready when they arrived. "Figured you two would work up a healthy appetite," he said, serving them each a hearty bowl of vegetable beef soup. He put a plate of grilled cheese sandwiches in the center of the table. "Help yourselves. There's apple cobbler on the counter cooling for dessert. I got some chores to tend to, so I'll just leave you two alone."

He winked broadly at Abigail and then at Luke before he headed back outside, letting the screen door slam behind him.

Abigail's narrow-eyed gaze dared Luke to say anything the least bit suggestive.

He opened his mouth and shut it once before he said, "Eat your soup. It's getting cold."

Abigail was more than happy to keep her mouth full eating, because then she didn't have to talk. She'd already found out more than she wanted to know about Luke Granger. It was obvious the man had spent his entire life surrounded by the wrong kind of women. No wonder he was so cynical about her gender. She had half a mind to prove to him over the next week that he was wrong. But that would mean getting more involved with him than she wanted to be.

But there was no reason why she couldn't talk to him, try

to change his mind. She didn't ponder too much on why it seemed so important to change his mind about women. But it was, so she might as well take advantage of the time she had with him to enlighten him on a few essential truths about the female sex.

Having come to this momentous decision, Abigail set down her spoon and said, "What attracted you most about the last woman you…uh…dated?"

Luke grinned, and she felt a flutter in the pit of her stomach. Considering what she knew, she couldn't possibly still be attracted to the man. She must just have eaten a mite too much of Shorty's soup.

"Are you sure you want to know that?" he answered.

Abigail nodded.

"Her looks."

"Well, there you have it," Abigail said with a great deal of satisfaction.

"Have what?"

"The reason why you've had so little success with women."

The grin disappeared. "I can have any woman I want," he countered.

"Oh. I didn't mean to suggest that you couldn't attract a woman," Abigail soothed. "Quite the contrary. I'm sure with your looks women fall all over themselves to get your attention."

Luke's eyes narrowed suspiciously. "What are you getting at?"

Abigail licked her lips nervously and said, "I only meant that you should spend a little more time getting to know a woman before you get more…uh…personally acquainted."

The grin was back, looking even more confident than before. "If that's an invitation, I accept."

Abigail's mouth fell open. "What?"

"That is what you're getting at, isn't it? You're ready to admit that you want to go to bed with me, but you'd like us to get to know each other better first. Hell, lady, that's fine with me."

Abigail's chair tumbled backward as she leapt to her feet. "That most certainly is *not* what I was getting at!"

Luke found her immensely appealing, with her chin up and her green eyes flashing and her fisted hands perched on her slim hips. He set his spoon down and leaned forward with his elbows on the table, one strong hand laced through the other. "I think the lady doth protest too much," he said in a quiet voice.

Abigail's face flushed scarlet.

Luke's brows lowered as a sudden thought struck him. He leaned back in his chair, put his laced hands behind his head and eyed her slowly from hip to hair. "How long has it been, Abby, since you made love to a man? One year? Two?"

Abigail's eyelashes swept down, and her flush deepened.

"Aw, Abby," he said softly. "It could be so good between us."

Abigail opened her eyes and, for an instant, let him see her vulnerability.

"You look like a deer caught in a set of headlights."

Abigail wrapped her arms around herself, amazed at how well he'd read her fear of getting emotionally involved with a man...with him. A second later another set of arms surrounded her, strong arms, comforting arms, as she was pulled back into Luke's embrace.

"Don't be afraid, Abby," he murmured in her ear. "I won't let you get hurt. I—"

Abigail turned and put her hands against his chest to keep some space between them. "You don't understand." This wasn't what she wanted. Tenderness was too frightening. "Please don't do this, Luke."

Instead of letting her go, he tightened his hold. "Talk to me, Abby. Tell me what you're feeling."

"I feel foolish," she admitted with a tad more honesty than she'd intended. She stopped struggling. Luke was stronger than she was. She wasn't going to get away until he let her go.

She looked up at him, searching his face, not sure what she was hoping to find. She couldn't understand or explain her undeniable physical attraction to him. Yet, somehow, she had to find the words to make him keep his distance. "I've already told you that to me, making love is more than a means of satisfying sexual desire. So what do you want from me? Sam was a very special man. Living with Sam, loving him, was so wonderful because we had a lifetime of good memories together. How can I ever find that with another man?"

"By sharing the rest of your life with another man," Luke answered. "By making new memories to carry with you."

Startled by what he'd suggested, Abigail met Luke's smoky-eyed gaze. "That presupposes I can find another man I could love as much as Sam." Her eyes searched his as she admitted in a sad voice, "I don't think that's possible."

Suddenly he freed her.

"I'm sure as hell not volunteering for the job."

Abigail was confused by his vehemence and had no idea how to respond to it.

Luke never gave her the chance. "The only kind of memories I'm interested in creating with you are the kind that involve hot and heavy sex," he said. "You touching me, and me touching you, in ways that make us writhe with ecstasy in each other's arms. I'm talking about me being so deep inside you, filling you so full, that there isn't room for memories of another man's touch.''

Luke had meant to frighten Abigail away, and he saw from the way she shrank from him that his tone of voice, and the ruthlessness of his words, had done their job. For a moment there, things had gotten a little scary. *Making memories.* That was the kind of fairy-tale hope that had gotten him married once upon a time. He wasn't about to travel down that trail again. There were too many pitfalls to lay a man low.

Abigail was watching Luke, so she saw the moment his gray eyes turned soft and yearning. He wasn't the callous bastard he wanted her to think he was. But as suddenly as it had appeared, the softness was gone from his eyes, and they were a bleak, flinty gray again.

''Well, Abby, you've heard my offer. What do you say?''

For a moment Abigail was tempted to say yes, just to call his bluff. But that wasn't honest, and more than anything, she wanted to be honest with Luke Granger. It seemed too few women had been.

''I have to say no, Luke,'' she answered in a low voice. ''But if you're willing, maybe we can make a different kind of memories in the next week that I can take along with me when I go back to Helena.''

Luke frowned. ''What did you have in mind?''

''I'd like to be your friend. And I'd like you to be mine.''

Luke made a dismissive sound in his throat. ''I don't have any women friends.''

''Maybe it's time you did.''

''We don't have a damn thing in common to talk about,'' he said.

''I'm not so sure about that,'' Abigail replied with a twinkle of mischief in her eye. ''We could always debate the merits of cattle over sheep ranching in Montana.''

"There isn't much you could say to convince me raising cattle makes as much sense as raising sheep," Luke said.

Abigail smiled. "We can discuss it between visits to the other sheep ranchers in the area. Shall we go?"

Without realizing quite how it had happened, Luke found himself ensconced in a deep conversation—some might have called it an argument—with Abigail over the advantages of raising a two-crop animal like sheep, versus raising cattle.

Sheep provided income both from wool in the spring and from lambs for slaughter in the fall. Meanwhile, cattle were raised for beef, the price of which fluctuated so much a rancher could be in clover one year and deep in Dutch the next.

Before he knew it, they'd arrived at Cyrus Alistair's ranch. Cyrus had died several months before and left a plot of land and about five hundred sheep to a grand-niece of his from back East. Luke tried to remember her name, but it wouldn't come.

What he could remember was how mad his best friend, Nathan Hazard, had been when Cyrus refused to let him buy the land, even when the ornery old cuss knew he was dying. This piece of property sat square in the middle of Nathan's sheep ranch, and Cyrus had been a thorn in Nathan's side for the fifteen years since the young man had come home from college and taken over the running of the ranch from his invalid father—who had been Cyrus's sworn enemy.

From what Luke had heard, the young woman who'd inherited the land from Cyrus was a greenhorn through and through. She'd been making mistakes—big mistakes—running the place that would soon have her so far in hock to the bank that she'd be more than willing to sell out to Nathan just to keep from losing her shirt.

"Oh, my God," Abigail said at her first sight of the ranch.

If she'd had any doubts about how well-run Luke's sheep ranch was, she only had to take one look at the place at which they'd just arrived.

The small wooden pens, called jugs, for holding the new lambs and their mothers were broken down. A stack of dead lambs had been piled beside the barn. There were numerous mudholes on the road leading to the house that should have dried out by now—if there had been any drainage ditches dug. Fields that should have been planted with winter feed were lying fallow. This place was a disaster in the making.

Abigail angrily eyed the stack of dead lambs. How could anyone expect a wolf—or any predator for that matter—to ignore that kind of invitation? When she met this rancher, whoever it was, she was going to give him a good piece of her mind. "What did you say this rancher's name is? I can't believe he let his place get run down like this."

"I didn't. And *he* is a *she*."

Startled, Abigail turned to Luke and said, "I suppose you're going to say the reason the place looks like this is because a woman's trying to manage it. I can't believe that's all there is to it. Something must be wrong."

Luke cleared his throat. "Well, actually the problem is she's a greenhorn. Doesn't know the first thing about what she's doing."

"I'm sure that as a good neighbor you offered her what help you could," Abigail said.

Luke shifted uneasily in his seat. "Well, you see, my friend Nathan, he—"

"I don't want to hear your excuses," Abigail said, cutting him off. She shoved the pickup door open and stepped down into a mud puddle. "Let's get this over with."

The moment Abigail saw the young woman, her heart went out to her. She was dumping slops into the pigpen, wearing bibbed overalls, a plaid wool shirt, galoshes on her feet, and a Harley's Feed Store baseball cap on her brown hair, which hung in two thick braids over her shoulders. She had an open, freckled face, but it was pale and drawn-looking. She was so tall, nearly six feet, and looked so physically strong that Abigail wondered why she hadn't made a better go of it.

"Hello," Abigail said, extending her hand. "Abigail Dayton, Fish and Wildlife."

A hesitant smile greeted Abigail's outstretched hand. The woman pulled a filthy glove off her hand, and an almost equally grimy and newly callused hand grasped Abigail's fingers. Abigail found herself wondering what she could do to help this woman succeed, where she was so obviously failing.

"My name's Harriet Alistair," the woman said in a surprisingly husky voice. She climbed over the top of the pigpen, instead of going through the gate, which was broken and had been wired shut. "People mostly call me Harry," the woman said as she joined them.

Harry. What a perfectly awful name for a woman, Abigail thought. There was nothing the least bit feminine about it. Although, to be honest, Harry couldn't be called your typical female. She defied description, not to mention the traditional role of a woman in the West, which was to stand by—or behind—her man.

When Harry looked inquiringly at Luke, he held out his hand and said, "I'm Luke Granger. Your neighbor to the south. Sorry I haven't been over to see you sooner but...I've been busy."

The excuse sounded lame to Luke's ears, and worse, he knew it wasn't the truth. He could have made time if he'd wanted to. Nathan had asked him to stay away, and in deference to his friend, he had. But he was starting to wonder how Nathan could leave this poor woman to fend for herself.

Luke could see that despite her size and apparent strength she was exhausted.

Abigail saw the same thing as they all walked toward the small log cabin that served as a ranch house. "I've come to ask if you've seen any wolves around here."

Harry stopped dead in her tracks, and her brown eyes rounded as big as saucers. "Wolves?"

Abigail saw that she'd frightened the woman and hurried to reassure her. "They aren't any danger to you," she explained. "As a matter of fact, there hasn't been a single recorded incident of a wild wolf seriously injuring or killing anybody in North America."

"Ever?"

"Ever," Abigail confirmed.

Harry's brow furrowed in disbelief. "But wolves are so— ferocious!"

Abigail laughed as she followed Harry toward the back door of the dilapidated, and rather primitive, log ranch house, with Luke trailing behind them, a forgotten man.

"You're probably remembering all those fairy tales you heard as a child. 'The Three Little Pigs and the *Big Bad Wolf,'* 'Little Red Riding Hood and the *Big Bad Wolf,'* 'Peter and the *Big Bad*'—well, you get the idea. It just isn't so. The wolf is about the shyest creature around. That's why, aside from the fact that there aren't too many left anymore, you don't often see them."

Abigail controlled a gasp when they stepped into the kitchen. Total chaos. About a half-dozen bum lambs slept on wadded blankets in the corner of the unfinished wooden floor. The sink was piled high with dishes. The painted yellow cupboards hung open and appeared nearly bare of food. The counters were covered with cans of formula and nippled Coke bottles used to feed the lambs. It was easy to see why the tall woman looked so exhausted.

Harry stared at the mess without seeming to know what to do next, and Abigail felt angry for what the woman must be feeling right now, and frustrated by her inability to do anything to really help.

"I'd love some coffee," Abigail said. "Wouldn't you, Luke?"

Luke was also appalled. He'd had no idea the woman was in such distress. He remembered how Nathan had said he planned to "hang that damned tenderfoot out to dry." Luke felt guilty. In a voice meant to be encouraging to his new neighbor, he said, "Sure, uh…Harry, I'd love some coffee." It felt strange calling a woman by a man's name.

Having some direction, Harry set to with a will. While she was working, Luke and Abigail settled themselves at a chrome kitchen table strewn with numerous brochures. The depth of Harry's ignorance was apparent from the titles: *Sheep Raising for Beginners, Harvesting, Preparing and Selling Montana Wool* and *Wintering Montana Ewes.* It was also apparent she was trying to learn the economics of the business from such titles as: *Making Your Farm Flock Pay* and *Managing Winter Sheep Range for Greater Profit.*

Harry Alistair wasn't a total fool if she recognized her own ignorance. But from the look of things, Abigail was pretty sure Harry was going to go bust long before she learned how to turn a profit managing sheep.

"I still find it hard to believe that wolves are as harmless to humans as you're suggesting," Harry said as she set down mugs of hot coffee in front of them. "If so, how did all those fairy tales ever get started? They must have had some basis in fact."

Abigail shrugged. "I suppose they might have started because wolves usually run in packs of ten to fifteen. That's an intimidating number of teeth to run into on a dark night. And they're ferocious hunters—of ungulates."

"Ungulates?" Harry said, slipping into a chrome-legged chair with a torn red plastic seat.

"Hooved animals—deer, elk and moose. Fairy tales have done the wolf a great disservice. I've learned over the years that wolves aren't the monsters of fairy tale legend. They're simply another predator that has to kill to survive."

Harry's smile reappeared, and the slight gap between her two front teeth gave her a winsome look. "What you're saying is a real relief. I've been meaning to learn how to shoot a gun in case I had trouble with predators, but—"

Abigail rose out of her chair like an avenging angel. "You can't *shoot* a gray wolf! They're endangered, and they're protected."

"I'm sorry," Harry said, her face a picture of despair. "I didn't know. There's so much I don't know!"

Abigail couldn't help responding to the other woman's wretchedness. She reached out a hand to comfort Harry, who'd hidden her face in her hands to conceal what, Abigail supposed from the hiccoughing sounds, had to be tears.

"I'm the one who's sorry," Abigail said. "Whenever I start talking about wolves, I tend to get on my high horse."

Abigail peeked at Luke to see if he'd heard that admission, and sure enough he was eyeing her ruefully. "Anyway, all I wanted to find out today was whether you'd seen any wolves, and I take it that you haven't."

Harry dropped her hands to her lap and stared at them as she answered, "No, I haven't. And I don't care if I ever do."

"You shouldn't leave those dead lambs lying around, then," Abigail warned. "Or you're liable to see a wolf sooner than you'd like."

Harry lifted her face to reveal misery etched in the furrows of her brow. "I...I don't know what to do with the lambs," she admitted.

Luke's lips thinned into a severe line. Nathan or no Nathan, he wasn't going to let this woman go unassisted. "I'll take care of burying them," he said.

"But I can't afford to pay—"

"Neighbors don't have to pay one another for lending a helping hand," Luke said. "If you two will excuse me, I'll see to those lambs right now."

"Is he always like that?" Harry asked when Luke was gone. "So helpful, I mean?"

"I don't know," Abigail answered. "I only met him this morning."

While Luke worked outside, Abigail had a chance to find out how and why Harry Alistair had decided to try to make a go of her great-uncle's sheep ranch. Once Abigail had heard the story, she had a great deal of respect for what Harry was trying to do. And a great deal of trepidation that she was doomed to fail.

The whole time Harry was talking, Abigail stayed busy, washing the dishes in the sink, gathering up the brochures on the table and closing cupboard doors. Slowly, but surely, the kitchen took on some semblance of order.

"Maybe you should accept this Nathan Hazard fellow's offer to buy you out," Abigail said.

"Never!" Harry retorted. "I'll let the place go to rack and ruin first. That man is the meanest, ugliest son of a bitch who ever—"

Harry stopped in the middle of her tirade as Luke Granger opened the kitchen door and stepped inside. "All finished. We have time to visit another ranch or two before supper if you're up to it," he said to Abigail.

Abigail turned and grasped Harry's hands. "I wish you luck, Harry." She knew the tenderfoot rancher was going to need it.

Luke turned to Harry and said, "If you're ever in trouble, you call me. I'll be glad to do what I can."

Harry's freckles disappeared as she blushed. "Thank you, Luke. I wouldn't want to be indebted to you for more than I could repay."

Luke slanted a glance at Abigail and said with a perfectly straight face, "Just doing my neighborly duty, Harry. Be seeing you."

Once they were back in the pickup and on their way, Abigail heaved a big sigh.

"What was that for?" Luke asked.

"She isn't going to make it, is she?"

"I doubt it," Luke admitted.

"It was kind of you to offer help."

"It was the least I could do," Luke replied, uncomfortable with the knowledge that he could have done a lot more, a lot sooner. And doubly uncomfortable with the warm feelings he got inside from Abigail's compliment. "Looked to me like you did your own share of helping."

"I couldn't do much," she replied with a troubled look. "Just washed a few dishes and stacked a few brochures. It sounded to me like somebody named Nathan Hazard is doing his damnedest to see that Harry fails."

"She doesn't need much help in that direction," Luke said.

"How can you say such a thing?"

"Because, unfortunately, it's true. It's another case of survival of the fittest, Abby. If she can't make a go of it, she should leave the land for someone who can," Luke said bluntly. "That's the way it's always been. That's the way it always will be."

Abigail shoved her fingers through her hair agitatedly. "It seems so sad. Harry told me she's never succeeded at anything she's ever tried. She was so determined when she came here to finally turn her life around.'' Abigail sought Luke's gaze. ''Isn't there anything anybody can do to help her?''

Luke's lips pressed into a thin line. He didn't like the way that look in Abigail's eyes affected him. He'd only met the woman this morning, and already he found himself wanting to please her. As much as he wanted to refuse to help, he found, after another look at those tear-threatened green eyes, that he couldn't. ''I can have a talk with Nathan Hazard,'' he said.

''You know him?''

''Harry's 'son of a bitch' is my best friend.'' Luke grimaced. ''He isn't as bad as she paints him. I'm sure if I talk to him, we can work something out.''

''I'd like to have a word or two with Harry's nemesis myself,'' she said, her eyes glinting with determination. ''Point me in the right direction.''

''That's his place down there by the river. Before you jump in with both feet, Abby, maybe I ought to warn you about Nathan Hazard.''

''What about him?''

''I think he's what you women fondly call a male chauvinist pig.''

Abigail's lips curved into an amused smile. ''And you're not?''

''Can't hold a candle to Nathan,'' Luke answered

Abigail sent a calculating look in Luke's direction. ''There's definitely more to you than meets the eye.''

''What makes you so sure?''

Abigail shrugged. ''A woman just knows these things.'' She had spent barely a day with the man, and already she was certain there were depths to him that he didn't want a woman to plumb. The minute Luke thought she might be slipping past the barriers he'd erected to keep her at arm's length, he became brusque and remote.

But a heartless man didn't help out a woman like Harriet Alistair and ask nothing in return. Or offer to take on his friend on her behalf. Or agree to put his lambs at risk to save a renegade gray wolf.

Abigail already liked what she'd seen of Luke Granger. She was determined to know the real man, the one beneath all the bitterness and disillusion caused by a lifetime of disappointment in his relationships with women.

She tried to convince herself that her interest arose from a desire to foster a budding friendship. But the pounding blood in her veins, and the shivers down her spine whenever the man came near her, left the purity of her motives in doubt. The situation was complicated because she felt obliged to be as open with Luke about herself as she wanted him to be with her. That entailed a certain gamble Abigail had to weigh carefully before she committed herself to getting more involved with the rancher.

When Sam had died, Abigail had sworn off taking risks. During the past three years, she hadn't let any man get close. She simply couldn't take the chance of losing any more of her heart.

But there was something about Luke Granger, some indefinable part of him that called out to some part of her. And despite the danger, Abigail didn't seem to be able to stop herself from taking just one more risk.

4

As the mating season approaches, all
interactions among pack members become more
intense and frequent, including friendly contacts
as well as conflicts and rivalries.

Abigail stared in awe at the tall, gorgeous male creature standing before her on the steps of a log house that was as huge, pristine and presentable as Harry's was tiny, dirty and decrepit.

"Howdy, ma'am," the man greeted Abigail in a deep, friendly voice. "Name's Nathan Hazard. What can I do for you today?"

This was Harry Alistair's mean, *ugly* son of a bitch? Nathan Hazard had sapphire blue eyes, thick, wavy blond hair that hung down over his blue work-shirt collar, powerful forearms that showed to advantage beyond his rolled-up sleeves, long legs encased in a pair of butter soft jeans and the sharp-planed face of a model in an upscale men's magazine. Abigail was struck speechless by his perfection. It was left to Luke to make the introductions.

"I'd like you to meet Agent Abigail Dayton from Fish and Wildlife," Luke said to his friend.

Nathan shook Abigail's hand, but when she remained mute he turned to Luke and said, "Last I heard you'd called Animal Damage Control about that wolf. What's going on?"

Luke flushed. "It's a long story. I—"

"Come on in and have a cup of coffee, and you can tell me all about it."

Before Abigail could protest that they had a lot of places to get to before the sun went down, and she only wanted to ask whether he'd seen any wolves, Nathan had ushered the two of them inside the A-frame house. He seated them on the corduroy couch and chair that faced a central copper-hooded fireplace, and relaxed into an ancient wooden rocker across from them.

On the interior walls, the pine logs of which the house was constructed had been left as natural as they were on the outside but were a lighter color because they hadn't weathered. The spacious living room was decorated in pale earth tones accented with navy. A tan, navy and rust braided rug snugged up under the furniture on the polished oak hardwood floor. The living room had a cathedral ceiling, with large windows at each end and on both sides, so that no matter where you looked there was a breathtaking view: the sparkling Boulder River bounded by cottonwoods to the east, the Crazy Mountains to the north, the snow-capped Absarokas to the south, and to the east, pasture dotted with ewes and their twin lambs, which had been joined by a grazing herd of twenty or so wild mule deer.

"This is beautiful," Abigail said in an awed voice. She couldn't decide which view she liked best. She craned her neck to check out the window behind her.

Luke and Nathan exchanged a knowing look. More than one woman had gotten starry-eyed over Nathan Hazard's house. But Nathan hadn't built the house to attract a woman; he was still a bachelor. From everything Luke knew about him, Nathan intended to stay that way. He had designed the house to please himself and built it because he liked beautiful things. Luke's friend had studied to be an architect before a farm accident fifteen years ago had left his father an invalid, and cut those dreams short.

"There you are, Katoya," Nathan said, as an old woman appeared with a tray containing three cups, a white ceramic pot and a sheep-shaped creamer and sugar bowl. "I was going to ask for some coffee for my guests, but I see you're a step ahead of me."

Abigail recognized the diminutive woman's features—her dark brown eyes, broad forehead, straight nose, high cheek-bones and thin-lipped mouth—as those of a Blackfoot Indian. Abigail had come to know many Blackfeet on the reservation that bounded Glacier National Park. The old woman's skin was a deep bronze and unlined, despite her great age, which was evidenced by her braided gray hair and gnarled fingers.

"I'm pleased to meet you, Katoya," Abigail said in the Blackfoot tongue. The woman's name meant Sweet Pine. The sweet pine was a fragrant balsam, sometimes mixed with grease and used by the Blackfeet as a perfume. It was a very romantic name, Abigail thought, and she wondered what kind of woman Katoya had been in her youth to earn it.

The old woman smiled with her eyes, rather than her mouth, and returned Abigail's greeting in Blackfoot. Then she turned to Luke and asked in English, "Is this your woman?"

Luke saw the amused look on Nathan's face as he waited to hear whether his friend would lay claim to the Fish and Wildlife agent. Luke let his gaze rove Abby's deliciously enticing body. What was he supposed to say? Wanting wasn't the same as possessing. If Abigail Dayton got her way, they would part as *friends*.

When Luke remained silent, the old woman shook her head and made another comment in the Blackfoot tongue.

Abigail turned beet red.

"What did she say?" Luke demanded when Katoya had left.

"Nothing," Abigail lied. *Only that Abigail's man was hungry—for more than food—and Abigail should feed him or he would find another who would.*

"I didn't know you knew how to speak Blackfoot," Luke said.

Confused by the rush of desire she'd felt at the Indian woman's words and needing desperately to put some emotional distance between herself and Luke Granger, Abigail arched a brow and said, "There are a lot of things you don't know about me."

"I'm ready and willing to learn. All you have to do is say the word," Luke said, focusing his gaze on Abigail.

Nathan grinned at the sight of the sparks flying between his two guests but resisted the urge to tease his friend. Instead, he interrupted Luke's visual seduction of the Fish and Wildlife agent by asking, "What caused your change of plans regarding the wolf?" Although, considering what he'd just seen, the answer seemed obvious. He covered his mouth to keep the laughter from erupting.

Luke kept staring at Abigail, refusing to release her from his sensual spell.

Abigail tore her gaze away from Luke and focused it on Nathan's face—which seemed a little rigid. She felt as though she'd escaped a terrible threat. She ought to feel relieved, but she felt more like crying. It had been a mistake to let her feelings get out of control like this. After Sam's death she'd grieved so long and so hard that it had been necessary to stop feeling, in order to get over her loss. She didn't want to feel pain again. She didn't want to feel anything again.

Abigail's forehead creased in confusion as she tried to

remember what Nathan had asked. Oh, yes, why was she here instead of someone from Animal Damage Control? To her consternation, she had to keep her hands clasped in her lap to keep them from shaking as she explained, "I convinced Luke to give me a chance to capture and relocate the wolf he sighted. I'm checking now to see if any other ranchers in the valley have sighted wolves or had problems with wolf depredation."

"Nope and nope," Nathan said. "But I'll be on the lookout and give you a call. Where can I reach you?"

"I'll be staying—"

"She'll be staying at my place," Luke interrupted.

Abigail felt as though the ground had fallen out from under her. She couldn't spend the night at Luke's house. In her current state of emotional upheaval, being a bedroom away would be too close for comfort. "It's not necessary—"

"You haven't got much time to catch that renegade," Luke said. "You'll have even less if you have to spend it driving back and forth to Big Timber."

What he said made a lot of sense. Surely she had enough self-control to resist Luke's overtures. She didn't fool herself that he wouldn't make them. All she had to do was reassert her desire to pursue a *friendship* with him.

"I'll be glad to accept your invitation." Abigail's sense of humor suddenly reasserted itself, and she managed to grin as she added, "If you're up to it, maybe we can have a good game of checkers after supper." She turned back to Nathan and said, "If you see any wolves, you can leave a message for me at Luke's place."

Luke exchanged a look with Nathan that spoke volumes. Both men understood, even if Abigail didn't, that Luke had plans to enjoy more than a game of checkers with Abigail Dayton after supper.

"By the way," Abigail said to Nathan. "We stopped off at Harry Alistair's place before we came here. She seems to be having a bit of trouble making a go of it." That was the understatement of the year.

A frown appeared on Nathan's face, and for a moment he looked every bit as mean and ugly as Harry had accused him of being. "That woman has no business trying to manage that ranch."

"I agree that she certainly needs some help. I'm surprised her neighbors haven't volunteered to provide some of it," Abigail said pointedly.

"She's an Alistair," Nathan retorted, as though that explained everything.

"What does that have to do with anything?" Abigail asked.

"Hazards have always hated Alistairs."

Abigail was incredulous. "Are you telling me you won't lift a finger to help Harry Alistair because of a *feud?*"

"That says it in a nutshell."

Abigail had a tremendous urge to call Nathan Hazard an idiot. But calling Nathan names wasn't going to convince him to help Harry Alistair. To hide her agitation she rose from the couch and walked over to the closest artifact—a bronze of a buffalo on a marble pedestal—and admired it.

The whole room was dotted with items of equal beauty, bronze sculptures and oil and watercolor paintings by famous Western artists. How could a man with a home this beautiful, who appreciated art this exquisite, act like such a narrow-minded idiot?

When she had control of her temper, Abigail turned to Luke and said, "He's your friend. Do you think you could talk him into changing his mind?"

Luke grimaced. Part of the reason he and Nathan had

become such fast friends and stayed that way was because both men adhered strictly to the unwritten Code of the West.

The Code was a set of rules that had evolved when men first began to drift West, away from secret pasts, and toward a bold new future in a land that could be as merciless as it was bountiful. It included laws such as *Never ask a man where he comes from,* and *Never draw a gun unless you mean to shoot.*

Part of that Code was *Never offer a man advice unless he asks for it.* Abigail was asking him to break that unwritten rule. Luke heaved a sigh.

Nathan heard the sigh and asked, "Something troubling you, Luke?"

That was all Luke needed to hear. Nathan had asked. He could broach the subject now without offense. Nathan had made Luke promise not to help Harry Alistair, and it was likely Nathan had made sure no one else in the valley would lend a helping hand, either. Luke wanted Nathan to back off from that stand and give the woman a chance.

He leaned forward and rested his forearms on his widespread knees. "I know you want to get rid of Harry Alistair, but I think you're going about it the wrong way," Luke said earnestly.

Nathan's jaw clenched before he said, "Oh? What's the right way?"

"Since you asked," Luke said, flashing a relieved grin, "I think you ought to help her make a go of the place and encourage the rest of her neighbors to do the same. Then—"

"Wait just a damn minute," Nathan said, slamming his coffee cup down onto the small antique table next to the rocker.

"No, you wait," Luke said in a steely voice that kept Nathan rooted in his chair. "When was the last time you saw Harry Alistair?"

"I saw her two months ago, the day she took over that old man's place," Nathan admitted.

"I suggest you make another visit. Take a good, long look around and see if you don't feel a little ashamed at the shabby way you've acted toward your new neighbor."

"I don't owe any Alistair a thing," Nathan argued.

"I've known you for a long time, Nathan," Luke said in a quiet voice. "But the way you've treated Harry Alistair is enough to make me question whether you're the kind of man I want to keep calling my friend."

Nathan's jaw worked as he absorbed Luke's hard words. "You're walking a narrow ledge, saying a thing like that."

"I wouldn't say it if I didn't mean it."

Nathan's eyes narrowed, his huge hands fisted, and his body tensed as though held under rigid control. "I think you'd better leave now."

Luke rose slowly, never taking his flinty gray eyes off his friend. "Come on, Abby. Let's get out of here. I think we've about worn out our welcome."

They were almost to the door when Nathan's voice stopped them. "Luke?"

Luke paused.

"I'll go see her again," he said quietly. "I won't promise more than that."

"That's all I'm asking," Luke replied. He ushered Abigail out the door and closed it firmly behind them.

Luke remained silent as Abigail drove them to the next ranch in her pickup. She made no attempt to start a conversation, because she was doing some thinking. How strange that Luke would risk a friendship of long standing for a woman he hardly knew. More proof he wasn't the heartless bastard he'd tried to convince her he was. She pursed her lips in contemplation. The question that came to mind was, why had he been so anxious to have her believe the worst of him?

"Penny for your thoughts?"

Abigail wasn't ready to confront Luke about his benevolent behavior—especially since she was certain he would only deny it. Instead she asked, "Do you think Nathan will go visit Harry Alistair?"

"He gave his word. He won't break it."

"Will he let the feud get in the way of helping her?"

Luke picked at a frayed cuff on his sleeve. "The Hazard-Alistair feud has been going on a long time. There's a lot of bad blood between them."

"Harry's from back East," Abigail protested. "She doesn't have anything to do with the feud."

"Nothing about a feud ever makes much sense. I do know Nathan Hazard. Once he sees Harry Alistair, he isn't going to be able to walk away from her without lending a helping hand, any more than I could."

Abigail glanced at Luke from the corner of her eye. She wondered if he realized what he'd just admitted. Here was strong evidence that Luke's professed attitude toward women was laced with a well-camouflaged streak of kindness and consideration. At any rate, Abigail hoped Luke was right about Nathan helping out. Because she wasn't going to forget the look of despair in Harry Alistair's brown eyes for a long, long time.

They stopped at two more ranches before dark, but no one had seen any wolves or suffered any wolf depredations. Abigail sighed with relief when Luke's wood-frame house came into sight, because the silence between them had gotten decidedly uncomfortable.

It wasn't the silence, exactly, that was the problem. Quite simply, Abigail had become aware of every move Luke made. She'd watched the denim stretch over his thighs as he set his ankle on his knee. She'd seen the corded muscle ripple in his arms when he took off his felt Stetson to run a hand through his thick black hair. She'd felt a growing tightness in her belly as his hair-dusted fingers scratched what she was certain was a washboard belly.

What made the whole experience so unnerving was that she hadn't felt the least physical interest in any other man since Sam had died—until this morning when she met Luke Granger. Right now her entire body was alive, quivering with awareness of the man who sat totally relaxed beside her. It was enough to make her scream. Which, of course, she would never do, being a sane, rational kind of person. All the same, she kept her teeth gritted to make sure no sound got out. Which was why the truck had been so quiet since they'd left the last ranch house.

Despite what Abigail might have thought, Luke was as conscious of her as she was of him. He'd kept his eyes straight ahead, knowing that to look at her was to desire her. But he could still smell her and feel her heat. His whole body felt on fire. He was burning alive, and the woman wanted to be his *friend.* He had to bite his lower lip to keep from laughing aloud. Which was why it had gotten so damned quiet on the ride home.

Luke bolted from the truck the instant they arrived at his ranch, saying he had to check on some things in the sheep buildings before he came inside. Abigail took advantage of the opportunity to take several deep, calming breaths before she headed into the house.

Apparently Shorty had done some cleaning during the day, because when Abigail walked through the front door of Luke's house, the items she'd had to step over at dawn had been removed from the living room floor. In fact, the furniture glowed with a rich sheen that reflected the licking flames crackling in the fieldstone fireplace.

Abigail was enchanted by the coziness of the small room. Nathan's house had been beautiful, but Luke's home possessed a warmth and charm that she found much more appealing.

Abigail could have made the same comparison between the two men. She found them both attractive. But somehow Nathan's astonishing handsomeness didn't cause her pulse to race the way Luke's striking features did.

"There you are," Shorty said as he entered the living room. "You ready to eat?"

"Hungry as a wolf," Abigail said with a grin.

Abigail turned when she heard the front door open, and her eyes locked with Luke's.

Luke swore under his breath. It had been foolish to think he could rid himself of the need for her simply by taking a brisk walk in the cold night air. His need wasn't going to go away until it was quenched. He pressed his lips flat. The sooner they ate, the sooner Shorty would retire to his room, and the sooner he could have what he wanted—needed— from Abigail Dayton.

"You got some supper on the fire?" he said to Shorty.

"Just been awaitin' for you two to get here," he replied.

The instant they entered the kitchen the three orphan lambs came running toward Luke, baaing a noisy greeting. Abigail smiled when he stooped to pet each one in turn.

"I just fed them greedy little bums," Shorty said. "So don't you worry none 'bout them. Just set yourselves down and eat 'fore everything gets cold."

"I've invited Abby to stay with us while she's hunting that renegade," Luke told Shorty once the three of them had sat down to eat the Mexican casserole Shorty had prepared.

"I sorta 'spected that might happen," Shorty said with a twinkle in his eye. "So I made up the bed in the spare bedroom upstairs and dusted around a little. You need anything, Miss Abigail, you just holler.''

''Thanks, Shorty.''

As far as Luke was concerned, it took an eternity for supper to get eaten. He would have stolen Abigail then, except she volunteered to help Shorty with the dishes, and that sly old coot welcomed the help, even though he could see Luke had his desire on a short leash. Then Abigail invited Shorty to join her for a cup of coffee and a game of checkers in front of the fireplace. Although Luke was gnashing his teeth by then, Shorty just shot him a smug look and said, ''I'd enjoy that right much. Gets so lonesome round here sometimes, I get to talking to myself.''

Shorty made a point of sitting across from Abigail on the leather couch, the game board on the coffee table between them. Luke was forced to sit in the chair across the room while they played three games.

He finally lost his patience when he saw Abigail's eyelids slip closed as she listened to the end of one of Shorty's yarns. ''I think maybe Abby has heard enough tall tales for one night.'' *But she's not done playing by a long shot.*

Abigail yawned. ''I suppose I'd better get to bed. We've got an early day tomorrow.''

Luke shot a killing glance at Shorty, who quickly gathered up the coffee cups from the end tables and said, ''I s'pose you two need to make plans for tomorrow. I'll drop these in the kitchen and go on to bed.''

Despite the coffee she'd just drunk, Abigail could hardly keep her eyes open. She yawned again. ''Lord, I can't believe how tired I am.''

''It has been a long day,'' Luke agreed. But *tired* was the last thing he was feeling.

Abigail was mesmerized by the sight of Luke's body flexing as he stood and stretched like a wolf ready for the hunt.

An instant later, that powerful body settled beside her on the couch. She looked into Luke's gray eyes and found a purely feral gleam.

The hairs prickled on her neck and gooseflesh rose on her arms. A wolf was on the prowl. And she was its prey.

Luke's hands lightly grasped her shoulders from behind, and he began to knead her aching muscles with his thumbs. "You must be sore from carrying that heavy pack this morning."

"Uh...a little." Suddenly Abigail wasn't the least bit tired.

Luke's hands moved up under Abigail's hair to massage her neck and sent a shiver down her spine.

"Caught a nerve?" he murmured in her ear.

Abigail shivered again and tried to laugh at her powerful reaction to Luke's touch. Her breath caught in her throat when his hands lifted her hair so he could kiss her nape.

Abigail shot off the couch as though she'd been bitten, leaving Luke with his empty hands hanging in the air. "I think I'd better go to bed now," she said.

Abigail started up the stairs without looking back but had only gotten halfway up when she realized she had no idea which bedroom was hers. She turned around and found Luke on the step below her.

"Abby, I—"

Abigail put a hand on his chest to keep him where he was. The feel of hard muscle under her fingertips set her pulse to pounding. "Don't come any closer."

"I want you, Abby."

She put the other hand against his lips. "And don't say anything."

He reached up ever so slowly and took the hand she held against his lips and turned it so he could kiss her palm, and then her wrist. "I want you."

Abigail's knees felt wobbly. He had to stop doing what he was doing or she wouldn't be responsible for the consequences. "Please don't say things like that."

"Why not?"

"I thought we were going to be friends."

"We are," he said with a smile.

"Friends don't—"

"Friends do."

Abigail moaned as Luke took one of her fingers into his mouth and sucked on it.

"I don't even know you," Abigail said, her whole body trembling as Luke bit the pad between her thumb and forefinger.

"You know everything you need to know about me."

"I doubt that," Abigail said breathlessly.

"Ask me anything."

"Do you have any social diseases?"

Luke's head jerked up in surprise. "Do I *what?*"

Well, that certainly broke the mood. "I mean," Abigail continued in a firm voice, "that a woman can't be too careful nowadays."

Luke smiled. "I don't have any social diseases," he said. "Anything else you'd like to know?"

"Uh...do you have any...uh...protection?"

"You're not protected?"

Abigail blushed and licked her lips. "No."

Luke swore under his breath and let her go. He shoved his fingers through his hair in frustration, then gripped the banister with both hands. She had as much as admitted she hadn't had a man since her husband had died, so there would have been no need for her to be protected. Unfortunately it had been so long since he'd had a woman, he didn't have any protection handy, either. Luke swore again. "I don't have a damn thing in the house."

Abigail breathed a sigh of relief.

"You don't have to act so damned happy about it," Luke said.

Abigail put a hand lightly on his shoulder. "You'll thank me for this in the morning."

Luke stared at her in disbelief and then laughed out loud. "Only a woman could make an idiotic statement like that."

"I don't want to have sex with you, Luke." She paused and added, "And I don't love you, so making love is out of the question." She softened what she'd said with a friendly smile and finished, "Now that we have that settled, tell me, which bedroom is mine?"

There was a moment of poignant silence before he said, "Last door on the left at the end of the hall."

Abigail leaned forward and pressed her lips lightly against Luke's, savoring the softness of his mouth. "Good night, Luke," she whispered.

Luke watched her hips sway as she walked up the stairs and imagined himself with his hands around her waist walking right behind her, her backside rubbing up against him. He groaned. His body was taking a real beating, and Abigail Dayton had barely laid a finger on him.

She'd also given him a lot of food for thought. She was the first woman in his memory who hadn't been willing to settle for sex. And he wasn't interested in more than that. Normally he would have kissed her goodbye and sent her on her way. Somehow that solution didn't even occur to him in relation to Abigail Dayton. It was entirely possible that he could seduce her; she was not indifferent to him. But knowing how she felt about sex...and making love...it was also clear that seducing her might cause her pain in ways he didn't want to contemplate. So where did that leave him?

With a lot of thinking to do.

"Abby?" he called up to her.

Her voice came down to him from the hallway upstairs.
"Yes, Luke?"

"Can you ride a horse?"

"Yes. Will we be riding tomorrow?"

"Yes. Good night, Abby."

"Good night, Luke."

Luke hoped that renegade wolf didn't get himself caught
in one of those traps Abby had laid today. Because he hadn't
finished stalking Abigail Dayton. Before he was done, he
would figure out a way to capture her—and make her his—
without committing his soul to do it.

5

*Male wolves generally initiate three times the
number of courtship actions as females do.*

Abigail stared with dismay and disgust at the trap she had
so carefully set the previous day. "It's sprung! Just like all
the others. That sneaky, three-toed renegade sprang my
traps. And he didn't leave so much as a hair behind to show
which way he went."

"I'd be willing to bet he lost that fourth toe in a steel
trap," Luke mused, "and learned a hard lesson he hasn't
forgotten."

"Damn his wily hide!"

Abigail stepped down off the bay horse she was riding
and strode over to pick up her leg-hold trap—the last to be
collected. The first trap had been sprung with no other sign
of the renegade than a soft paw track in the dust. The second
trap had likewise been sprung, but had contained a rabbit,
which had been half eaten by the wolf. The jaws of the third
trap had closed on a branch of juniper that had been dragged
across it.

Abigail hadn't really held out much hope that the fourth
trap, the one at the creek, would have caught the wolf, but
she was still disappointed to discover that the cunning renegade had dispatched her efforts as easily here as at the other
three sites.

"Has this ever happened before?" Luke asked.

"Not to me. Not like this. I mean, there have been traps

sprung by the wrong kind of animal, or by a branch falling from a tree, but I've never seen the likes of this. That wolf *deliberately* sprang these traps.''

''What now? Will you set the traps again?'' Luke asked.

''What good would that do?'' Abigail snapped. ''He would just spring them again.'' Abigail knew she shouldn't take out her frustration on Luke. It wasn't his fault the wolf was so smart. She slung the fourth trap into one of the saddlebags on the pack mule Luke led, which held all her supplies and the rest of the traps she'd collected. She wouldn't be needing her tranquilizer gun, or the cage she'd hoped to use on the wolf once it had been captured. Abigail leaned her forehead against the canvas pack and took a deep breath. ''I'm sorry. I'm not usually so short-tempered.''

The truth was, she hadn't gotten much sleep last night. She was tired and therefore cranky. She wanted to blame Luke for that, too, but in all honesty, once she'd left him behind on the stairs, she hadn't heard a peep out of him the rest of the evening. Abigail had lain in bed staring at the ceiling in the dark, wondering what would have happened if she had let him carry her upstairs to his bedroom, which it had turned out was across the hall from hers. Her fantasies had been vivid and uncomfortably sensual.

Abigail had been relieved to see the pale gray light of dawn. She'd dressed quickly and joined Luke for breakfast. He'd suggested they trailer horses and a pack mule up to the edge of the forest, since they could make better time getting to the traps on horseback.

Abigail was grateful now that she'd agreed. It would have been infinitely more frustrating to tramp back down the mountain on foot and empty-handed. ''I've got to get to a phone and call my office in Helena,'' she said.

Luke cocked an inquiring brow.

''I need to arrange to have a helicopter flown down here,

so I can do an aerial survey. If I can find the wolf, I may be able to tranquilize him from the air.''

''That would take some pretty fancy shooting,'' Luke said, standing in the stirrups to stretch his legs.

''I'm a pretty fancy shot,'' Abigail retorted, as she remounted. She was feeling singed by her failure to catch the wolf. She didn't need Luke throwing coals on the fire, questioning her ability.

''If this isn't a renegade,'' Abigail continued, ''if it's actually half of a breeding pair, there might be pups. The den, if there is one, won't be far from water, so I'll start my search along the East Boulder River and follow up along the creeks.''

As they rode back down the mountain, Abigail forced herself to concentrate on the beauty of the day, the sunshine, the piney air and the gorgeous wildflowers. It didn't help. She felt agitated and distraught. Why was she so upset that the wolf had sprung her traps? Of course, there was the concern that she might run out of time to capture the renegade.

But that wasn't really the problem. The truth was, she'd wanted to prove to Luke that she was good at what she did, and she'd been embarrassed by the failure of her best efforts. And anyway, why was it so important to her what Luke Granger thought? Abigail had been assiduously avoiding that question all morning. Because the answer was—

''How did you learn to speak Blackfoot so well?''

Abigail welcomed Luke's interruption with the same relief as a rodeo bronc rider who sees the pickup man coming after the eight-second buzzer sounds. She cleared her throat and said, ''I studied anthropology in college and wrote my senior thesis on the Blackfoot Indians. That's when I learned most of what I know. When Sam and I were assigned to Glacier National Park, I got back in touch with some of the

Blackfeet I'd met while in college and had a chance to practice what I knew.''

"Why become a park ranger when you have a background in anthropology? Why aren't you off somewhere
studying Indian artifacts?''

Luke watched Abigail's eyes take on a wistful look as
she said, "Actually, I was offered a graduate assistantship
to work with a noted anthropologist studying the origin of
the Blackfoot language. I had already decided to accept it
when my parents were killed.''

"So you married Sam Dayton instead of following your
dreams.''

Abigail frowned. "I never gave up my dreams.''

"So why aren't you studying Indian dialects right now,
instead of setting traps?'' Luke asked.

Abigail drew in a sharp breath. "Because there's such a
thing as being practical,'' she replied. "I have to earn a
living.''

"Sam didn't have life insurance?''

"It went to his parents.''

"You said you grew up on a cattle ranch. Didn't your
parents leave you anything?''

"My brother, Price, got the ranch. There wasn't much
else.''

"I didn't know you had a brother.''

Abigail smiled ruefully. "I told you before, there's a lot
you don't know about me.''

"Surely your brother would have been willing to help out
if you'd asked.''

"Price and I never really got along,'' Abigail said.

"I'd have guessed that with such loving parents, you and
your brother would be close.''

"Price was ten years old when I was born. By the time

he was twenty, he'd left home. We never had much to do with each other. By his choice, not mine," Abigail said.

"Yet he got the ranch. That hardly seems fair."

"Nobody said life is fair," Abigail returned. "Besides, Sam and I had other plans."

"You mean, Sam had plans, and you went along because you were married to him," Luke said with an insight that Abigail found frightening.

She heaved a frustrated sigh. "You just don't understand."

"I'd like to," Luke said in a soft voice. "Why don't you explain it to me?"

Abigail met Luke's gaze and found a wealth of warmth and comfort. They had reached a mountain meadow, so they could ride side by side. When Luke reached out a hand to her, it seemed the most natural thing in the world to clasp it.

"I suppose I didn't feel like I was giving up my dreams when I married Sam, because Sam had always been a part of those dreams. Abigail sighed. "Sometimes I wonder how my life might have been different if my parents hadn't died. I mean, I still believe I would have married Sam...eventually. Things don't ever turn out the way you expect, do they?"

Luke didn't answer, but it wasn't a question that called for an answer. They rode in silence for several minutes before he said, "I suppose I was curious about your broken dreams, because I've watched a few dreams of my own bite the dust. I wondered how you handled the disappointment."

"I try to look forward, instead of back," she said quietly. "I try to remember what Sam and I had together and forget everything else."

Abigail watched Luke's lips thin into a bitter line and his

eyes harden before he said, "Some things are hard to forget. Or to forgive."

"Like what?"

"Like your wife telling you in one breath that she's pregnant...and in the next, that she got rid of your child."

Abigail gasped and reined her horse to a stop. Her hand tightened on Luke's as their eyes met—his full of pain, hers full of compassion. The look in his eyes changed, the pain becoming a somber sadness as he accepted the comfort she offered. Then it changed again, to one of need. It felt as though a band constricted her chest, and she couldn't breathe. She started to pull her hand from Luke's, but he reached over and curled an arm around her waist, lifting her out of her saddle and onto his lap.

"Luke, I—"

He cut her off, his mouth seeking hers as though he were a man dying of thirst, and she was life-giving water. It was a kiss of resurrection, of rebirth, of new life. It was a kiss of hope.

Abigail met his touch with willing lips as her hands circled his neck and then slid up into his hair, knocking his hat from his head.

"Abby, Abby," Luke whispered between kisses. "I need you. I need your warmth. I need your touch."

Abruptly Luke stopped kissing her, as though he had suddenly realized what he'd said.

They were both breathing hard, and Abigail felt the sweet ache of desire in her belly and breasts. She was sitting across him in such a way that it was impossible not to know that Luke was also aroused. Yet he had stopped.

"What's wrong?" she asked softly.

Instead of speaking, he kissed her again. This kiss was different from the ones before. It still aroused, it still implored, but there was something missing. Abigail leaned back and searched Luke's face to try and discover what it was he'd given before, that he now withheld. He still wanted her. That much she could see. What was gone was the vulnerability, the *need,* that for a brief time had been naked in his eyes.

"Let me go," she said.

Luke felt the resistance in Abigail's body and searched out her expressive green eyes to see whether she meant what she'd said. Her eyes were troubled and showed no remnants of the desire that had been there only moments before. He let go of her and helped her slide off his horse onto the ground. Before she could remount, he slid his leg over the saddle and landed on the ground beside her. He casually reached down and retrieved his hat from the ground where it had fallen and replaced it on his head, pulling it down low, leaving his face shadowed.

"Would you care to tell me what just happened?" he said.

"I think I could ask the same question of you."

He rested his hands on her hips and brought her flush against him, so she could feel his need. "A moment ago you were willing," he murmured, nudging himself against the soft cradle of her thighs.

"I changed my mind."

"Maybe I can change it again," he said with a coaxing grin.

"Look, Luke," Abigail said in her most reasonable voice. "This isn't a good idea."

His mouth found the soft skin at her throat and nibbled there. "I think it's a very good idea."

"I have work to do," Abigail insisted, valiantly attempting to ignore what he was doing. "A wolf to catch before he eats any more of your sheep."

"He can help himself to dinner on me," Luke said as his lips trailed up the slender length of her neck.

"You don't really mean that," Abigail said in a breathless voice. "Be sensible, Luke."

He caught the lobe of her ear in his teeth and bit it gently.

The blood raced in Abigail's veins. Luke was making it devilishly hard to concentrate on what was important: her job. That was where she had found solace after Sam's death. That was where she would find solace when Luke was gone from her life. She was proud of what she did and how well she did it.

Luke's tongue dipped into her ear.

Abigail moaned deep in her throat, a keening sound of need.

"The grass is soft here," Luke crooned in a husky voice. "We'll have the sun on our skin, the wind caressing our naked bodies. When was the last time you made love with nothing more than the big blue sky above you, Abby?"

When Abigail jerked away with a wounded cry, Luke knew he'd hit a nerve. He took one look at her pale face and said with certainty, "You were with Sam."

When Abigail shuddered, Luke knew he was right. He also knew when he'd run into a wall he couldn't go around, a wall he couldn't go over. Sam Dayton, the wonderful. Sam Dayton, the heroic. He had about had his fill of Sam Dayton, the damned perfect ghost!

"You've got a phone call to make, and I've got business that needs tending. We'd better get going," he said as though it were she, and not he, who'd caused their delay getting down the mountain.

Before Abigail could voice a word to stop him, Luke put his hands on either side of her waist and lifted her back into the saddle. He remounted his chestnut in a smooth vault and kneed the gelding into a fast walk, tugging the pack horse along behind him.

Abigail followed Luke back to where they'd left the horse trailer without another word being spoken between them. She felt like hissing and spitting and clawing. It wasn't her fault Luke kept making passes at her that she didn't welcome.

You didn't enjoy his kisses?

I didn't want him to kiss me.

You didn't answer the question. Did you enjoy his kisses?

Yes.

So what stopped you?

Sam. Memories of Sam.

Maybe it's time to follow your own advice. Look forward, not back.

Abigail sighed so loudly that Luke stopped to stare at her before he shot home the bolt on the horse trailer, locking the three animals inside.

"I'm not going to ask what that was all about," he said. "Just get in the pickup, and let's get out of here."

The silent ride home gave Luke too much time to think. He'd surprised himself back there on the meadow. Where was the Luke Granger who had sworn he was never going to let another woman get under his skin? Hell, a few more minutes and they would both have been lying in the sweet, tall grass, bare-assed naked. And he still didn't have a damned bit of protection with him. He must be out of his mind. Crazy. Crazy with want. Crazy with *need.*

That thought brought him up short. Luke Granger didn't *need* a woman. He'd managed fine without the kind of pain and heartbreak *needing* a woman caused a man. He wasn't about to let this honey-blond, green-eyed seductress lure him into a trap he couldn't escape.

The instant they arrived at Luke's house, Abigail excused herself and headed inside to use the phone in the kitchen.

After Luke had unloaded the animals, he came in through the kitchen door to find Shorty putting away groceries. Abigail stood with her back to him, talking in a low voice on the phone.

"I got them 'necessary' supplies you wanted from the drugstore," Shorty said.

Luke's eyes widened in alarm when he saw what Shorty held in his hand. He gestured wildly for Shorty to hand the item to him.

Shorty held out the box of condoms and looked at it. "You didn't say how many to get," he said. "So I got a couple dozen. Hope that's enough." The twinkle in Shorty's eyes was evidence of his teasing.

During the course of her conversation on the phone, Abigail turned to face Luke, who flushed a dull red, praying that Shorty wouldn't hand the condoms to him while Abigail was watching. There was nothing to be ashamed about in caring enough to take precautions. It reminded him that when he'd been on the mountain with her, the thought of protection, of making sure she didn't get pregnant with his child, had been the last thing on his mind. He wasn't ready to consider what that might mean.

Only now Luke wished he hadn't involved Shorty by asking him to pick up the condoms for him. He could take whatever ribbing the old man gave him, but he didn't want Abigail embarrassed by the situation. He realized now that what had been all right with other women, wasn't all right where Abby was concerned. He wished he'd kept his intentions toward her more private. But Luke had no idea how to cut off Shorty's teasing without apprising Abigail of the problem. He gritted his teeth and prayed.

"I didn't realize these come in so many varieties," Shorty said. "I got an extra box, to make sure I got the right kind."

Shorty pulled another equally large box of condoms out of the paper bag. He held one box in each hand and grinned. "Here you go."

Luke scowled.

Abigail, thinking the look was for her, abruptly turned her back on him.

Luke took quick advantage of the moment, stuffing the two boxes of condoms back into the paper bag from which Shorty had withdrawn them. He chastised Shorty with a sharp look before he grabbed the bag and headed out of the kitchen. "I'll go put these away."

"You just do that," Shorty said with a chortle of glee. "Someplace where they won't be too hard to reach when the time is right."

Luke brushed against Abigail on his way out of the room, and both of them tensed. Luke clutched the bag to his chest and mumbled, "Medicinal supplies. Go in the bathroom upstairs. Always put them away myself to save Shorty the trip."

Abigail's brows rose in confusion.

Shorty guffawed.

Luke glowered ferociously at Shorty before stomping off up the stairs.

When Abigail finished her call she turned to Shorty and asked, "What was that all about?"

"'Spect you'll find out soon enough," he said with a secretive grin. "You gonna get that helicopter you want?"

"Not this afternoon," Abigail said. "Our regular pilot is ferrying somebody else around in another part of the state. He'll be here first thing in the morning."

"You got any plans for the rest of the day?" Shorty asked.

Abigail leaned back against the wall. "I have plans for the evening, but nothing this afternoon."

"What plans?" a voice beside her said.

Abigail turned to find Luke standing in the kitchen doorway. "I thought I'd take a drive tonight and see if I can howl up any wolf pups."

Luke breathed an inner sigh of relief. For a moment there he'd thought maybe she was going to meet someone—a man—in town. The ridiculousness of that possibility hit him a moment later, and he felt chagrined at the jealousy that had provoked such a thought. But she wasn't going anywhere tonight without him.

Luke had heard of howling up wolves, although he'd never tried to do it himself. It involved driving around dark forest roads and stopping at intervals to howl like a wolf. The human wolf howls, even though they weren't authentic, would be enough to set wolf pups to answering. It was the same principle as a town dog howling when it heard a siren. By locating the pups, Abigail would be able to pinpoint the den, and thus, the adult wolf or wolves. Assuming such a den with pups existed.

"If you don't have other plans, maybe you'd like to go with me this afternoon," Luke said.

"Go where?"

"Over to Harry Alistair's place." Luke grinned. "I got a call from Nathan early this morning asking if I could spare some time to help do repairs. I told him I'd get over there today if I could."

Abigail met his grin with one of her own. "I'm sure I could find something to keep me busy, too."

They ate a quick lunch before driving over to the Alistair ranch. The scene that greeted them wasn't exactly what they'd been expecting.

Nathan was bent over a tractor engine near the barn, his

shirt off and a fine sheen of sweat glistening on his broad shoulders. Harry was standing next to him, her fists on her hips, her face set in severe lines.

Abigail and Luke exchanged guilty glances. They were both responsible for Nathan being there. It didn't look like Harry was too happy about the situation.

"Hello, there," Luke said as he and Abigail approached the other couple.

"Hello," Harry muttered through clenched teeth. Her angry eyes remained on Nathan.

Nathan kept his head down and his hands busy. "I ran into a little problem," he said. "The tractor needs some work before I can do anything about that fallow field."

"Anything I can help with?" Luke asked Nathan.

Harry whirled on him, and Luke was stunned by the fierce light in her brown eyes. "You can turn that truck around and drive right back out of here."

"We came to help," Abigail said.

"I don't need your charity," Harry said in an anguished voice. "I don't need—"

Nathan suddenly dropped his wrench on the engine with a clatter and grabbed Harry by the arm, forcing her to face him. "That'll be enough of that!"

"Just who do you think you are?" Harry snarled. "I didn't ask you to come here. I didn't ask you to—"

"I'm doing what a good neighbor should do," Nathan replied.

"Right! Where was all this neighborliness when I had lambs dying because I didn't know how to deliver them? Where was all this friendly help when I really needed it?"

"You need it right now," Nathan bellowed, his grip tightening. "And I intend to give it to you."

"Over my dead body!" Harry shouted back.

"Be reasonable," Nathan said. "You need help."

"I don't need it from you," Harry replied stubbornly.

"Maybe you'd let us help," Abigail said, stepping forward to place a comforting hand on Harry's other arm, wanting to separate the two combatants and not sure how to accomplish it.

Harry's shoulders suddenly slumped, all the fight going out of her. She bit her quivering lower lip and closed her eyes to hold back the threatening tears. Then her shoulders came up again, and when her eyes opened, they focused on Nathan Hazard, flashing with defiance. "I want you off my property, Nathan Hazard. Now. I…" Her voice caught in an angry sob, but her jaw stiffened and she finished, "I have things to do inside. I expect you can see yourself off my land." Harry turned and marched toward the tiny log house without a single look back to see if he had obeyed her command.

Abigail shot a condemnatory look at Nathan. "I think I'll go see if there's anything I can do in the house to *help*." She pivoted and headed for the log house after Harry.

"What the hell happened here?" Luke demanded of his friend. "I asked you to come see the woman to help her out, not to make her mad…or cause her pain."

Nathan turned away from Luke and bent over the tractor engine searching for the lost wrench, which he quickly found. "She doesn't want my help," he said, tightening a bolt that was already as tight as it was ever going to be.

"There's such a thing as tact," Luke said dryly. "You don't have to force help down her throat."

"I don't think she'll take it any other way," Nathan said, his eyes bleak. He turned and leaned a hip against the tractor, wiping his greasy hands on what had once been a clean blue chambray shirt. "I don't understand that woman at all," he complained to Luke. "All I did was tell her a few things she was doing wrong and—"

"You did what?"

"I just told her..." Nathan stopped scrubbing at his hand with the shirt. "I shouldn't have been so blunt, I suppose..."

"You suppose?" Luke said incredulously.

"Aw, hellfire, Luke. I don't know a damn thing about talking to a woman. Just enough to say please and thank you and hand me my hat, I'll be going now. How was I supposed to know I'd hurt her feelings?"

"I'll agree there's no understanding a woman," Luke said, rubbing the back of his neck, "but surely you could do a better job of hanging on to your temper."

"I don't know about that," Nathan admitted in a raw voice. "Every time I get around that woman my self-control flies out the window. I can't even talk to her without getting into an argument. She's so damned stubborn—"

"And I suppose you're not," Luke interrupted.

"But I'm right, and she's wrong," Nathan protested righteously.

Luke burst out laughing and leaned against the tractor beside his friend. His laughter suddenly died in his throat. He rubbed his eyes with the heels of his hands. "Oh, my friend, I know exactly how you feel."

Nathan raised a speculative brow. "Abigail Dayton?"

He nodded.

"What do I do now?" Nathan asked, truly bewildered.

"Hell if I know," Luke said, shaking his head. He looked toward the house where Abigail had disappeared with Harry. "Maybe you'd better go back to square one and start over."

"I wish I'd never met Harry Alistair," Nathan said vehemently.

Luke opened his mouth to say the same thing about Abigail Dayton and snapped it shut again without speaking. He turned his back on Nathan and stared out over the fallow field they had come here to plow. His life in the past ten years had been a lot like that field.

Then Abby had come along, determined to make him see that love could grow where it had lain dormant for far too long. Luke could feel the slash of new furrows in his heart. Abby had planted seeds there. Luke wasn't sure whether he wanted to nurture them, or let them die. He only knew things weren't the same anymore. Not since Abigail Dayton had come into his life.

"Give it another try," Luke advised Nathan. "Maybe you'll have better luck next time." It was advice that could apply equally well to his own situation. If only he weren't too set in his ways, too damned stubborn, to take it. After all, what did he have to lose?

His heart.

In the past, when things had gone wrong, he'd picked up the broken pieces of his heart and slowly, carefully, put them back together again. What he had left was a fragile organ that couldn't take another break without shattering once and for all. Luke couldn't take the chance. He couldn't endure that kind of pain again. The past had taught him hard lessons, and he'd learned them well. He wasn't about to give any woman, not even Abigail Dayton, the chance to make a suffering fool out of him again.

6

*Once a wolf begins howling, other pack
members show a strong tendency to approach
that animal and join the chorus.*

Abigail turned her face to the night sky, took a deep breath,
and let out a long, loud, ululating sound.

"Aaaaaoooooohhh."

She paused, waiting for a response, then howled again.

"Aaaaoohhooohhhooohh."

Luke felt a chill down his spine. She did a pretty good
imitation of a wolf. "Don't you feel a little silly doing
that?"

Abigail grinned, her teeth showing white in the moon-
light. It was the fourth or fifth stop they'd made, so she'd
already done quite a bit of howling. "It's kind of fun, actually," she said. "You ought to try it."

"I'd feel ridiculous."

"I promise not to laugh."

Luke thought about it for a moment. "If you tell a single
soul I did this, I'll deny it."

"Your secret is safe with me." Abigail crossed her heart
with her finger. "Cross my heart and hope to die."

Luke stared at her warily for another moment, then turned
to stare off into the darkness of the forest. They were standing next to Abigail's truck on the side of a dirt road in the
mountains. He looked both ways for headlights or lights
from a ranch house that would indicate anyone else might

be close enough to hear him if he decided to indulge in this foolishness. He had to be insane to even think about howling at the moon.

He took a deep breath, turned his face to the sky, and produced a low, throaty sound.

"Aaaaaooooooo."

Abigail bit her lips to keep from laughing. He sounded more like a wounded bear than a wolf. "Try again," she urged. "Think of every wolf howl you ever heard on the Late-Late Show. Then relax, and let the sound come out."

"I feel stupid."

"You're doing fine."

Luke shifted his stance uneasily. He felt like a kid again, not a thirty-five-year-old man. He found himself grinning. So, who said an old man like himself couldn't have fun like a kid?

He shook his hands as though he were getting ready for some bulldogging, took several deep breaths, as though he were about to leave the chute on a wild bronc, and cleared his throat as though in preparation for some serious cowboy crooning. Then he turned his face upward until it was bathed in moonlight, opened his mouth and let the sound issue forth.

"Aaaaoohhohhooooohhhh."

Abigail's mouth dropped open in amazement. She held her breath, waiting for the sound to die. "That was wonderful! You sounded just like a wolf. Do it again."

Luke grinned boyishly. "I think I'll stop while I'm ahead."

Abigail laughed. "All right. I'm ready to call it a night, anyway. If there had been any pups around here, they'd have joined us by now. I guess we'd better head back."

"I'm sorry this didn't work," Luke said as he and Abigail turned toward her pickup.

Abigail shrugged. "It was worth a try to howl up some pups. But it looks like you're probably right, and we're looking for a lone wolf. At least you haven't lost any more sheep today."

"Maybe the wolf has moved on. Headed north or south out of the area," Luke said.

"That's always a possibility," Abigail conceded. "It's just as likely this renegade has established a territory around here. I'll have to keep looking until I know for sure."

"Or until your ten days are up," Luke said in quiet voice.

Abigail stopped in her tracks and turned to face him. "I'm grateful for what you're doing, Luke. Not many ranchers would be willing to risk losing stock to save a gray wolf."

He stuck his hand in his back pockets. "My motives aren't quite as generous as you're making them sound."

"Oh?"

"I have to admit the thought of spending time in your company influenced my decision."

"Oh."

"I haven't made any secret of my attraction to you, Abby."

"I'm only here to do a job—"

"And doing it very well. But you know what they say, all work and no play... How would you like to go for a swim?"

"A swim?" Abigail laughed. "It's got to be around fifty degrees tonight."

"More like forty-five. But I know a great place to swim that's not too far off. We could be there in under an hour. What do you say?"

"I don't have a suit."

"You don't need one."

"I beg your pardon?" Abigail asked with an arched brow.

"I'm not suggesting we go skinny-dipping—although I

must say the idea has great appeal,'' Luke said with a roguish grin.

Abigail had to agree, although she was surprised at herself for entertaining such thoughts.

Luke continued, ''I have a friend who'll provide swimsuits at the place I'm suggesting we go.''

''Now I'm intrigued,'' Abigail said. ''You mean you aren't going to spirit me off to a frigid mountain stream?''

''Not hardly. If you grew up in Bozeman, you must have heard of the hot springs at Chico,'' he said.

''I've heard about them, but I've never been there.''

''There's not much to see—a restaurant and bar built around a pool that's filled with water from a natural hot spring, so you can swim all year round. It's all tucked in a little niche in Paradise Valley, south of here.''

Abigail thought of Luke wearing nothing more than a pair of swimming trunks.

Luke imagined Abigail in nothing more than a form-fitting swimsuit.

''I have to admit it sounds like it might be fun,'' Abigail remarked.

Luke put a hand on the small of her back, urging her into her pickup. ''Come on. I'll drive.''

''You realize I'll probably regret this tomorrow,'' Abigail said.

''How so?''

''Dawn comes early when I'm on the job.''

''I won't keep you up too late. Besides, this will relax all those tight muscles you've gotten climbing up and down mountainsides for the past two days.''

It took almost an hour to get to Chico, where Luke quickly found his friend, the chef at the restaurant, and obtained suits for himself and Abby. She barely got a look at the tiny white French-cut swimsuit before Luke showed her into the dressing room to slip it on.

Abigail stared at herself in the mirror of the dressing room. The tank-style swimsuit left absolutely nothing to the imagination. Maybe if she were quick enough she could slip into the water before Luke got a good look. Her skin prickled from the cold the instant she stepped outside into the chilly night air.

"You'd better hurry up and get in," he said.

Luke's appreciative gaze warmed her, and she felt a coiling sensation in her belly. His eyes focused on her breasts, and her nipples hardened into tight buds that strained against the slick fabric.

As quickly as she could, Abigail slipped into the pool, actually sighing aloud in pleasure as the warm water covered her to the shoulders. Steam rose near the surface as the hot water met the cold air.

"This is wonderful," she murmured to Luke as he swam through the water to her side. "It's everything you promised and more."

"I can't believe what you were hiding under that old flannel shirt," Luke said, openly admiring her.

His heated gaze made Abigail's blood simmer. Looking for a way to defuse the situation, she said in a teasing voice, "My, what big eyes you have, Mr. Granger."

For a moment she was afraid Luke wouldn't remember the tale of Little Red Riding Hood and take his cue, but he grinned and promptly replied, "The better to see you with, my dear."

Abigail smiled in response. For the life of her she couldn't remember what came next. So she improvised, "My, what big...hands you have, Mr. Granger."

Luke stalked closer to her through the shallow water. Suddenly he reached out and captured her in his arms. With a smug grin he announced, ''The better to catch you with, my dear.''

Abigail laughed, but it was a decidedly breathless sound. When she saw Luke's eyes were filled with mirth, she felt safe saying, ''My, what a furry chest you have, Mr. Granger.''

She laid her hand on the black curls above his heart. She felt his muscles tense under her fingertips. His lips curled in a sensuous smile that revealed white teeth in the moonlight, reminding Abigail of another of the lines from the fairy tale. In an attempt to get things back to a more humorous vein she said, ''My, what big teeth you have, Mr. Granger.''

There was a long pause. Finally in a very quiet voice he answered, ''The better to bite you with, my dear.''

This time it was Abigail who tensed. She stood perfectly still as Luke slowly lowered his head to her shoulder and grazed her flesh with his teeth. A ripple of pleasure ran down her spine.

Abigail would have given a lot for the appearance of the fairy-tale woodchopper with his ax. Instead, she tore herself from Luke's grasp with a nervous laugh and fled with a strong, splashing kick toward the lighted area at the deep end of the pool. Luke wasn't as likely to try to make love to her there, where they could be plainly seen from the picture windows of the bar. An audience would surely deter his amorous overtures.

Or so she thought.

Abigail was still breathing hard when Luke caught up to her at the far end of the pool. He didn't give her the opportunity to escape him again. One hand slipped around her waist, pulling her up snug against him, so their practically naked bodies were flush, their legs entwined in the warm water, while his other hand reached for the edge of the pool to keep them afloat. He nudged her up against the tile wall and held her there with the length of his body, putting one hand on either side of her on the edge of the pool, effectively trapping her there.

Abigail gasped. "Luke. There are people watching. We can't—"

He cut her off with a kiss, his lips claiming hers with an urgency that she quickly matched, her hands slipping around his neck to pull him close. His hips pressed against hers, and she could feel his arousal. She ended the kiss, leaning her head against his shoulder, trying to get her rioting senses back under control.

"I don't usually do this with an audience," she said.

"Me, neither," he answered with a crooked grin. Under the water, out of sight, one of his hands slid slowly upward along her ribs until he finally cupped her breast, the budding tip pressing against the palm of his hand.

Abigail didn't want the pleasure to end. But she knew that any minute someone might come out onto the pool area from the bar and see them. That thought made her put her hand atop his. "Luke, you have to stop. Someone might see us. Someone will—"

"No one can see what I'm doing, Abby. Just keep talking and—"

A masculine voice jolted them when it spoke practically beside them. "Hey, Luke. I thought that was you."

Luke pulled Abigail closer, hiding the state of their joint arousal from the sight of the intruder. "Hello, Nathan. Fancy meeting you here."

Abigail hid her face against Luke's chest. She heard the frustration in Luke's voice, but silently blessed Nathan Hazard for the timely interruption. To her chagrin, she'd been all too easily ensnared by the sexual lure Luke had thrown out to her.

"Who's that with you?" Nathan asked.

There was a brief hesitation before Luke said, "It's Abby."

"Abby?"

"Abigail Dayton," Luke bit out.

"From Fish and Wildlife?" Nathan asked, astonished.

"Yes, Nathan," Abigail said, realizing there was no sense hiding her head like an ostrich in the sand. She turned to face him. "It's me. Luke and I are relaxing a few tired muscles."

Nathan grinned. "Yeah. Sure."

A female voice called from the doorway. "Nathan?"

Luke turned to look, but the light was behind the woman, her face invisible in the shadows. She was wearing an off-the-shoulder dress with a skirt made of some filmy kind of material. The light behind her showed off a fantastic figure and a dynamite pair of legs. He turned back to his friend. "Who's that with you?"

"Uh..."

The woman stepped out into the pool area and made her way over to them. "Nathan, is it Luke? Oh, hello. It is you. Nathan thought he recognized you."

It was Luke's turn to stare. "Harry?"

Harriet Alistair smiled. "Nathan tried to convince me to take a swim, but I was too chicken. How's the water?" she asked Abigail.

"Marvelous," Abigail replied. She was stunned to see Harry and Nathan together, all animosity between them apparently forgotten. She was afraid to ask them how they'd solved their differences for fear of raising an issue that might put them at each other's throats again.

Luke was not so subtle. "I thought you two hated each other's guts."

Nathan stuck a hand in the trouser pocket of his Western suit pants. "Uh. We called a truce for tonight."

"Just for tonight?" Abigail inquired.

"Nathan promised me a dinner of the best rack of lamb in two counties. I was willing to forego killing him for the pleasure," Harry said, throwing a quick smile in Nathan's direction.

"Why don't you two dry off and join us for a drink?" Nathan invited.

Luke glanced longingly at Abigail. It was obvious the other couple wasn't going to leave them alone. He was tempted to excuse himself and Abby and retreat to the privacy of the truck. But he had a feeling he wouldn't find the same Abby waiting for him once she was wearing jeans and a flannel shirt again.

He dreaded the thought of spending the next hour sitting on the opposite side of the truck from her, smelling her, feeling her presence, seeing her soft, smooth skin, and knowing all the time that when they arrived home they would most likely retire to their separate beds. They might as well stay and have a drink with Harry and Nathan. The later he and Abby started home, the more tired he would be when they got there, and the better he would sleep—if he ever fell asleep with her just across the hall.

"Fine," Luke said at last. He gave Nathan a penetrating stare, and his friend picked up on Luke's hint.

"Why don't we go inside and wait for Luke and Abby," he said, taking Harry's arm and leading her back toward the bar.

"We'll join you soon," Abigail promised. She turned back to Luke and said, "This seems to be a pretty popular spot for seduction. Do you come here often?"

Luke paused so long before answering, that Abigail decided she didn't want to hear his answer. "It doesn't matter. I—"

"Wait, Abby." Luke caught her before she could swim away. "I've never been here to swim with another woman. I don't know why. I just—I guess I never thought it would be much fun. But with you, after what we did tonight...I mean the howling and all...I imagined being here with you would be exciting, exhilarating. And it was."

His hand stroked across her bare shoulder. He grasped her nape and pulled her toward him. His mouth lowered to cover hers briefly, tantalizingly. "Ah, Abby. Everything is exciting with you."

Abigail shivered, despite the heat of the water. She stared up into Luke's desire-darkened eyes, knowing that if she didn't get away soon, she would be lost. She was in danger of losing her heart to a man who had no heart to give in return. She turned and swam quickly to the ladder and climbed out of the pool.

Luke watched her leave, wondering how he'd ever let things go so far. What was happening to him? When had he ever acted so silly with a woman and enjoyed himself so much? When had he ever had so much fun with a woman who excited and tantalized him at the same time?

Abigail Dayton wasn't like the other women he'd known. But he was afraid to trust what he'd found with her. It was too good to be true. There had to be a catch somewhere. So they'd done a little howling at the moon together. So what? That was no reason to let down barriers that had been up for longer than he could remember.

"You still in the water?" Nathan growled.

"What are you doing back out here? Where's Harry?"

Nathan slumped into one of the wrought-iron chairs beside the pool. "She went home."

Luke levered himself out of the pool, grabbed the towel

he'd left on a chair and began to dry off. "What the hell happened?"

"That fool woman is so thin-skinned—"

"What exactly did you say to her?"

"What could possibly be wrong with telling a woman she's attractive?" Nathan demanded.

"That's all you said? That she's an attractive woman?"

"I may have said something about her working too hard, because her hands were a little callused for a lady," Nathan admitted.

"What else?"

Nathan chewed on his lower lip in concentration. "I might have mentioned she shouldn't spend so much time in the sun, because her nose was freckled like a kid's."

"Anything else?" Luke asked dryly.

"I said she ought to sell her place to me and get back to being a woman."

Luke groaned.

"What was wrong with that?" Nathan asked belligerently.

Luke laughed and shook his head in disbelief. "If you don't know, Nathan, I don't think I can explain it to you."

"You can laugh at me all you want, so long as you give me a ride home."

"A ride?"

"The damned woman took my car when she left," Nathan grumbled.

Luke's laughter died. He couldn't very well leave Nathan stranded an hour's drive from home. But he'd looked forward to having Abigail to himself.

At that moment Abigail showed up dressed in her jeans and flannel shirt, her wet hair brushed back from her face. She looked so fresh and clean Luke wanted to put his cheek to hers and hold her close. He was suddenly very grateful for Nathan's presence.

There was something about Abigail Dayton that kept sneaking past defenses he'd kept strong for the past ten years. He would have to keep a careful watch on his feelings when he was around her, to make sure she didn't get past his guard. That way lay more trouble than he was willing to risk.

"Hi, Nathan. Luke. Where's Harry?" Abigail asked.

"She left," Nathan said flatly.

"Oh?"

"We're going to give Nathan a ride home," Luke said.

"Oh."

"Do you two still want to stay for a drink?" Nathan asked.

"I don't," Abigail said. "Do you, Luke?"

"No. We might as well head home."

Abigail was grateful for Nathan's presence in the pickup. Having a third person in the cab broke the tension between her and Luke. The more she talked to Nathan, the better she liked him. She wanted to ask him what had happened between him and Harry Alistair, but discretion kept her silent. She sincerely hoped he and Harry would work out their differences.

By the time they dropped Nathan off, Abigail was having a hard time keeping her eyes open. She leaned her head back against the leather seat, and against her will, her mind drifted back to her time in the pool with Luke. The touch of his hand, the taste of his mouth, the hard feel of his body against the softness of hers. Abigail turned her head to study Luke.

"See anything you like?"

"I like everything I see," she said. "I had a lovely time, Luke. Thank you for taking me."

Luke pulled the truck to a stop in front of his ranch house. "It was my pleasure, Abby."

Luke knew he should get out of the truck immediately, but he liked the way she was looking at him. He liked the way her low, sultry voice sounded in his ears. He liked Abigail Dayton way too much. He leaned over and pressed his lips to hers.

Abigail was expecting the kiss, and yet she was still surprised by the thrill she experienced at the firm touch of his mouth and the gentle caress that followed as his lips brushed hers. She kissed him back, capturing his lower lip in her teeth and nibbling gently, then letting her tongue trace the edge of his mouth. She felt the tension building, the need, the want.

And the fear that kept her from giving more.

Luke had never been kissed like this by a woman, with such restraint, when he was sure she wanted more, needed more. He wanted what she withheld. He wanted all of her. His mouth came seeking again, his tongue came searching, for what, he wasn't even sure.

Abruptly Abigail sat up, tearing her mouth from Luke's. "I have to go inside." She shoved open the door to the pickup and headed quickly toward the ranch house, with Luke on her heels.

"Abby."

The call of his voice sent her scurrying. She reached the back door to Luke's house and shoved it open. It was warm and welcoming inside, but she didn't stop to enjoy the atmosphere, just fled up the stairs two at a time toward the second floor and the safety of her room.

Luke caught her in the upstairs hallway and enfolded her in his embrace. Abigail didn't fight him, just dropped her forehead to his chest and waited for him to speak.

"Why are you running from me?" he asked in a ragged voice.

"I don't want to feel the things you make me feel, Luke. I don't want to leave a part of myself here when I go."

Luke didn't know what to say to that.

"Let me go, Luke."

He stepped away, letting his hands fall to his sides. "You have to live for today, Abby," he said. "We may not have tomorrow."

"That's the big difference between us," Abigail said. "You can't imagine a relationship with tomorrows. I can't imagine a relationship without them."

Abigail left Luke standing in the hall and closed the door to her bedroom firmly behind her. The differences between them were too great. He was like the renegade she sought, an independent creature, destined to travel the paths of life alone.

She needed more from a man. She wanted what she'd had with Sam. Luke could never give her that, so she had to stay away from him. Her very life depended on it.

7

*When stalking, the wolf sneaks as close
to the prey as it can without making it flee.*

Sometime during a sleepless night, Abigail made up her mind to keep Luke at a stiff arm's length from now on. She'd enjoyed herself the previous evening much too much. It would be dangerous to let things progress to their natural conclusion. Abigail shivered at the thought of her naked skin pressed close to Luke's, of his hands on her breasts and belly.

In the past, Sam's face had intruded on such thoughts, saving her from folly. All she saw now were Luke's gray eyes, burning with desire for her.

Abigail smelled bacon cooking as she descended the stairs for breakfast. Surprisingly her appetite didn't seem to have suffered. She was starving. She dropped a large collection of gear in the living room before she headed for the kitchen.

"You look bright-eyed and bushy-tailed this morning, Miss Abigail," Shorty greeted her. "Have a seat, and I'll pour you some coffee. Bacon's ready, just need to drop some bread in the batter, and French toast is coming right up."

"Where's Luke?"

Shorty gave Abigail a speculative look as he handed her a mug of coal-black coffee. "He's up and gone."

"Gone?" Abigail felt bereft and grimaced at her fickle feelings.

"Said he'd be back 'fore you was to leave, and not to worry."

"I wasn't worried," she said too quickly, confirming for Shorty that she had been.

"Heard Luke whistling this morning," Shorty commented.

"Oh?"

"Don't whistle less'n he's happy. You must be good for him."

"Don't look for what isn't there, Shorty," Abigail warned, pouring maple syrup onto the golden French toast the old man had set in front of her.

Shorty served up a plate of French toast for himself and sat down at the table across from Abigail. "You denying you're attracted to Luke?"

Abigail fidgeted nervously with her fork. "That's none of your business."

"I don't want Luke hurt," Shorty said, his gaze intent on the French toast he was cutting up. "Luke's wife dragged him up, down and sideways over the years they was married. Didn't think he'd ever let himself care for another woman."

The implication Abigail heard was that Luke cared for her. But Shorty was wrong. That was the whole problem, as she saw it. Luke wasn't about to let himself care for a woman...any woman. The best way to protect herself from getting hurt was to stay away from him. "I think you're mistaken about Luke's feelings," she said.

Shorty looked up, his solemn eyes intent on her. "Don't hardly think so."

They were interrupted by the sound of the front door opening. "What's all this stuff?" Luke called from the living room.

Abigail was about to yell a reply when Luke arrived at

the doorway to the kitchen and said, "You have enough stuff in here to survive a month of Sundays in the wild."

Shorty retrieved a plate of French toast that he'd kept warm in the oven and said to Luke, "Sit down and eat."

Luke wasn't the least bit hungry, but he did as he was told, his eyes never leaving Abigail's face. She was beautiful. Funny how he hadn't noticed that when he first met her. He smiled inwardly. Even funnier how he hadn't thought she was his type. He wanted her more than any other woman he'd ever known. Luke knew he'd better get his mind off Abigail or he'd end up having to keep his napkin on his lap after he got up from the table.

"Are you planning to haul all that gear with you in the helicopter?" he asked.

"If I sight the wolf and can't get him with the tranquilizer gun, I plan to have the copter pilot set me down as close to the wolf as possible, so I can track him on foot."

"Hope you packed some warm clothes. Weather report says there might be snow," Luke said.

"I've got everything I need," Abigail replied. "You don't have to worry about me."

"It's my old bones I'm thinking about," Luke said with a grin. "I'd better go pack some long johns."

"There's no need for you—"

He was out of the kitchen and up the stairs before Abigail had a chance to voice her objection. How could she feel threatened by a man who grinned like that? But she did. The grin was a tiny facet of the charming man who was urging her to succumb to his desires. Abigail simply had to resist that charm.

"He's a good man to have along on a hunt," Shorty said as he cleared the table.

"Except he seems more interested in hunting a two-legged species than in tracking the wolf," Abigail muttered.

She heard the distant whir of the helicopter and rose to carry her plate to the sink.

"You 'member what I said," Shorty reminded as he took the plate out of her hands. "You take care of that boy. He's got a patched-up heart inside that big chest of his, make no mistake about it."

Abigail sighed. "You don't play fair, Shorty."

Shorty chortled. "Ain't fair to get as old as I am, either. But it sure beats my other choice all to heck."

That made Abigail laugh, and she kissed the old man on his weathered cheek. "I've got to go. You take care of yourself. Don't worry about me." Then, because she'd been affected by what he'd said, amended, "Us. Don't worry about us." She kissed him quickly on the other cheek and hurried out of the room.

Shorty concentrated on the sudsy dishwater, as though the two bright pink spots on his cheeks didn't exist. That sweet woman was going to make Luke a good wife. If he knew Luke, wolf or no wolf, it would all be decided before they came down out of those mountains.

Abigail ran smack into a broad chest at the kitchen door, and Luke's arms wrapped around her to keep her from falling. There they were, breast to breast, with the sun barely up in the sky. So much for keeping Luke at arm's length, Abigail thought as a shiver skittered down her spine. She stared up into Luke's face and watched a smile form, revealing the attractive dimple in his cheek. Lord, the man positively reeked with charm.

"The helicopter's here," Abigail said. "We have to go."

"I heard it," Luke answered. But he didn't release her.

Abigail pushed against his chest, seeking freedom. "It's time to go, Luke."

It was the fear in her voice, rather than what she said or did, that made Luke drop his arms and step back, allowing

Abigail through the doorway. She hurried past him and began to gather up equipment in the living room. He crossed
his arms over his chest and leaned back against the frame
of the doorway, watching her. She was moving quickly, ef-
ficiently, but make no mistake about it, she wanted out of
his house. And away from him.

Well, he wasn't going to let her get away. He would give
her a little space, if that was what she needed. But they were
going to be together, sooner or later. He didn't mind waiting
a little while. She could run as much as she wanted, but he
would follow. Eventually she would discover, and accept,
that there was no escape.

"Hi, Geoff," Abigail greeted the copter pilot. The door
had been taken off on the passenger's side. A web rope
across the opening and a belt around her waist were all that
would keep her from falling when she leaned out the door
to use her tranquilizer gun. The lack of restraint had frightened her the first few times she'd gone up. Actually, it
frightened her every time. But it was part of her job, so she
suffered through it.

Luke had his own misgivings about the danger involved
in what Abby was about to do, but he took his cue from
her. She seemed confident she could handle the situation.
He wasn't about to let her see his fear for her.

She started to lift her bags through the open space where
there should have been a door, into the back of the copter,
but Luke took them from her and did it himself. He helped
her into the seat next to the pilot, then lifted his own things
inside and settled himself into the seat behind her. A moment later they were in the air and wearing radio headsets
so they could talk to one another.

Almost immediately, Abigail turned back to Luke to point
out a large herd of mule deer grazing on his land alongside

his sheep and realized that among the gear stacked beside him was a hunting rifle. "Why did you bring that gun?"

Luke unbuckled his seat belt and sat forward as he answered her. "There are other dangers in the mountains besides wolves, Abby. We may need it."

She didn't agree, but she didn't argue. Instead, she turned back around and directed Geoff where she wanted him to go, using a grid map on which she'd sectioned off the areas around the confirmed wolf kill.

Geoff angled the helicopter sharply as he banked for a turn, and one of Luke's bags started to fall out through the open space on Abigail's side. Luke took one look at the disappearing bag and realized the *condoms* were in there.

Abigail was startled when she saw the bag sliding toward the copter doorway. Before she could react, Luke made a death-defying grab for the bag and only caught it when half his body was hanging out of the copter. Her heart leapt to her throat when it seemed he was going to fall out.

Geoff saw what was happening and banked the opposite way. With corded muscles rippling in his back and shoulders, Luke made a superhuman effort to pull himself back inside the copter. An instant later it was all over. Luke was safe in his seat, the bag clasped to his side.

Abigail was furious. "You could have been killed!" she yelled. "What's in that bag that makes it worth dying for?"

Luke couldn't help the grin that split his face. "Medical supplies," he shouted back. "*Necessary* medical supplies."

When Luke laughed, Abigail realized the man had thoroughly enjoyed every second of danger. It was a good thing she didn't love him. The woman who did was in for a lifetime of such hair-raising adventures. Abigail envied her every moment of it.

She turned back around in her seat and concentrated on looking for the wolf, which was, after all, the reason she'd come here in the first place. A few minutes later, Abigail saw the remains of a half-eaten deer. She leaned back and spoke to Luke. "Looks like this renegade likes deer better than he does sheep."

"Let's hope so," Luke replied.

They'd been in the air over an hour when Abigail sighted the wolf. "There he is!" Although her voice was excited, she kept her actions calm. She'd spent most of the trip with the tranquilizer gun in her lap, loaded and ready for action, knowing she might have to act fast.

They knew when the wolf felt threatened, because it began to run. Ordinarily there were enough treeless spaces, firebreaks and meadows, that Abigail would be able to tranquilize a wolf as it ran across an open area. Unfortunately this renegade stayed in the low brush, never giving her a clean shot.

"He's done this before," Luke murmured.

"What?" Abigail said distractedly.

"Look at him," Luke said, his voice full of admiration. "He knows we're trying to get him to bolt into the open. And he isn't going to do it. Abby, that is one smart wolf."

"He's going to be one smart *dead* wolf, if I can't reach him. Animal Damage Control won't need to get close to put a bullet in him."

"We'll catch him, Abby," Luke reassured her, laying a hand on her shoulder. "It just doesn't look like he's going to make it easy for us."

It was amazing how comforting Abigail found the touch of Luke's hand. Such a little thing. In that instant the feelings of loneliness she'd endured since Sam's death vanished. Abigail felt almost sick when she realized what that must mean. It wasn't smart to care so much for a man who wouldn't care for her. She jerked away from his touch, making sure he knew she wanted free of him.

Luke was confused by her rejection. And, though he would never have admitted it, he was also hurt.

Abigail was immediately sorry for overreacting but was saved from destroying whatever she'd accomplished by pulling away, when Luke settled back into his seat.

They followed the wolf long enough to be sure he wasn't going to break into the open. Finally Abigail said to Geoff, "Look for a meadow, someplace open where you can get the copter down. I'll have to track this wolf on foot. Tell my office I'll be out of touch until I catch him."

Soon after that, Luke and Abigail were waving Geoff off and distributing between themselves the supplies Abigail had brought.

"I'll carry that," Luke said, when Abigail put the two-man dome tent in her pack.

She started to argue but merely shrugged and let him have it. He was bigger and stronger. He could carry more. They were both toting heavy loads when everything was divided, but Abigail was used to it. "We'll head toward the last sighting and pick up the trail there."

Luke didn't question the way Abigail took the lead. He found himself admiring her determination as much as he admired the wiliness of the wolf that eluded her. It would be interesting to observe Abigail's tactics with the wolf. He was bound to learn something about capturing an elusive spirit that might be useful to him in his pursuit of Abby.

Abigail shivered as a blast of Arctic air hit the sweat on the back of her neck. The weather was already turning frigid, a forerunner of the promised snow. "I don't think the snow will be entirely a bad thing," she remarked. "It'll certainly make tracking the wolf easier."

Luke smiled wryly. It would take quite an optimist to find something good about being on foot in the mountains with a storm threatening. The lowering gray storm clouds were considerably worse by the time he suggested they think about setting up a camp.

Abigail shook her head no. Panting with the uphill climb, she replied, "The wolf will look for a place to sit this out. I'd like to find him before he goes to ground."

Luke saw it first, a gray shadow in the undergrowth. "Abby," he whispered.

She followed his pointing finger and found what she'd been searching for—a gray wolf. He was magnificent, nearly six feet from the tip of his nose to the tip of his tail and about a hundred pounds, Abby estimated. The wolf's pelt was a light gray, with darker fur along the center of his back and tail. His legs, ears and muzzle were tawny.

Despite the fact wolves rarely threatened humans, Abigail hadn't forgotten that a wolf's fangs could be more than two inches in length, and its powerful bite was capable of ripping through four inches of moose hide and hair, or snapping off the tail of a full-grown steer as cleanly as a knife. Abby hadn't realized she was holding her breath until she released it in a rush.

She slowly eased her pack down off her shoulders and took the tranquilizer gun in both hands, sighting down the scope. In that instant, the wolf lifted its head.

"He knows we're here," Luke said in a quiet voice.

"One...more...second...." Abigail squeezed gently on the trigger.

The wolf bolted the instant she fired. A second later he'd disappeared into the forest.

"Missed! Damn it, I missed!" Abigail was furious with herself. The hunt would be all over now if only she'd hit what she'd aimed at.

"He was already spooked," Luke said. "You didn't have much of a shot before he ran."

"But I did have a shot," Abigail said. "And I missed."

"Every hunter misses now and then."

"I don't. Not very often, anyway," she conceded. "Now that he's running we probably won't get another chance at him before the storm hits." Her grip tightened on the gun. "I couldn't afford to miss."

"No sense crying over spilled milk," Luke said practically.

Abigail tried to hang on to her anger. As long as she was angry she could refuse the much-needed comfort Luke was offering. Instead of answering him, she loaded up her pack and marched off after the wolf.

Luke shook his head at Abby's contrariness as he followed in her footsteps. "Have you always been this hard on yourself?" he asked as they headed farther up the mountain.

It would be completely churlish, almost childish, not to answer him. She dropped back to walk beside Luke and admitted, "Ever since I was a little girl I've always wanted to be the best at whatever I did."

"And were you?"

"Yes." When he arched a disbelieving brow she amended, "At least, enough of the time that I got to be pretty sure of succeeding no matter what I tried to do."

"Maybe I should be asking if you ever failed at anything," Luke said with a wry twist of his mouth.

Abigail kept her face carefully blank as she said, "A few things." She hadn't been able to keep the people she loved from dying. First her mother and father. Then Sam.

To avoid having to elaborate, she asked, "How about you? Apparently you've been a pretty successful sheep rancher. Was there ever anything you really wanted that you didn't manage to get for yourself?"

"I have to admit, I usually get what I go after, too," Luke answered, catching her gaze and refusing to release it.

Abigail felt the threat, but was helpless to escape it.

Luke felt himself sinking into a bottomless well of emotion. He hadn't felt these feelings for years—if ever—and he didn't want to feel them now. The urge was there to say more to her, to admit that he hadn't been entirely truthful. He hadn't always gotten everything he'd wanted. He hadn't been very good at getting a woman to love him. Not his mother. Not his wife. Not any of the women he had known.

Without realizing it, they'd both stopped walking. Luke probed Abigail's eyes, as though he might find evidence of what lay in her heart. Here was a woman he thought might offer him the love he'd always wanted—if he gave her the chance.

But that didn't seem like such a smart thing to do. What if he was wrong? What if she was just like all the others? It was safer to take what he could get. They could share some good times together. When she was gone there would be others. There always were.

Abigail saw the kiss coming. She wanted it. Her body trembled in expectation. But she mustn't allow it to happen. She ducked her head as his mouth reached hers and headed away at a quick pace.

"We'd better keep moving," she said. "Once the snow starts falling we'll have to stop for the day. I want to cover as much ground as I can before then."

The next couple of hours were spent climbing in rugged terrain. Abigail followed the trail left by the wolf, which cut across the East Boulder River, ever closer to the summer pastures where Luke's sheep grazed. Luke moved with her like a shadow. She was aware that a virile male was stalking her, even as she stalked the wolf.

Luke's eyes rested often on Abigail, and whenever she looked over her shoulder to see if he followed, he made a point of letting her know he was there, watching, waiting

for the opportunity to take what she'd avoided giving earlier.
She would be his before the night was done.

Late in the afternoon, snow began falling in large, beautiful flakes that made the forest look like a winter wonder-
land.

Abigail stopped and stuck out her tongue to catch several
flakes. "Umm. They're cold."

Luke watched as snowflakes gathered on her eyelashes
and drifted across her cheeks. He wanted to kiss them off.
As he closed the distance between them, her head jerked
upright, and she stared warily at him. He fought to control
the need, the desire to touch her. He didn't want to frighten
her away. Take it one step at a time, he told himself. One
small step at a time.

It was a magical snowfall. Slowly and silently the soft
white powder blanketed the earth. Before long, Abigail was
forced to concede that they weren't going to catch up to the
wolf. "We might as well quit for the day," she said. "I
saw a spot a few minutes back that might be a good place
to camp."

"If you don't mind hiking another five minutes, there's a
hunting cabin where we can spend the night," Luke said.

"With real beds?" Abigail said, her eyes lighting.

"A real bed and a couple of chairs in front of a woodstove," he replied with a smile.

"I'm sorry you had to haul that tent all day for nothing,
but a roof and a stove sounds great to me. Lead on."

Night came swiftly in the mountains. By the time they
arrived at the cabin, there was barely light to see.

"How charming!" Abigail said when she spotted the tiny
A-frame cabin. She was even more pleased when she
stepped inside. "Why, it's lovely. You didn't tell me it was
so nice," she said. "You even have running water!"

"It's a private getaway. A place where I can come to be by myself and think," Luke confessed.

Abigail looked around the cabin, with its rustic wooden bed and table and chairs, a black woodstove along one wall and a kitchen area along another. A tiny niche she saw held a bathroom with indoor plumbing—wonder of wonders! The cabin had everything needed for comfort in a single room. The curtains and the bedspreads were all a masculine red-and-black plaid. There was a bearskin beside the double bed. The wooden chairs in front of the stove faced a window through which it was still possible to see snow falling in the last rays of evening light.

"I can't believe this," Abigail said, shaking her head with astonishment. "If I had a place like this, I'd never leave it."

"If I had a woman like you to share it with me, I'd have no cause to leave it, either."

Abigail lowered her eyes to hide her reaction to Luke's comment. She didn't want to be tempted. And being alone with Luke in this place was all too tempting.

Luke was startled by what he'd said, but realized it was the truth. Abigail filled a void he hadn't known existed. He had her in his lair. What was he going to do about it?

"Abigail," Luke said softly. "Come here."

8

*The stage of the hunt that immediately
follows the stalk is the encounter. This is the point
at which prey and predator confront each other.*

"I don't think that's a very good idea," Abigail said in a shaky voice.

"What are you afraid of, Abby? I won't bite," Luke teased.

"I might," Abigail snapped back.

Luke eyed her as a predator might its prey. He could see that Abigail felt the tension, too. The need. It was there, shimmering between them. He could wait. They needed time to rest and to satisfy their physical hunger. Then they could concentrate on the desire that arced between them. He was already aroused just looking at her, anticipating what was to come. It was a sweet ache and one which he hoped Abby would assuage before the night was done.

"We might as well get settled in before it gets any darker. I'll take care of the fire, if you'll handle dinner," Luke said.

Abigail was immediately suspicious. Luke was acting as though he hadn't just made a pass at her. He *had* made one, hadn't he? It hadn't been her imagination, had it? Oh, he was clever all right, pretending like he wasn't watching, like he'd given up the thought of touching her, tasting her, thrusting himself deep inside her. Abigail knew better. She wasn't about to let down her guard.

Luke laid a fire in the woodstove while Abigail fixed a

pot of coffee. They both chose cold rations she'd brought along rather than having to cook and wash dishes.

Abigail moved warily around Luke, keeping her distance. But it wasn't a large cabin, and they kept brushing against each other. Every time they did, Abigail felt a frisson of excitement that left her wanting. Luke teased, he taunted, with the barest of touches, never enough that she could say, "Stop that," but enough to make her conscious of him, of what was to come.

At last they sat before the woodstove sipping a second cup of coffee. Abigail had her feet tucked up under her, almost relaxed, when Luke asked, "Did you ever do this with Sam?"

"Do what?" she asked.

"Spend the night together alone in the forest."

Abigail chose to make a joke of what he'd said, because to treat it seriously was too unsettling. "Sam and I spent a lot of time together in the forest," she said with a forced laugh. "After all, we were forest rangers."

"That's not what I meant."

"Maybe what you meant is none of your business," Abigail said.

"I'm making it my business," Luke replied, never taking his eyes off hers.

Abigail was feeling trapped again. She didn't understand why he was so interested in her relationship with Sam. She found it painful to dredge up those memories. But Luke's forceful gaze demanded it.

She took a deep breath and said, "Sam and I often camped together in the forest, usually in a tent. We both loved the sight of the stars and moon overhead when we...made love. Is that what you wanted to hear?"

It was what he'd expected—another eulogy to the memory of a perfect man. How could he possibly compete? Luke set his coffee cup on the small table beside his chair, threaded his hands together and leaned forward with his arms on his thighs. "I'm only a flesh-and-blood man, Abby, with all the faults and foibles we humans possess. I'm not perfect like Sam. But I want you. I want to share whatever the night brings with you."

The fact that Abigail was tempted to take him up on his offer left her shaken and defensive. "Sam had a heart. Sam was capable of loving. That's what made being with him special. I'm not willing to settle for less."

"I have a—" Luke clamped his teeth. He didn't have to prove anything to her. But he wasn't willing to back down, either. "The truth is, that it's much safer to put yourself in the grave with Sam than to keep on living, isn't that it, Abby?"

Abigail's face paled. She carefully set her coffee cup on the table between them, to avoid the urge to throw it in his face. She struggled at the same time to get to her feet. "How dare you!"

She didn't know she was going to hit him until her hand had already streaked out. Luke rose and caught her wrist the instant before her palm reached his face. He pulled her around the table to confront him.

"Too close to the truth for comfort, Abby?" he said quietly. "You've put Sam on a pedestal and kept him there rather than let another man get close. Why is that, Abby?"

He caught her chin, so she had no choice except to meet his gaze. His eyes demanded the truth from her. "What's really holding you back, Abby?"

"I'm scared," she said at last. "I'm scared." Abigail had never acknowledged her fear to anyone in words—not even to herself. Admitting to Luke that she was afraid made her feel tremendously vulnerable.

Luke drew Abby into his arms. Her head rested on his

shoulder as her body shuddered to contain sobs she refused to set free. "You don't have to be scared, Abby. I'm here. I won't let anything bad happen to you."

She clutched fistfuls of his shirt and said, "You don't understand. I don't want to love any man ever again—and lose him. I don't want to go through that kind of pain again. I couldn't bear it. Now do you understand?"

"I understand, Abby. I do." Luke held her in his arms, offering comfort, but she was inconsolable. "I'm not going to die, Abby," he murmured. "Not for a good long while, anyway." He was kissing her cheeks, her eyes, her forehead, caressing her back and shoulders with his hands.

"It's happened before," she said. "It could happen again." She tried to escape his embrace, to escape the pain and fear, but he wouldn't let her go.

"Are you telling me that I matter to you, Abby?"

"Oh, Luke."

He saw her answer in her eyes. At that moment, something happened inside him. The wall that had encased his heart crumbled, leaving him as vulnerable as the woman he held in his arms.

When Luke reached for the snap on Abby's jeans, her hand was there to stop him. He never took his eyes off her face, just moved her hand aside. Slowly, surely, he unsnapped her jeans and then unzipped them, pushing the material away so he could slide his hand down inside and cup the heart of her.

Abigail felt the heat pooling between her thighs. When her legs would no longer support her, she raised her arms to encircle Luke's neck.

"Luke," she whispered.

"What?"

She didn't say anything, simply began unsnapping his shirt, one pearl button at a time. She pulled the shirt out of his jeans along with the long johns underneath, exposing a chest full of black curls.

Luke hissed in a breath of air when she rubbed her cheek against his chest and gasped when she found a nipple with her teeth. An instant later he heard the snap on his jeans and watched as Abby's eyes were drawn to the line of dark, downy hair that ran from his navel downward.

Luke withdrew his hand and lifted her onto the thigh he thrust between her legs. His hands cupped her buttocks as he pulled her toward him. The pressure caused Abigail to groan.

Luke leaned his cheek against hers, and Abigail felt the harsh rasp of a day's growth of beard. She wanted this. She wanted him. But there were things that had to be considered before they allowed themselves to go any further.

"Luke, we have to be responsible," Abigail said with more regret than she realized he could hear. "We're out here in the middle of nowhere and, much as I'm tempted, it's better that we don't start something we can't finish. What I mean to say is, I have no more protection now than I had two days ago."

"I do," Luke said.

Abigail swallowed hard. "You do?"

Luke nodded his head toward the bag that had nearly gone out the helicopter door.

"Oh, my God," she whispered, as realization dawned. "Medical supplies."

"*Necessary* medical supplies," he said with a wolfish grin. "There's plenty of protection, Abby. That doesn't have to stop us. But maybe there's some other reason—"

"There's nothing else, Luke. Except..." She was reluctant to admit that she was afraid she wouldn't meet whatever expectation he might have in a lover. Instead she said, "It's been a while since...I mean..."

Luke thrust his hands into her hair. "I know it's been a long time since you've made love, Abby." He leaned down to kiss the roses that appeared on each cheek. "I'll be gentle and take it slow, as slow as you want."

Abigail was too conscious of Luke's thigh between her legs, of his hand tangled in her hair, to think rationally. "Oh, Luke," she said. "I do want you, only..."

"Only what?"

"There are good reasons why we shouldn't do this."

Luke's thumbs caressed her temples as he asked, "Are you going to bring up that nonsense again about me dying?"

"It isn't nonsense," she said. "I don't want to care for anyone, Luke. I—"

He put his lips to hers to quiet her. "Shh. Shh. Take it easy. We'll talk about all that later. We have something else to do right now. I want to be close to you, Abby. I want to be deep inside you, touching a part of you I can't touch any other way."

Abigail tried for a smile, and though her lips quivered, she managed one. "I don't think this is a good idea. It's not you, Luke. I mean, if I were going to do this with anyone, it would be you...."

"That's good to hear."

"But since Sam died, I haven't wanted to make love to anyone."

Luke gathered her hands into his own. "I'm not asking for your love, Abby," he said in a quiet voice. His hands tightened to keep her from speaking. "I want something entirely different from you."

"Sex," Abigail said.

"Yes, sex." There was more he wanted from her. But he wasn't going to ask for it.

Abigail thought about what he had said, and what he hadn't. He wasn't offering love. And he didn't expect it in return. Abigail didn't let her head make the decision; she left it to her heart. She took a deep breath and said, "All right, Luke."

Abigail had thought she knew what she was doing. When they stood naked in the firelight before each other, she wasn't so sure. She trembled as Luke's callused fingers caressed her bare shoulder, followed by his mouth in the hollow above her collarbone. His hands caught her waist, and his searching fingers slipped up onto her ribs, his thumbs tracing them from center to edge and back again. His fingertips moved upward, circling her breasts, teasing again, but leaving her unsatisfied.

Abigail's hands found the fur pelt on Luke's chest, and she dug her fingers into the black curls. She leaned into him, scraping her flesh deliciously against his skin.

Luke held her close, enjoying the feel of their two bodies aligned from breast to thigh. His hands cupped her buttocks and pulled her close, and he leaned into the embrace, wanting to be closer still.

"This is torture," Luke said, his forehead resting against hers. "I can't touch you enough, can't hold you enough. Can't—"

Abigail's hands framed his face, lifting it until she could see the fierce wanting in his eyes. "Touch me, Luke. Hold me. I want you so much."

His lips captured hers, his tongue plundering her mouth, taking what he wanted, what he needed. He stopped kissing her long enough to lift her into his arms, make a brief detour to collect the necessary protection, and carry her to bed, where he quickly joined her on the flannel sheets.

Sensations. Abigail reveled in them. Smooth skin over hard muscle. Sweat and heat. Controlled power. The gentleness of a strong man's caress.

Sensations. Luke had never known a woman who affected

him as she did. Softness. Curves that fit in his hands. Dampness and heat. A woman's tenderness that reached deep inside him to warm the coldness there.

"Abby, Abby, let me inside."

He opened a foil packet, but she took it from him. "Let me." Slowly, using both hands, she led him to the center of her desire and guided him inside. Suddenly, she was filled with him.

A deep, guttural groan of pleasure and satisfaction rose from his chest.

"Oh, Luke." Abby's voice was filled with awe. "I feel so full. It...it feels so good."

She held him close, trying to touch enough, to taste enough to last a lifetime, though the fire between them raged so hot she was certain nothing could ever put it out.

The tension built as they performed the dance of wolves, the ritual of mating.

"Give yourself to me, Abby."

"Luke, kiss me, please."

"Here, Abby. Touch me here."

"Luke, hold me. Love me."

"Abby, baby, I can't wait much longer...."

"Sweetheart, I can't wait...."

Then they were flying, soaring together, their bodies arched, shuddering with ecstasy. It was a trip to the heavens, a visit to a paradise that few ever know, two souls joined as their bodies find in each other their perfect human complement.

Abigail lay gasping for breath. Luke lay beside her, his broad chest rising and falling in an effort to catch up to his racing pulse.

It was never like this with Sam. The thought came before Abigail could repress it. And with it the knowledge that what she felt for Luke, what she had felt from virtually the first moment she'd seen him, was far stronger than what she'd experienced with Sam, whom she'd known nearly all her life. She wanted to cry. She wanted to shout hosanna. She closed her eyes and lay perfectly still, as though to deny the emotions roiling inside her.

It was never like this with any other woman. Luke knew he'd found more than sexual fulfillment in Abby's arms. He was terrified. He was ecstatic. He couldn't marry her. He couldn't let her go. He didn't know what to do.

At that moment, Abigail turned her back to him, and he knew that whatever he felt, whatever he decided for the long term, at this moment he wanted to hold her in his arms. He turned on his side and pulled her close, to spoon her against him.

"Luke, I—"

He cut her off with the pressure of his hand on her belly. "Don't say anything tonight, Abby. Just sleep. We'll talk about this in the morning."

He knew she must be feeling as excited, upset and confused about what had happened between them as he did. Something special *had* happened between them. But if he admitted his feelings to Abby tonight, she'd have a hold on him that he couldn't escape. He didn't trust the love he felt. It had betrayed him before.

"Go to sleep, Abby."

Abigail clenched her jaw. She hadn't expected a declaration of love. And he hadn't disappointed her. She certainly wasn't going to shed any tears over him. It was better this way. It would hurt to lose him now, but not as much as it would hurt if she let him into her life.

Something warm and hot fell on Luke's arm, the one he had around Abby. A tear. She was crying. He tried to harden his heart against her pain. He'd done it before with other women. He could do it again.

Only this time, things were different. This time, he felt her pain.

He turned Abigail in his arms and tucked her head under his chin, holding her close, feeling his body heating again, even though it had been so recently sated.

"All right, Abby. I'll say it." Angrily he admitted, "I care for you. Is that what you wanted to hear? But it isn't going to change anything. I won't marry you. I'm never going to marry again. I'm not cut out for it. When you catch this renegade wolf, when you're finished here, that's it. We part ways."

He wasn't going to use the word love. Love had never been a good thing in his life. Abby would have to settle for caring. It was the best he could offer.

Abigail heard what Luke had said. And what he had not said. "I'll take what I can get," she whispered.

Her lips caressed his neck, his chest, his cheek, his eyelids, and finally his mouth. It was a kiss that expressed her love, the love he didn't want...and refused to return.

The banked fires between them burst into flame and burned hot again. Their hands roamed, seeking out the places they'd learned could give pleasure.

"Luke, Luke, stop," Abigail begged in a breathless voice.

"What? What's wrong?" Luke had trouble rising from the well of pleasure into which she had taken him.

"I...uh..."

"What is it, Abby?"

She hid her face against his chest and said, "I've always wanted to make love on a bearskin rug. Do you suppose..."

The rich sound of masculine laughter filled the cabin. "Say no more."

An instant later, Abigail's buttocks were lying nestled on the bearskin rug beside the bed, and Luke's body mantled hers.

"Now, where were we?" Luke asked with a roguish grin.

"I believe you were making love with me. Your mouth was right here." Abigail pointed to the hollow above her collarbone.

"So I was," Luke said, his mouth lowering to her skin.

Abigail groaned, a harsh sound that grated up from deep within her. It was the first of many sounds of pleasure that followed throughout the night.

9

---

*The chase is the stage of the hunt
in which the prey flees and the wolf follows.*

Abigail had lied to Luke. Simply knowing he cared was not enough. She wanted everything he had to give. She wanted his love.

Despite all the precautions she'd taken over the past three years not to get involved, she had, in a matter of days, fallen into a trap she hadn't seen until its jaws had closed around her. She should have been more wary. The consequences of loving were frightening, and Luke had already told her the price she would have to pay for her foolishness. Contemplation of a life without him left her feeling desolated.

She forced herself to concentrate on tracking the wolf. Once her work was done she could escape the pain of loving a man who refused to love her back.

The weather was considerably warmer, all the way up in the mid-sixties, making it a pleasure to walk in the mountains. They had picked up wolf sign early, and Abigail had high hopes they would find the renegade today. The snow was melting quickly under a warm sun, and there were only patches of white to be found.

What attracted Abigail's eyes was a patch of snow stained yellow. She went on one knee and scooped her gloved hand down under the top layer of snow. She carefully brought a handful of the stained snow up to her nose, which wrinkled when it caught a pungent scent.

"I assume you did that for a purpose," Luke said, eyeing her askance. "What did you find out?"

"The wolf was here." She held the snow out for him to sniff, and as he did she explained, "Elk and deer smell like the grass and trees they eat, pleasant. Wolves smell rank and gamy."

"Definitely wolf," Luke agreed with a wrinkle of his nose.

Abigail dropped the snow and dusted her gloved hand against her jeans. "He's not far ahead of us."

Her words proved to be true. They both spotted the wolf at the same instant, but Luke was quicker to react. The picture of the wolf poised over the dead carcass of one of his sheep spurred him to action. He had his rifle raised and aimed, his finger tight on the trigger, when Abigail's cry of horror made him pause.

"Stop! Don't shoot. Please, Luke." Her hand gripped his arm, tightening as he sighted down the barrel.

Luke's jaw worked as he gritted back the fury he felt toward the fleeing wolf, which was threatening his livelihood. He made the mistake of looking at Abigail, and the pleading expression in her wide green eyes caused him to swing his rifle away in disgust.

Abigail breathed a sigh of relief and brought her shaking hand up to rake it through her disheveled blond hair. "Thank you," she said.

"For what?" he spat. "You're running out of time, Abby. That renegade isn't going to let you catch him. Some wild things can't be caged. The only way to stop him is to put a bullet in him."

"I'm not giving up!" Abigail replied in a voice made more fierce by the fact that she feared he was right. "I'll catch him, and I'll cage him. He is not a lost cause, Luke."

Any more than you are, she thought. She was not a quitter. She wasn't going to give up on the wolf. She wasn't going to give up on Luke, either. He was capable of loving. She just had to convince him of that fact.

Luke wasn't sure what to make of the determined look in Abby's eyes or her militant stance, with her hands fisted on her hips. But he didn't intend to argue with her. He simply stalked off toward the dead sheep, with Abigail hard on his heels.

When they got a good look at the sheep carcass and examined all the evidence to be found, it was Abigail's turn to rant. "It's a good thing you didn't shoot, because that wolf didn't kill this sheep!" she said. "Most likely it was coyotes. Now, aren't you glad I stopped you?"

Luke saw Abby was expecting an apology. But he wasn't going to give it to her. He hadn't said anything he didn't still believe. "Maybe that renegade didn't kill this sheep, but he's sure developing a fine taste for mutton. You better find him, Abby, and find him quick. If I get my sights on him again—"

"You'll hold your fire like you did this time," Abigail cut in. "My ten days aren't up, Luke. If you shoot that wolf—which I'll remind you is a *protected* endangered species—I'm going to see that you're prosecuted to the full extent of the law."

"So, my innocent little lamb is a big, bad wolf in disguise," Luke murmured with a reluctant grin. "All right, Agent Dayton. Lead on. This wolf hunt is getting downright interesting."

By sundown, another of Abigail's precious ten days was gone, and she hadn't done more than catch another brief glimpse of the wolf she'd come to trap.

That evening, they found a nice level spot in an open area where they could set up the tent. Fortunately the weather was in the low fifties, comfortable enough for sleeping outdoors. It was the sleeping *arrangements* that Abigail was finding awkward. Luke insisted it made sense to zip their two sleeping bags together.

"The space inside the tent is small enough that we'll both be more comfortable if we make one bed that fills the whole space," he explained.

Abigail didn't argue, but not because she thought what he said made any sense. She wanted to lie close to Luke. She wanted to savor whatever time she had with him. She wanted a chance to convince him that they belonged together.

Luke wasn't sure what imp had prompted him to zip their sleeping bags together, but he couldn't be sorry for the result, as he watched Abby ease her jeans down her legs and slip between the down covers.

He'd spent the day in an agony of wanting her, knowing that she'd be leaving him soon to return to her life in Helena. Where she might meet another man. Where she might marry and have the children that ought to be his.

Luke's thoughts were both irritating and confusing. He didn't love her. He damn sure didn't want to marry her. Why should he care what happened to her after she left the valley?

He stripped down to his long johns and crawled into the sleeping bag beside Abby. Where he promptly recalled every delightfully sensuous moment of the previous night spent loving her. And realized that from the moment he'd wakened that morning, with the sound of Abigail singing in the tiny shower in his mountain cabin, he'd thought of little else but loving her again.

The howl of a wolf, sad and mournful, raised goose bumps on Abigail's arms. "That's him," she whispered in the darkness.

"Most likely," Luke agreed.

"He sounds so alone."

"I know how he feels."

"What did you say?"

Luke turned on his side toward Abigail. Enough moon-light filtered through the tent walls for him to see shapes, but no more. He reached out a hand and cupped her cheek. "I think maybe I've been lonely a long time, Abby. Only I didn't realize it until last night."

Abigail put her hand over Luke's and turned her head slightly so she could kiss his callused palm. "What was different about last night?"

"You filled a hole inside me that I didn't even know was there."

Abigail took Luke's hand in both of hers and brought it down to cup her breast. "Touch me, Luke. Take what you need."

The heavy swell of her breast in his hand felt right, it felt good. He caressed her, but there was too much cloth in his way. Slowly, giving her a chance to object, he began to unbutton her wool shirt. When it was off, he reached down and pulled her long john shirt up over her head. By the time he was finished, breathless moments later, he had stripped them both bare. He pulled her toward him, to feel the soft-ness and the heat of her against his nakedness.

Abigail moaned as the tips of her breasts nestled in the crisp mat of hair that covered Luke's chest. She rubbed her-self from side to side, enjoying the feel of their two bodies, hard and soft, brushing against each other.

Luke grasped her buttocks and pulled her belly against the part of him that was hard with need.

Her hand reached down to cup him and Luke groaned and put his hand against hers to hold her there. He was so soft and so hard, both at the same time, that Abigail de-lighted in the contrast.

"Luke?" she murmured.

"What, Abby?" he said breathlessly as his tongue laved the heavy pulse where her throat and jaw met.

"Did you remember to bring in...the...protection."

Luke smiled against her skin. "I have all the necessary medical supplies at hand," he assured her.

Abigail released a moan of pleasure as Luke's tongue and teeth nipped her earlobe and then soothed the pain. There was an urgency to his loving that hadn't been there before—as though he might not have another chance, and he had to make enough memories to last forever.

His mouth trailed down from her throat to her breasts and from there to her navel. His tongue followed his hands as he reveled in the taste of her. His mouth found the fount of life and drank of the sweetness there.

Abigail gripped Luke's hair as her body rose up to meet his mouth and tongue. The sensations were unbelievable. She reached out to him with her body and with her soul, hoping he would take all she was offering.

"Luke, I want you inside me. Fill me up."

He did. And found himself fulfilled as well. Being inside her, moving inside her, his body joined with hers, as their hearts pounded in chests gasping for air, lifted him to some higher plane of being.

"Abby," he gasped. "Baby, slow down. Not so fast. Make it last. Make it last forever."

Abigail tried to make it last. But the rising tension wouldn't wait. Couldn't be stopped. It flowed up and over and around her, making her body tense like a tightly strung bow, until she thought she might snap. "Luke," she cried. "I can't bear it. It's too much."

Her face contorted with pleasure too great to bear. Her fingernails dug crescents in his back, and her legs clamped tight around his buttocks, refusing to release him, as she climaxed, shuddering again and again.

Luke thrust savagely inside her, wanting to be a part of the joy. He envied the sheen of happiness that bathed her glowing face.

Abby's arms grasped his nape and pulled him down to join her mouth to his, taking his soul, giving her soul in return.

Luke tensed and growled in guttural satisfaction as his body spilled its seed into hers. Then, exhausted, he lay upon her, as their bodies heaved to carry air to struggling lungs.

Abigail welcomed Luke's heavy weight atop her, but despite her protest, he rolled to his side and pulled her into his arms.

"Abby, Abby. It's so good between us. It's never been so good for me."

"I feel the same. It was —oh, Luke!" she wailed in sudden realization.

Luke jerked up, afraid he'd somehow hurt her. "What is it, Abby? What's wrong?"

"We forgot about protection."

"Protection?" He was only confused an instant before it dawned on him what she meant. There was no empty foil packet lying anywhere in the vicinity.

He rubbed his forehead in consternation. "Lord, Abby, I don't know what happened. I planned— I'm never irresponsible about things like that. I know better than to get caught in that kind of female trap—"

Abigail tore herself from his arms, rising quickly to her knees. "Don't worry," she said, both angry and hurt. "I wouldn't think of trying to trap you. I'm a big girl. I'm as responsible as you are for making sure 'mistakes' don't happen. So don't you worry about anything."

She lay down in a huff and pulled the sleeping bag up over her shoulder.

Luke reached out a hand to touch her, and she yanked her shoulder away. "Don't touch me. I'm tired. I want to go to sleep."

Luke didn't know what to say. He'd really made a mess of things with Abby tonight. He wasn't the kind of man to forget something as important as protection. So what had gone wrong? The thought of his child growing inside her...it was something he hadn't realized how much he wanted.

Who had he been trying to force into a decision—himself, or Abby? He couldn't think about that right now. He'd be smart to get some sleep. He had a feeling tomorrow was going to be a very long day.

Luke was right about the very long day, which seemed even longer in the face of Abby's silence. She wasn't speaking to him except when absolutely necessary. They were close to the wolf. He could smell it, feel it. Any moment he expected to see the gray renegade again.

They heard the wolf before they saw it. It was battling another animal, and the vicious sounds coming from the throats of both beasts were frightening in their savagery.

Luke and Abigail approached the glade in the forest cautiously, Abby with her tranquilizer gun ready, Luke with his rifle in hand. When they reached the site of all the noise, they were treated to a stunning spectacle. The magnificent gray wolf was doing battle with a yearling grizzly bear, while in the background six wolf pups stood in the opening to a den, yipping with excitement.

"It's the renegade—and *he's* a *she*. A mother!" Abigail said, her heart pounding with excitement. It wasn't hard to figure out what had happened to cause the fight between the bear and the wolf. The wolf had buried a cache of uneaten meat near the den. The bear had apparently dug it up and been eating it when the wolf returned. Feeling her pups threatened, she'd attacked.

Abigail was stunned by the ferocity of the female wolf. Her teeth bared, she confronted the bear, which outweighed her by nearly two hundred pounds. What she lacked in weight, she made up in mobility, running circles around the bear, biting and retreating. But the bear wasn't going anywhere. It swiped at the wolf with deadly claws and revealed sharp canines of its own when the wolf snapped at it with powerful jaws.

Abigail looked at Luke, not sure what to do. If she tranquilized one animal and then missed her shot at the other, she'd be condemning one to a savaging by the other. Yet she now had the wolf in her sights—along with her six pups, and she couldn't let the three-toed renegade escape.

"I'll distract the bear," Luke said.

Memories of how Sam's body had been mauled rose before her. "No. Don't put yourself in danger. It's not worth it." She grabbed his arm to keep him from moving. "Please, Luke. I couldn't bear it if anything happened to you."

"I couldn't *bear* it, either," he said with a grin. "I'll be careful, Abby. Don't worry about me. Besides, I've got my gun if anything goes wrong." He didn't have to tell her he would shoot to kill if it became necessary. "Once I have the grizzly distracted, you can tranquilize the wolf."

Abigail's heart was in her throat as Luke moved off into the underbrush. She had no idea how he planned to distract the bear, but she was horrified when she saw him come up behind the bear and jab it with a tree branch.

The bear turned to confront its new tormentor with a roar. Luke quickly retreated, but the wolf took advantage of the opportunity to attack the bear from the rear, and the grizzly turned back once again to its four-legged nemesis.

"Luke," Abigail shouted. "Forget it. We'll come back later."

"No. This will work." He jabbed again, and this time the bear took several steps toward him. When it did, Abigail distracted the wolf by showing herself.

"Hello, there, you beautiful renegade, you," she said. The wolf was paralyzed for an instant as their eyes locked, green to gold.

Luke poked at the yearling grizzly's nose, to which the beast took great exception.

When the grizzly went up on its hind legs, Abigail forgot all about the wolf, awed by the fearsome sight of the bear which, while still far from grown, was nevertheless an impressive foe. She immediately raised her tranquilizer gun to shoot the grizzly, as Luke slowly, carefully, backed away from the towering beast.

Before Abigail could fire, the unexpected happened. The wolf abruptly attacked the towering bear from behind. Startled, the grizzly dropped down on all fours to flee—straight toward Luke. Luke didn't have time to back up, or even to turn and run, before the bear was on him.

Abigail didn't stop to think, she just ran toward Luke, shouting at the top of her lungs, her only thought to save him, even at the cost of her own life. Her advance caused the pups to retreat inside the den and the mother wolf to flee. The grizzly heard the noise behind it and turned, rising once more on two legs. Abigail stared up at the bear's terrifying jaws, frozen with fear.

"Don't move, Abby," Luke said in a quiet voice. "Don't move an inch."

"I'm all right, Luke. I'm going to use the tranquilizer gun. I can't miss. He'll be out like a light in a very few minutes." She took a deep calming breath. She knew how long *a few minutes* could be. "If he isn't," she continued, "I expect you to come to the rescue."

Luke knew Abigail had a better chance with the tranquilizer gun than he did with a bullet. He might not kill the bear with his first shot, and an enraged grizzly would be infinitely more dangerous.

Abigail slowly raised the gun to her shoulder, took aim and fired.

The grizzly dropped on all fours when the dart hit him. At the same moment, Luke prodded him from behind again, and the grizzly pivoted and headed toward Luke.

Luke backed up slowly, letting the bear come toward him. Abigail's aim had been true. They took turns baiting the bear for the few hazardous minutes until the dart took effect. At long last, the grizzly staggered and fell.

Luke edged around the bear and came running toward Abby, who was still standing in front of the wolf den. He pulled her into his arms and held her tight. "Are you all right? You're not hurt?"

"I'm fine. What about you?" Abigail was still clutching her tranquilizer gun but frantically ran her free hand over Luke, making sure he hadn't been hurt.

"I'm fine, thanks to you. You could have been killed pulling a stunt like that! Whatever possessed you to do something so crazy?" he demanded.

"Look who's talking!" She hung on to her anger because it was all that kept her from crying with relief. "I've never heard of anything so idiotic as baiting a bear like that."

"It worked, didn't it?"

"What if it hadn't? You'd be dead, and I'd be heartbroken!" She realized that her worst fear had almost been realized...again. "Oh, Luke. You could have been killed!"

Luke pulled her into his arms. In her agitation she had said that losing him would leave her *heartbroken*. He was certain she hadn't meant to reveal so much. Yet Luke didn't remark on her words for fear she would deny their significance. He merely calmed her by saying, "I'm fine, Abby. I'm okay."

All he could think, as he held her in his arms, was how his heart had frozen when he'd seen her come running toward both wolf and grizzly, risking her life to save his.

He opened his mouth to say I love you and shut it again. People said things, felt things, in moments of crisis that weren't real. This was one of those times when it would be better to wait before speaking.

So he didn't say what he was thinking. He merely held her until her trembling stopped, and said, "You realize, of course, that you've scared off the wolf you came here to catch."

"She'll be back," Abigail said with certainty. "She's not going to abandon her pups. And we'll be waiting. It's only a matter of time now. That renegade is as good as trapped."

Luke had the uncomfortable feeling she could have said the same thing about him. She'd captured his heart, and with it, his mind and soul. If she left him, *when* she left him, she would take them with her. He'd been lonely before she came into his life. He'd be devastated when she was gone. Yet he couldn't bring himself to say the words that would keep her with him.

"I'll take the wolves to a relocation area in Glacier National Park and collar the female there," Abigail explained, as though she already had the renegade caged. "Then I'll be heading back to Helena. I want to thank you for all your help."

Luke stared at the hand she held out to him and then looked into her solemn green eyes. She hadn't forgiven him for last night. And she was denying—by ignoring—the words of love she'd so recently uttered. Apparently, she was going to leave with things still unsettled between them.

Like hell she was!

"We have some unfinished business before you go anywhere," he said in a rough voice.

"Oh? Like what?"

Luke's fisted hands landed on his hips. "Like maybe you're carrying my baby inside you right now, that's what!"

Abigail's hand slipped down to cover her womb. She'd known it was the right time of month for her to get pregnant. She had no explanation for why she hadn't stopped Luke to make sure she was protected. Except she'd been certain he was going to let her walk out of his life, and if this was all she could have of him she'd been determined to take it.

"Are you suggesting we get married because I might be pregnant?" Abigail asked.

Luke stared at her, opened his mouth to say the words, and then couldn't get them out. It was why his parents had married, and their marriage had been a disaster. "That's not a good reason for two people to marry."

"I agree," Abigail said with a sad smile. "People should marry because they love each other and want to spend their lives together —two halves, making one perfect whole."

She was leaving it up to him. All he had to say was three words, and he could take her home and spend the rest of his life with her.

"I'm sorry, Abby. I don't think I can love anybody," Luke confessed, his voice laced with regret.

"You're wrong, Luke. But I guess you'll have to find that out for yourself. If you do, *when you do,* you know where to find me."

She turned and walked away. She wasn't going far, just to collect the equipment they needed to set up camp. But she might as well have been headed for Timbuktu, he felt such a sense of loss.

Because she'd already taken the first steps out of his life.

10

Wolves mate for life.

Luke and Abigail hauled the unconscious bear some distance away from the wolf den and watched to make sure the grizzly wasn't attacked by some other forest animal before it regained consciousness. Once they were sure the bear was on its feet again, they returned to the wolf den.

Not far from the opening of the den they found the remains of the three-toed wolf's mate. There was a bullet hole in the gray wolf's hide. Apparently the male wolf had come back here to die. Abigail exchanged a poignant glance at Luke.

"I didn't shoot him, Abby."

"Somebody did."

"I can't deny that. I can even make a pretty good guess how it happened. There's a lot of misunderstanding about wolves out there, Abby. You certainly have your work cut out for you."

Abigail turned sad eyes on Luke. "I only hope that what I'm doing will make a difference."

"It will," Luke assured her, taking her hands in his.

Luke's touch was comforting, but it reminded her of all she would soon be denied. She broke away and said, "We'd better find a place to conceal ourselves. That she-wolf won't come back until she thinks we're gone."

As Abigail had predicted, late in the afternoon the renegade returned to her pups. From a hiding place downwind,

Abigail was able to dart the wolf with the tranquilizer gun, and while it was unconscious, cage it in the collapsible wire cage, much like a dog traveling cage, she'd brought along. The pups were still small enough that Abigail merely used gloves and slipped them into the cage with their mother.

Abigail had counted on having to carry the cage with the hundred-pound wolf back down the mountain, but the extra weight of the pups was going to complicate matters. She was trying to figure out the best way to distribute the weight of the animals between them when Luke pulled out a portable phone and began dialing.

"What are you doing?"

"Getting us a ride home." He contacted the closest rancher and asked him to phone Shorty, giving him directions where to meet them. Then he tucked the phone back into his bag again. "You look surprised," he said to Abby.

"I am. And pleased," Abigail added with a rueful smile. "I should have thought of that myself. I sure wasn't looking forward to hauling that she-wolf and her pups all the way down the mountain."

"It'll be a long enough hike to get to the road," Luke said.

As quickly as that, they ran out of things to say to each other. Abigail stared for a moment, then turned away and busied herself packing up the last of her equipment, which she hefted onto her back. They ran a pole through the cage to provide an easier means of distributing the wolves' weight. Fortunately the walk to the road, while grueling, was short.

As they sat waiting by the side of the road for Shorty to arrive, the silence became oppressive.

When Abigail couldn't stand the quiet tension any longer she asked, "How does Shorty know where to pick us up?"

"I told him to come to the spot where we killed the timber rattler last summer."

Abigail quickly lifted her feet and looked around the ground under the dead log on which she was perched. "Are there a lot of snakes up here?"

"Enough. It's a little early in the season for them to be active, though."

Once again, the silence descended.

Abigail wanted to ask whether she was going to see Luke again, and whether he thought there was any chance for a future between the two of them. But Luke had already made his feelings plain. She wasn't going to get a different answer simply by asking him again.

Luke chewed on his lower lip, wondering if he was making a big mistake letting Abby walk out of his life. The more he thought about it, the more he thought that what had happened between them must simply have been born out of the unique situation into which they'd been thrust together. He'd known the woman for less than a week! Surely a love that was meant to last a lifetime took longer than that to take seed and grow. Thanks to his foolishness, however, there was another seed that might take root and grow.

He cleared his throat and said, "If you find out—if you're...if there's a baby, I expect you to call me."

Abigail had her knees tucked up to her chest, with her arms hugging them, "If I'm pregnant, it'll be my business and not yours."

"Like hell it will!" Luke said, grabbing Abigail by the arm and yanking her to her feet. "If you're pregnant, that child is mine, too. I'll be part of the decision—"

"We've already agreed it would be foolish to get married because of a baby, Luke," Abigail said, trying to reason with him. "I don't see what purpose it would serve to—"

"Nobody's killing another child of mine!" he snarled.

Abby stared at him in horror. "Is that what you think? That if I were pregnant with your child, I'd get rid of it?"

"Wouldn't you?" he challenged, his voice cold and hard with fury.

As his wife had done, she suddenly realized. Her heart went out to him for the pain he'd suffered in the past. How could any woman have hurt him so much?

"I love you, Luke. I know you don't believe me or understand what that means, but it's true. I would love a baby we made together. I could never kill it."

He wanted to call her a liar. All women were liars. They only said what they thought a man wanted to hear. Except, what Luke saw in Abby's deep green eyes was honesty. What he heard in her voice was sincerity. Confused, he let go of her and stalked away.

Abby sat down on the log again, rubbing her arms where Luke had held her in anger.

He paced back and forth in front of the log like a caged animal, never coming to rest.

Abigail saw his distress but had no idea how to pacify the savage beast in him. "I owe you a great deal, Luke," she said at last.

"For what?" he said, halting in front of her.

"For showing me that I don't have to be afraid of loving again. That it's better to have loved and lost, than never to have loved at all."

Luke snorted. "Hogwash."

"We'll see," she said.

"What's that supposed to mean?"

"That I'm not sorry for loving you, even if you can't love me back. That I don't regret this time with you, even if I can't have more. Not that I don't wish for more," she said wistfully.

"Be honest, Abby," Luke said, putting his foot up on the

log beside her and, bracing his arm on his thigh, knowing he was crowding her. "All we had going for us was damned good sex."

Abigail shook her head sadly. "It was much more than that, Luke. Maybe the reason you don't recognize what we had together is because you've never been in love—really in love—before. But I have."

"With Sam the Magnificent."

"With Sam," she continued doggedly. "What I feel for you is so much more, so much greater, than what I felt for him, that I know it can't be a lie."

She would have said more except the honking of a truck horn—Shorty in Luke's pickup—interrupted her.

Abigail had thrown caution to the winds. She'd spoken from the heart. What Luke chose to do with that information was anybody's guess. She was expecting heartache, and he didn't disappoint her.

"All I want from you," he said, talking quickly to get everything said before Shorty arrived, "is a promise that you'll call me if you find out you're carrying my child. That's all. Nothing else. Do you understand?"

"Yes, Luke," Abigail said in a quiet voice. "I understand all too well."

"So you'll call me."

"No, Luke, I won't. It's going to be painful enough to leave you. I won't let you back into my life to hurt me again."

"Damn it, Abby, I—"

"Hey, Luke, Miss Abigail. You two ready for a ride?" Shorty yelled.

Luke swore loudly and creatively as he grabbed his and Abigail's bags and slung them into the back of the pickup. He removed the carrying pole and loaded it, then hefted the cage with the wolf and her pups onto the tailgate and shoved it onto the bed of the pickup, daring Abigail to help him.

Abigail stood and watched, angry with the stubborn man who refused to admit he loved her—because she felt sure he did. Well, she wasn't going to go into a decline and die when she left him behind. She'd picked up the pieces before and kept on living. She could do it again.

Shorty saw from the body language between Luke and Miss Abigail that the romance he'd hoped was budding between them had come to naught. He was sorry for that. Shorty did his best to keep a conversation going on the drive away down the mountain, but it was clear the two of them were pretty distracted.

He caught a couple of searing looks between them that gave him some hope that all was not lost. If the two of them were having this much trouble leaving each other, time apart might allow them to reconsider. He was willing to bide his time. Meanwhile, he'd be sure to provide Luke with lots of reminders of his time with Miss Abigail.

After the wolves and Abigail's equipment had been reloaded onto her own truck, she gave Shorty a quick buss on the cheek goodbye. Then she turned to Luke and said, "Thank you again...for everything."

Luke wanted to pull her into his arms, to hold her tight, to kiss her, to thrust himself inside her and make them one. *He wanted to keep her with him.* That thought frightened him so much that he said a curt, "Goodbye, Abby," pivoted on a booted heel and stalked off.

Tears welled in Abigail's eyes as she watched him walk away. Realizing that Shorty was watching, she dabbed at her eyes with her sleeve and said, "Thanks again, Shorty." Then she turned and ran to her truck. Gunning the engine, she raced down the dirt and gravel drive.

"Be seein' you," Shorty yelled after her. He turned and

squinted an eye in the direction Luke had retreated. "I do believe I'll be seein' ya."

Abigail made one stop before heading home. When she drove up to Harry Alistair's tiny log cabin she saw that numerous improvements had been made in the condition of the property. Harry was out in the pigpen again, and as Abigail walked up, Harry left it through the gate, which had been repaired.

"I came to say goodbye," Abigail said. "And to see how you're doing. It looks like things have changed around here for the better."

"Come on up to the house for a cup of coffee," Harry said, taking off her cap and wiping her brow with her sleeve, "and I'll tell you all about it."

"I can only stay a few minutes," Abigail said. "I need to get these wolves back to Helena tonight." She gestured toward the wolf and her pups, which were in the back of the pickup.

Harry came over to admire them. "She's beautiful. They're all beautiful. Where will you take them?"

"There are already some breeding pairs in the Bob Marshall Wilderness in Glacier National Park. After she's radio-tagged, I'll look for a place with good water and rendezvous spots for her pups and leave her there."

Abigail looked around at all the changes for the better in Harry's property. "I'm dying of curiosity, Harry. How did you manage all these improvements so fast?"

Harry pulled off her gloves and leaned a hip against the fender of Abigail's pickup. "I've got a new ranch manager—Nathan Hazard," she said bitterly.

"You don't sound too happy about it," Abigail noted.

"Would you be happy if help was forced down your throat?" Harry said. "I needed a loan from the bank because—well, because I had a little cash-flow problem. John Wilkinson at the bank wouldn't make the loan unless Nathan Hazard agreed to help me manage my place. Said otherwise I was too much of a credit risk.''

''Won't this arrangement give you a chance to learn what you need to know to get along on your own?'' Abigail asked.

''You bet it will! The day I sell my crop of lambs and pay off that loan, is the day I see the backside of Nathan Hazard for good.''

Privately Abigail thought Harry seemed a little more upset than the situation warranted. But maybe there was more going on between Nathan and Harry than met the eye. ''I wish you luck, Harry,'' Abigail said, extending her hand for the other woman to shake.

''Thanks, Abby,'' Harry said, grasping Abigail's hand in hers and pumping it twice. ''It means a lot to me to have you for a friend. If there's ever anything I can do to help you out, give me a call.''

''I might just do that,'' Abigail replied. ''Meanwhile,'' she said, ''make sure you don't leave any wolf bait lying around.''

''You got it,'' Harry said, returning Abby's smile. ''So long, Abby.''

Luke had thought he knew what it was like to live with a broken heart. That was before he fell in love with Abby and let her walk out of his life. More like chased her out of his life, he admitted.

Here he was, six weeks later, standing on the darkened doorstep to her wood-frame house in a quiet residential section of Helena, working up the courage to ring the doorbell and ask her to be his wife. He had never been more afraid of anything in his life.

What if she says no?

Luke rang the bell twice, but there was no answer. He looked in through the lace-curtained window, and saw there was a light on in the kitchen. She had to be there. The phone had been busy when he'd tried to call from her office and let her know he was coming. Her boss had said she had gone home sick.

Luke didn't want to think what that might mean. After all the things he'd said, if she did turn out to be pregnant, it was going to be even harder to convince her to marry him. Not that he would let that stand in his way.

He leaned against the bell and let it ring. If she was in there, he wasn't going to allow her to ignore him.

Abigail was on the phone with a rancher in Kalispell who had sighted a pair of wolves and was worried about his stock. She ignored the doorbell because she wasn't expecting anyone, and because she hated door-to-door salesmen. But the constant ringing didn't stop.

"Could you hold on just a moment," she said to the rancher on the phone. "I'll be right back."

She ran to the door and threw it open, prepared to lambaste the party at the door. She was astonished to find Luke Granger standing there, hat in hand.

"Your boss said you came home sick," Luke said. "Why aren't you in bed?"

"It was only an upset stomach," she replied.

Luke's eyes narrowed and dropped to her belly.

Abigail's hand protectively covered her womb. "What are you doing here, Luke?"

"I want to talk to you. Let me in."

"I think we've said everything we have to say to one another." She tried closing the door.

A second later he was inside with the door shut behind him.

Abigail backed away from him. "I'm busy, Luke."

"You don't look busy to me," he said, his eyes roaming over her from head to foot and back again. He'd been starved for the sight of her and couldn't get enough of looking at her. She hadn't been getting enough sleep. There were dark circles under her eyes. And she'd lost weight. She couldn't afford to get any thinner. She needed to eat if she was pregnant. *Pregnant.* He swallowed hard. Was she?

Abigail felt uncomfortable under Luke's perusing gaze. But she was looking, too. His cheeks were even more hollow than before. He didn't look well. Or happy. Why had he come? Why didn't he speak? "I was talking to someone on the phone," she said, heading back toward the kitchen. "If you'll wait—"

Luke was right behind her as she picked up the phone.

"Hello, Harley," she said. "Just someone at the door."

"Who's Harley?" Luke demanded. While he'd been going out of his mind without her, it sounded like she'd already found another boyfriend!

"Excuse me a minute, Harley," Abby said. She put the phone against her chest to muffle the sound and hissed, "Who I talk to is none of your business, Luke Granger. Now, I'll thank you to—"

Luke took the phone out of her hand and said, "Who the hell is this?"

"Harley Frederickson," a surly voice answered. "Who the hell is this? I got wolf trouble, and I need help. Put Abby back on the phone."

"Agent Dayton's got some wolf trouble of her own to deal with first," Luke responded, never taking his eyes off Abby. "She'll call you back tomorrow."

Luke hung up the phone and leaned a hip against the kitchen counter.

"That is the most high-handed—"

Luke pulled her into his arms and kissed her. It was a kiss that said *I love you and I need you.* Abby was breathless when he finally released her.

"Are you pregnant?" he asked.

"That is none of your—"

He kissed her again, in case she hadn't gotten the message. *I love you. I want to make babies with you. I want us to spend our lives together.* Only he thought the words, he didn't say them.

"Are you pregnant?" he asked again, his voice husky with feeling.

Abigail searched his eyes. She didn't want the baby to make a difference. She didn't want a marriage he would come to regret. "What if I am?"

"We'll get married." Luke knew immediately, when her body stiffened in his arms, that he'd said the wrong thing. "Aw, hell, Abby," he said, releasing her and forking a hand through his hair. "That came out all wrong. That isn't why I came here. The baby, I mean. If there is a baby, I mean. Aw, hell."

Abigail found hope in his confusion. "Why did you come here, Luke?"

"I came because I need you like I need water to drink and sunshine on my face and the sight of the mountains at daybreak. I can't live without you, Abby. I want you to be my wife."

It was the longest declaration of love Luke had ever made to a woman in his life. His pulse was galloping when he was finished. He'd put his heart in her hands. It was in her power to crush it.

"Oh, Luke," Abigail said, as a single tear slipped onto her cheek.

"Is that a yes or a no?" he croaked.

She took a step into his open arms and grasped him tightly

around the waist. "That's yes. Yes, I love you. Yes, I'll be your wife. Yes, I'll be the mother of your children."

Luke kissed her then, and neither of them said anything for a good long while. Until Luke remembered that she'd never said for sure whether or not she was pregnant.

"Uh, Abby—about the baby..."

"Yes, Luke?"

"Yes?"

"I'm pregnant." Abby didn't have to see Luke's face. She could feel his reaction. His whole body tensed before his arms tightened around her.

"I'm glad," he whispered. "I'm so glad."

"What made you change your mind, Luke?" Abigail whispered as she held him close, loving the feel of being held in his arms.

Luke chuckled. "I'm sure Shorty will take the credit."

"Oh? What did he say?"

"That if I wasn't as dumb as the sheep I raised, I'd make you my wife."

Abigail laughed. "Good advice."

"And Nathan's sure to claim he's the one who brought about my change of heart."

"Nathan?"

"He said if I didn't come here and propose to you, he was going to do it for me."

Abigail laughed. "I take it you haven't been the easiest man to be around lately."

"You might say that," he agreed. "By the way, I promised Nathan he could be my best man."

"Oh, dear."

"Some problem with that?"

"I thought I'd ask Harry to be my maid of honor."

Luke smiled down into Abby's mischievous green eyes. "That's going to ensure an eventful wedding."

"You're avoiding my question," Abigail said. "What made you change your mind?"

"I love you, Abby." It was amazing how right the words sounded, now that he'd actually spoken them aloud. "Once I admitted that to myself, everything fell into place. I knew I would never be happy unless you were part of my life."

The kiss came naturally, out of feelings that rose up from deep inside him.

Abigail was moved by his gentleness, aroused by his ferocity. She began undoing the buttons on Luke's chambray shirt. "What are your neighbors going to think when they find out you're marrying a woman who's devoted to saving wolves?"

Luke grinned. "I don't know about them, but I'd say when it comes to catching renegades, you really know your business."

"I hope you know I don't ever intend to let you go."

"I sort of expected that."

"Oh?" she asked, as her lips teased his.

"I read somewhere that wolves mate for life. Is that true, Abby?"

"Oh, yes," she sighed. "They mate forever and ever and—"

He didn't give her a chance to say more, just joined her mouth with his, telling her of his love in the most elemental way. Still, he might have considered howling with joy—if his mouth hadn't been otherwise delightfully occupied.

*   *   *   *   *

A WOLF IN SHEEP'S CLOTHING

ACKNOWLEDGMENTS

The Do's and Don'ts for the Western Tenderfoot at the beginning of each chapter come from *The Greenhorn's Guide to the Woolly West* by Gwen Petersen, and are used with permission of the author. I am also indebted to Gwen for the invaluable background information provided in her equally hilarious guide to ranch life, *The Ranch Woman's Manual.* Both books are available from Laffing Cow Press in Cheyenne, Wyoming. I would also like to thank Jim Rolleri of the County Extension Service in Big Timber, Montana, for generously parting with every brochure on sheep ranching he could find in his files. Finally, I would like to thank Jim Overstreet, a banker in Big Timber, Montana, who was kind enough to have lunch with me at The Grand and suggest the sort of financial foibles to which a sheep man can be prone.

1

What do newcomers find abounding in Woolly West towns?
Answer: Quaintness and charm.

Nathan Hazard was mad enough to chew barbed wire. Cyrus Alistair was dead, but even in death the old curmudgeon had managed to thwart Nathan's attempts to buy his land. Cyrus had bequeathed his tiny Montana sheep ranch to a distant relative from Virginia, someone named Harry Alistair. For years that piece of property had been an itch Nathan couldn't scratch—a tiny scrap of Alistair land sitting square in the middle of the Hazard ranch—the last vestige of a hundred-year-old feud between the Hazards and the Alistairs.

Nathan had just learned from John Wilkinson, the executor of the Alistair estate, that Cyrus's heir hadn't let any grass grow under his feet. Harry Alistair had already arrived in the Boulder River Valley to take possession of Cyrus's ranch. Nathan only hoped the newest hard-nosed, ornery Alistair hadn't gotten too settled in. Because he wasn't staying. Not if Nathan had anything to say about it. Oh, he planned to offer a fair price. He was even willing to be generous if it came to that. But he was going to have that land.

Nathan gunned the engine on his pickup, disdaining the cavernous ruts in the dirt road that led to Cyrus's tiny, weather-beaten log cabin. It was a pretty good bet that once Harry Alistair got a look at the run-down condition of Cyrus's property, the Easterner would see the wisdom of selling. Cyrus's ranch—what there was of it—was falling down. There weren't more than five hundred sheep on the whole place.

Besides, what could a man from Williamsburg, Virginia, know about raising sheep? The greenhorn would probably take one look at the work, and risk, involved in trying to make a go of such a small, dilapidated spread and be glad to have Nathan take it off his hands. Nathan didn't contemplate what he would do if Harry Alistair refused to sell, because he simply wasn't going to take no for an answer.

As he drove up to the cabin, Nathan saw someone bounce up from one of the broken-down sheep pens that surrounded the barn. That had to be Harry Alistair. Nathan couldn't tell what the greenhorn was doing, but from the man's agitated movements it was plain something was wrong. A second later the fellow was racing for the barn. He came out another second later carrying a handful of supplies. Once again he ducked out of sight in the sheep pen.

Nathan sighed in disgust. The newcomer sure hadn't wasted any time getting himself into a pickle. For a moment Nathan considered turning his truck around and driving away. But despite the Hazard-Alistair feud, he couldn't leave without offering a helping hand. There were rules in the West that governed such conduct. A man in trouble wasn't friend or foe; he was merely a man in trouble. As such, he was entitled to whatever assistance Nathan could offer. Once the trouble was past and they were on equal footing again, Nathan could feel free to treat this Alistair as the mortal enemy the century-old feud made him.

Nathan slammed on the brakes and left his truck door hanging open as he raced across the snowy ground toward the sheep pen on foot. The closer Nathan got, the more his brow furrowed. The man had stood up again and put a hand behind his neck to rub the tension there. He was tall, but the body Nathan saw was gangly, the shoulders narrow. The man's face was smooth, unlined. Nathan hadn't been expecting someone so young and...the only word that came to mind was *delicate,* but he shied from thinking it. He watched the greenhorn drop out of sight again. With that graceful downward movement Nathan realized what had caused his confusion. That was no man in Cyrus Alistair's sheep pen—it was a woman!

When Nathan arrived at her side, he saw the problem right away. A sheep was birthing, but the lamb wasn't presenting correctly. The ewe was baaing in distress. The woman had dropped to her knees and was crooning to the animal in a low, raspy voice that sent shivers up Nathan's spine.

The woman was concentrating so hard on what she was doing that she wasn't even aware of Nathan until he asked, "Need some help?"

"What? Oh!" She looked up at him with stricken brown eyes. Her teeth were clenched on her lower lip and her cheeks were pale. He noticed her hand was trembling as she brushed her brown bangs out of her eyes with a slender forearm. "Yes. Please. I don't know what to do."

Nathan felt a constriction in his chest at the desperate note in her voice. He had an uncontrollable urge to protect her from the tragic reality she faced. The feeling was unfamiliar, and therefore uncomfortable. He ignored it as best he could and quickly rolled up his sleeves. "Do you have some disinfectant handy?"

"Yes. Here." She poured disinfectant over his hands and arms.

Nathan shook off the excess and knelt beside the ewe. After a quick examination, he said flatly, "This lamb is dead."

"Oh, no! It's all my fault."

"Maybe not," Nathan contradicted. "Can't always save a case of dystocia."

"What?"

"The lamb is out of position. Its head is bent back, not forward along its legs like it ought to be."

"I read in a book what to do for a problem delivery. I just didn't realize..." She reached out a hand to briefly touch the lamb's foot that extended from the ewe. "Will the mother die, too?"

"Not if I can help it," Nathan said grimly. There was a long silence while he used soapy water to help the dead lamb slip free of the womb. Almost immediately contractions began again. "There's another lamb."

"Is it alive?" the woman asked, her voice full of hope.

"Don't know yet." Nathan wanted the lamb to be born alive more than he'd wanted anything in a long time. Which made no sense at all. This was an Alistair sheep.

"Here it comes!" she exclaimed. "Is it all right?"

Nathan waited to see whether the lamb would suck air. When it didn't, he grabbed a nearby gunnysack and rubbed vigorously. The lamb responded by bleating pitifully. And Nathan let out the breath he hadn't known he'd been holding.

"It's alive," she said in a tear-choked voice.

"That it is," Nathan said with satisfaction. He cut the umbilical cord about an inch and a half from the lamb's navel and asked, "Where's the iodine?"

Nathan helped the ewe to her feet while the woman ran to fetch a wide-mouthed jar full of iodine. When she returned he held the lamb up by its front legs and sloshed the jar over the navel cord until it was covered with iodine. He set the lamb back down beside its mother where, after some bumping and searching with its nose, it found a teat and began to nurse.

Nathan glanced at the woman to share the moment, which he found profoundly moving no matter how many times he'd seen it. Once he did, he couldn't take his eyes off her.

She was watching the nursing lamb, and her whole face reflected a kind of joy he had seldom seen and wasn't sure he had ever felt. When the lamb made a loud, slurping sound, a laugh of relief bubbled up from her throat. And she looked up into his eyes and smiled.

He was stunned. Poleaxed. Smitten. In a long-ago time he would have thrown her on his horse and ridden off into the sunset. But this was now, and he was a civilized man. So he simply swallowed hard, gritted his teeth and smiled back.

Her smile revealed a slight space between her front teeth that made her look almost winsome. A dimple appeared in her left cheek when the smile became a grin. Her bangs had fallen back over her brows, and it took all his willpower not to brush them back. Her nose was small and tilted up at the end, and he noticed her cheeks, now that they weren't so pale, were covered with a scattering of freckles. Her lips were full, despite the wide smile, and her chin, tilted up toward him, seemed to ask for his touch. He had actually lifted a hand toward her when he realized what he was about to do.

Nathan was confused by the strength of his attraction to the woman. He didn't need—refused to take on—any more obligations in his lifetime. This was a woman who looked in great need of a lot of care and attention. This kind of woman spelled RESPONSIBILITY in capital letters. He shrugged inwardly. He had done his share of taking care of the helpless. He hadn't begrudged the sacrifice, because it had been necessary, but he was definitely gun-shy.

When he chose a woman to share his life, it would be someone who could stand on her own two feet, someone who could be a helpmate and an equal partner. He would never choose someone like the winsome woman kneeling before him, whose glowing brown eyes beseeched him to take her into his arms and comfort her.

Not by a long shot!

Nathan bolted to his feet, abruptly ending the intense feeling of closeness he felt with the woman. "Where the hell is Harry Alistair?" he demanded in a curt voice. "And what the hell are you doing out here trying to handle a complicated lambing all alone?"

His stomach knotted when he saw the hurt look in her eyes at his abrupt tone of voice, but he didn't have a chance even to think about apologizing before a spark of defiance lit up her beautiful brown eyes and she rose to her feet. Her hands balled into fists and found her hipbones. She was tall. Really tall. He stood six foot three and she was staring him practically in the eye.

"You're looking for Harry Alistair?" she asked in a deceptively calm voice.

"I am."

"What for?"

"That's between him and me. Look, do you know where he is or not?"

"I do."

But that was all she said. Nathan was damned if he was going to play games with her. He yanked the worn Stetson off his head, forked an agitated hand through his blond hair and settled the cowboy hat back in place over his brow. He placed his fists on his hips in a powerful masculine version of her pose and grated out, "Well, where the hell is he?"

"*He's* standing right here."

There was a long pause while Nathan registered what she'd said. "*You're* Harry Alistair?"

"Actually, my name is Harriet." She forgave him for his

rudeness with one of those engaging smiles and said, "But my friends all call me Harry."

She stuck out her hand for him to shake, and before he could curb his automatic reaction, he had her hand clasped in his. It was soft. Too damn soft for a woman who hoped to survive the hard life of a Montana sheep rancher. He held on to her hand as he examined her—the Harry Alistair he had come to see—more closely.

He was looking for reasons to find fault with her, to prove he couldn't possibly be physically attracted to her, and he found them. She was dressed in a really god-awful outfit: brand-new bibbed overalls, a red-and-black plaid wool shirt, a down vest, galoshes, for heaven's sake, and a Harley's Feed Store baseball cap, which meant she'd already been to Slim Harley's Feed Store in Big Timber. Nathan hadn't realized her hair was so long, but two childish braids fell over each shoulder practically to her breasts.

Nothing wrong with them, a voice inside noted.

Nathan forced his eyes back up to her face, which now bore an expression of amusement. A flush crept up his neck. There was no way he could hide it or stop it. His Swedish ancestors had bequeathed him blue eyes and blond hair and skin that got ruddy in the sun but never tanned. Unfortunately his Nordic complexion also displayed his feelings when he most wanted them hidden. He dropped her hand as though it had caught fire.

"We have to talk," he said flatly

"I'd like that," Harry replied. "After everything we've just been through together, I feel like we're old friends, Mr.—Oh, my," she said with a self-deprecating laugh. "I don't even know your name."

"Nathan Hazard."

"Come on inside, Nathan Hazard, and have a cup of coffee, and we'll talk."

Nathan was pretty sure he could conduct his business right here. After all, how many words did it take to say "I want to buy this place?" Only six. But he was curious to see the inside of Cyrus Alistair's place. He had heard the tiny log cabin called "rustic" by those who had actually been inside, though they were few and far between.

Against his better judgment Nathan said, "Sure. A cup of coffee sounds good."

"I don't have things very organized," Harry apologized.

Nathan soon realized that was an understatement. Harry took him in through the back door, which led to the kitchen. What he saw was *chaos*. What he felt was *disappointment*. Because despite everything he had already seen of her, he'd been holding out hope that he was wrong about Harry Alistair.

The shambles he beheld in the kitchen of the tiny cabin— dishes piled high in the sink, half-empty bottles of formula on the counters, uneaten meals side by side with stacks of brochures on the table, several bags of garbage in one corner, and a lamb sleeping on a wadded-up blanket in the other—confirmed his worst fears. Harry Alistair needed a caretaker. This wasn't a woman who was ever going to be anyone's equal partner.

Harry had kicked off her galoshes when she came in the door and let them lie where they fell. Her down vest warmed the back of the kitchen chair, and she hooked her Harley's Feed Store cap on a deer antler that graced the dingy, wooden-planked wall.

Poor woman, he thought. She must have given up trying to deal with all the mess and clutter. He hardened himself against feeling sympathy for her. He was more convinced than ever that he would be doing her a favor by buying Cyrus's place from her.

While he stood staring, Harry grabbed some pottery mugs

for the coffee from kitchen cupboards that appeared to be all but bare. He was able to notice that because all the cupboards hung open on dragging hinges. As quickly as she shoved the painted yellow kitchen cupboards closed, they sprang open again. And stayed that way. She turned to him, shrugged and let go with another one of her smiles. He stuck his hands deep into his pockets to keep from reaching out to enfold her in his arms.

Not the woman for me, he said to himself.

The walls and floor of the room consisted of unfinished wooden planks. A step down from "rustic," he thought. More like "primitive." The refrigerator was so old that the top was rounded instead of square. The gas stove was equally ancient, and she had to light the burner with a match.

"Darned thing doesn't work from the pilot," Harry explained as she set a dented metal coffeepot on the burner. "Make yourself at home," she urged, seating herself at the kitchen table.

Nathan set his Stetson on the table and draped his sheepskin coat over the back of one of the three chrome-legged chairs at the Formica table. Then he flattened the torn plastic seat and sat down. The table was cluttered with brochures. One title leaped out at him—"Sheep Raising for Beginners." He didn't have a chance to comment on it before she started talking.

"I'm from Williamsburg, Virginia," she volunteered. "I didn't even know my great-uncle Cyrus. It was really a surprise when Mr. Wilkinson from the bank contacted me. At first I couldn't believe it. Me, inheriting a sheep ranch!

"I suppose the sensible thing would have been to let Mr. Wilkinson sell the place for me. He said there was a buyer anxious to have it. Then I thought about what it would be like to have a place of my very own, far away from—" She jumped up and crossed to the stove to check the coffeepot.

Nathan wanted her to finish that sentence. What, or whom, had she wanted to escape? What, or who, had made her unhappy enough that she had to run all the way to Montana? He fought down the possessive, protective feelings that arose. She didn't belong to him. Never would.

She was talking in breathless, jerky sentences, which was how he knew she was nervous. It was as though she wasn't used to entertaining a man in her kitchen. Maybe she wasn't. He wished he knew for sure.

Not your kind of woman, he repeated to himself.

"Do you have a place around here?" Harry asked.

Nathan cleared his throat and said with a rueful smile, "You could say I have a place that goes all around here."

He watched her brows lower in confusion at his comment. She filled the two coffee mugs to the very brim and brought them carefully to the table.

"Am I supposed to know what that means?" she asked as she seated herself across from him again.

"My sheep ranch surrounds yours." When she still looked confused he continued, "Your property sits square in the center of mine. Your access road to the highway runs straight across my land."

A brilliant smile lit her face, and she cocked her head like a brown sparrow on a budding limb and quipped, "Then we most certainly *are* neighbors, aren't we? I'm so glad you came to see me, Nathan—is it all right if I call you Nathan?—so we can get to know each other. I could really use some advice. You see—"

"Wait a minute," he interrupted.

In the first place it wasn't all right with him if she called him Nathan. It would be much more difficult to be firm with her if they were on a first-name basis. In the second place he hadn't come here to be neighborly; he had come to make an offer on her land. And in the third, and most important place, he had *absolutely no intention of offering her any advice.* And he was going to tell her all those things...just as soon as she stopped smiling so trustingly at him.

"Look, Harry-et," he said, pausing a second between the two syllables, unable to make himself address her by the male nickname. "You probably should have taken the banker's advice. If the rest of this cabin looks as bad as the kitchen, it can't be very comfortable. The buildings and sheds are a disgrace. Your hay fields are fallow. Your access road is a mass of ruts. You'll be lucky to make ends meet let alone earn enough from this sheep ranch you inherited to enjoy any kind of pleasant life. The best advice I can give you is to sell this place to me and go back to Virginia where you belong."

He watched her full lips firm into a flat line and her jaw tauten. Her chin came up pugnaciously. "I'm not selling out."

"Why the hell not?" he retorted in exasperation.

"Because."

He waited for her to explain. But she was keeping her secrets to herself. He was convinced now that she must be running from something...or someone.

"I'm going to make a go of this place. I can do it. I may not be experienced, but I'm intelligent and hardworking and I have all the literature on raising sheep that I could find."

Nathan stuck the brochure called "Sheep Raising for Beginners" under her nose and said, "None of these brochures will compensate for practical experience. Look what happened this afternoon. What would you have done if I hadn't come along?" He had the unpleasant experience of watching her chin drop to her chest and her cheeks flush while her thumb brushed anxiously against the plain pottery mug.

"I would probably have lost both lambs, and the ewe, as well," she admitted in a low voice. She looked up at him, her brown eyes liquid with tears she was trying to blink away. "I owe you my thanks. I don't know how I can ever repay you. I know I have a lot to learn. But—" she leaned forward, and her voice became urgent "—I intend to work as hard as I have to, night and day if necessary, until I succeed."

Nathan was angry and irritated. She wasn't going to succeed; she was going to fail miserably. And unless he could somehow talk her into selling this place to him, he was going to have to stand by and watch it happen. Because he *absolutely, positively,* was *not* going to offer to help. There were no ifs, ands or buts about it. He had been through this before. A small commitment had a way of mushrooming out of control. Start cutting pines and pretty soon you'd created a whole mountain meadow.

"Look, Harry-et," he said, "the reason I came here today is to offer to buy this place from you."

"It's not for sale."

Nathan sighed. She'd said it as if she'd meant it. He had no choice except to try to convince her to change her mind. "Sheep ranching involves a whole lot more than lambing and shearing, Harry-et." He was distracted from his train of thought by the way the flush on her cheeks made her freckles show up. He forced his attention back where it belonged and continued. "For instance, do you have any idea what wool pool you're in?"

She raised a blank face and stared at him.

"Do you even know what a wool pool is?"

She shook her head.

"A wool pool enables small sheepmen like yourself to concentrate small clips of wool into carload lots so that they can get a better price on—" He cut himself off. He was supposed to be proving her ignorance to her, not educating it away. He ignored her increasingly distressed look and asked, "Do you have any idea what's involved with docking and castrating lambs?"

This time she nodded, but the flush on her face deepened.

"What about keeping records? Do you have any accounting experience?"

"A little," she admitted in a quiet voice.

He felt like a desperado in a black hat threatening the schoolmarm, but he told himself it was for her own good in the long run and continued, "Can you figure adjusted weaning weight ratios? Measure ram performance? Calculate shearing dates? Compute feed gain ratios?"

By now she was violently shaking her head. A shiny tear streaked one cheek.

He pushed himself up out of his chair. He braced one callused palm on the table and leaned across to cup her jaw in his other hand and lift her chin. He looked into her eyes, and it took every bit of determination he had not to succumb to the plea he saw there. "I can't teach you to run this ranch. I have a business of my own that needs tending. You can't make it on your own, Harry-et. Sell your land to me."

"No."

"I'll give you a fair—a generous—price. Then you can go home where you belong."

She was out of his grasp and gone before he had time to stop her. She didn't go far, just to the sink, where she stood in front of the stack of dirty dishes and stared out the dirt-clouded window at the ramshackle sheep pens and the derelict barn. "I will succeed. With or without your help."

She sounded so sure of herself, despite the fact that she was doomed to fail. Nathan refused to admire her. He chose to be furious with her instead. In three angry strides he was beside her. "You're as stubborn as every other hard-nosed, ornery Alistair who ever lived on this land!" He snorted in disgust. "I can sure as hell see now why Hazards have been feuding with Alistairs for a hundred years."

She whirled to confront him. "And I can see why Alistairs chose to feud with Hazards," she retorted. "How dare you pretend to be a friend!" She poked him in the chest with a stiff finger. "How dare you sneak in under my guard and pretend to help—"

"I wasn't pretending," he said heatedly, grabbing her wrist to keep her from poking him again. "I *did* help. Admit it."

"Sure. So I'd be grateful. All the time you only wanted to buy my land right out from under me. You are the lowest, meanest—"

He wasn't about to listen to any insults from a greenhorn female. A moment later her arm was twisted up behind her and he had pulled her flush against him. She opened her mouth to lambaste him again and he shut her up the quickest, easiest way he knew. He covered her mouth with his.

Nathan was angry, and he wasn't gentle. That is, until he felt her lips soften under his. It felt like he'd been wanting her for a long time. His mouth moved slowly over hers while his hand cupped her head and kept her still so he could take what he needed. She struggled against his hold, her breasts brushing against his chest, her hips hard against his. That only made him want her more. It was when he felt her trembling that he came to his senses, mortified at the uncivilized way he'd treated her.

He abruptly released the hand he had twisted behind her back. But instead of coming up to slap him, as he'd expected, her palm reached up to caress his cheek. Her fingertips followed the shape of his cheekbone upward to his temple, where she threaded her fingers into his hair and slowly pulled his head back down.

And she kissed him back.

That was when he realized she was trembling with desire. Not fear. Desire. With both hands free he cupped her buttocks and pulled her hard against him. For every thrust he made, she countered. He was as full and hard as he'd ever been in his life. His tongue ravaged her mouth, and she responded with an ardor that made him hungry for her. He spread urgent kisses across her face and neck, but they didn't satisfy as much as the taste of her, so he sought her mouth again. His tongue found the space between her teeth. And the inside of her lip. And the roof of her mouth. When he mimicked the thrust and parry of lovers, she held his tongue and sucked it until he thought his head was going to explode.

When he slipped his hand over her buttocks and between her legs, she moaned, a sound that came from deep in her throat and spoke of an agony of unappeased passion.

And the lamb in the corner bleated.

Nathan lifted his head and stared at the woman in his arms. Her brown eyes were half-veiled by her lids, and her pupils were dilated. She was breathing as heavily as he was, her lips parted to gasp air. Her knees had already buckled, and his grasp on her was all that kept them both off the floor.

Are you out of your mind?

He tried to step away, but her hand still clutched his hair. He reached up and drew her hand away. She suddenly seemed to realize he had changed his mind and backed up abruptly. Nathan refused to look at her face. He already felt bad enough. He had come within a lamb's tail of making love to Harry-et Alistair. He had made a narrow escape, for which he knew he would later, when his body wasn't so painfully objecting, be glad for.

"I think it's time you left, Mr. Hazard," Harry said in a rigidly controlled voice.

He couldn't leave without trying once more to accomplish what he'd come to do. "Are you sure you won't—"

The change in her demeanor was so sudden that it took him by surprise. Her expression was fierce, determined. "I will not sell this land," she said through clenched teeth. "Now get out of here before—"

"Goodbye, Harry-et. If you have a change of heart, John Wilkinson at the bank knows how to get in touch with me."

He settled his hat on his head and pulled it down with a tug. Then he shrugged broad shoulders into his sheepskin-lined coat. Before he was even out the kitchen door Harry Alistair had already started heating a bottle of formula for the lamb she had snuggled in her arms. It was the first time he'd ever envied one of the fleecy orphans.

The last thing Nathan Hazard wanted to do was leave that room. But he turned resolutely and marched out the door. As he gunned the engine of his truck, he admitted his encounter with Harry-et Alistair had been a very close call.

Not the woman for you, he reminded himself. *Definitely not the woman for you.*

2

Are there bachelors in them thar hills?
Answer: Yep.

Once the lamb had been fed and settled back on its pallet, Harry sank into a kitchen chair, put her elbows on the table and let her head drop into her hands. What on earth had she been thinking to let Nathan Hazard kiss her like that! And worse, why had she kissed him back in such a wanton manner? It was perfectly clear now that she hadn't been *thinking* at all; she'd been feeling, and the feelings had been so overwhelming that they hadn't allowed for any kind of rational consideration.

Harry had felt an affinity to the rancher from the instant she'd laid eyes on him. His broad shoulders, his narrow hips, the dusting of fine blond hair on his powerful forearms all appealed to her. His eyes were framed by crow's-feet that gave character to a sharp-boned, perfectly chiseled face. That pair of sapphire blue eyes, alternately curious and concerned, had stolen her heart.

Harry wasn't surprised that she was attracted to someone more handsome than any man had a right to be. What amazed her was that having known Nathan Hazard for only a matter of hours she would readily have trusted him with her life. That simply wasn't logical. Although, Harry supposed in retrospect, she had probably seen in Nathan Hazard exactly what she wanted to see. She had needed a legendary, bigger-than-life Western hero, someone tall, rugged and handsome to come along and rescue her. And he had obligingly arrived.

And he had been stunning in his splendor, though that had consisted merely of a pair of butter-soft jeans molded to his long legs, Western boots, a dark blue wool shirt topped by a sheepskin-lined denim jacket, and a Stetson he had pulled down so that it left his features shadowed. The shaggy, silver-blond hair that fell a full inch over his collar had made him look untamed, perhaps untamable. Harry remembered wondering what such fine blond hair might feel like. His lower lip was full, and he had a wide, easy smile that pulled one side of his mouth up a little higher than the other. She had also wondered, she realized with chagrin, what it would be like to kiss that mouth. Unbelievably she had actually indulged her fantasies.

Harry wasn't promiscuous. She wasn't even sexually experienced when it came right down to it. So she had absolutely no explanation for what had just happened between her and the Montana sheepman. She only knew she had felt an urgent, uncontrollable need to touch Nathan Hazard, to kiss him and to have him kiss her back. And she hadn't wanted him to stop there. She had wanted him inside her, mated to her.

Her mother and father, not to mention her brother, Charlie, and her eight uncles and their dignified, decorous wives, would have been appalled to think that any Williamsburg Alistair could have behaved in such a provocative manner with a man she had only just met. Harry was a little appalled herself.

But then nothing in Montana was going the way she had planned.

It had seemed like such a good idea, when she had gotten the letter from John Wilkinson, to come to the Boulder River Valley and learn how to run great-uncle Cyrus's sheep ranch. She loved animals and she loved being out-of-doors and she loved the mountains—she had heard that southwestern Montana had a lot of beautiful mountains. She'd expected opposition to such a move from her family, so she'd carefully chosen the moment to let them know about her decision.

No Alistair ever argued at the dinner table. So, sitting at the elegant antique table that had been handed down from Alistair to Alistair for generations, she had waited patiently for a break in the dinner conversation and calmly announced, "I've decided to take advantage of my inheritance from great-uncle Cyrus. I'll be leaving for Montana at the end of the week."

"But you can't possibly manage a sheep ranch on your own, Harriet," her mother admonished in a cultured voice. "And since you're bound to fail, darling, I can't understand why you would even want to give it a try. Besides," she added, "think of the smell!"

Harry—her mother cringed every time she heard the masculine nickname—had turned her compelling brown eyes to her father, looking for an encouraging word.

"Your mother is right, sweetheart," Terence Waverly Alistair said. "My daughter, a sheep farmer?" His thick white brows lowered until they nearly met at the bridge of his nose. "I'm afraid I can't lend my support to such a move. You haven't succeeded at a single job I've found for you, sweetheart. Not the one as a teller in my bank, not the one as a secretary, nor the the one as a medical receptionist. You've gotten yourself fired for ineptness at every single one. It's foolhardy to go so far—Montana is a long way from Virginia, my dear—merely to fail yet again. Besides," he added, "think of the cold!"

Harry turned her solemn gaze toward her older brother, Charles. He had been her champion in the past. He had even unbent so far as to call her Harry when their parents weren't around. Now she needed his support. Wanted his support. Begged with her eyes for his support.

"I'm afraid I have to agree with Mom and Dad, Harriet."

"But, Charles—"

"Let me finish," he said in a determined voice. Harry met her brother's sympathetic gaze as he continued. "You're only setting yourself up for disappointment. You'll be a lot happier if you learn to accept your limitations."

"Meaning?" Harry managed to whisper past the ache in her throat.

"Meaning you just aren't clever enough to pull it off, Harriet. Besides," he added, "think of all that manual labor!"

Harry felt the weight of a lifetime of previous failures in every concerned but discouraging word her family had offered. They didn't believe she could do it. She took a deep breath and let it out. She could hardly blame them for their opinion of her. To be perfectly honest, she had never given them any reason to think otherwise. So why was she so certain that this time things would be different? Why was she so certain that this time she would succeed? Because she knew something they didn't: *she had done all that failing in the past on purpose.*

Harry was paying now for years of deception. It had started innocently enough when she was a child and her mother had wanted her to take ballet lessons. At six Harry had already towered over her friends. Gawky and gangly, she knew she was never going to make a graceful prima ballerina. One look at her mother's face, however, and Harry had known she couldn't say, "No, thank you. I'd rather be playing basketball."

Instead, she'd simply acquired two left feet. It had worked. Her ballet instructor had quickly labeled her irretrievably clumsy and advised Isabella Alistair that she would only be throwing her money away if Harriet continued in the class. Isabella was forced to admit defeat. Thus, unbeknownst to her parents, Harry had discovered at a very early age a passive way of resisting them.

Over the years Harry had never said no to her parents. It had been easier simply to go along with whatever they had planned. Piano lessons were thwarted with a deaf ear; embroidery had been abandoned as too bloody; and her brief attempt at tennis had resulted in a broken leg.

As she had gotten older, the stakes had gotten higher. She had only barely avoided a plan to send her away to college at Radcliffe by getting entrance exam scores so low that they had astonished the teachers who had watched her get straight A's through high school. She had been elated when her distraught parents had allowed her to enroll at the same local university her friends from high school were attending.

Harry knew she should have made some overt effort to resist each time her father had gotten her one of those awful jobs after graduation, simply stood up to him and said, "No, I'd rather be pursuing a career that I've chosen for myself." But old habits were hard to break. It had been easier to prove inept at each and every one.

When her parents chose a husband for her, she'd resorted to even more drastic measures. She'd concealed what looks she had, made a point of reciting her flaws to her suitor and resisted his amorous advances like a starched-up prude. She had led the young man to contemplate life with a plain, clumsy, cold-natured, brown-eyed, brown-haired, freckle-faced failure. He had beat a hasty retreat.

Now a lifetime of purposeful failure had come home to roost. She couldn't very well convince her parents she was ready to let go of the apron strings when she had so carefully convinced them of her inability to succeed at a single thing they had set for her to do. She might have tried to explain to them her failure had only been a childish game that had been carried on too long, but that would mean admitting she'd spent her entire life deceiving them. She couldn't bear to hurt them like that. Anyway, she didn't think they'd believe her if she told them her whole inept life had been a sham.

Now Harry could see, with the clarity of twenty-twenty hindsight, that she'd hurt herself even more than her parents by the choices she'd made. But the method of dealing with her parents' manipulation, which she'd started as a child and continued as a teenager, she'd found impossible to reverse as an adult. Until now. At twenty-six she finally had the perfect opportunity to break the pattern of failure she'd pursued for a lifetime. She only hoped she hadn't waited too long.

Harry was certain she could manage her great-uncle Cyrus's sheep ranch. She was certain she could do anything she set her brilliant mind to do. After all, it had taken brilliance to fail as magnificently, and selectively, as she had all these years. So now, when she was determined to succeed at last, she'd wanted her family's support. It was clear she wasn't going to get it. And she could hardly blame them for it. She was merely reaping what she had so carefully sowed.

Harry had a momentary qualm when she wondered whether they might be right. Maybe she was biting off more than she could chew. After all, what did she know about sheep or sheep ranching? Then her chin tilted up and she clenched her hands in her lap under the table. They were wrong. She wouldn't fail. She could learn what she didn't know. And she would succeed.

Harriet Elizabeth Alistair was convinced in her heart that she wasn't a failure. Surely, once she made up her mind to stop failing, she could. Once she was doing something she had chosen for herself, she was bound to succeed. She would show them all. She wasn't what they thought her—someone who had to be watched and protected from herself and the cold, cruel world around her. Rather, she was a woman with hopes and dreams, none of which she'd been allowed—or rather, allowed herself—to pursue.

Like a pioneer of old, Harry wanted to go west to build a new life. She was prepared for hard work, for frigid winter mornings and searing summer days. She welcomed the opportunity to build her fortune with the sweat of her brow and the labor of her back. Harry couldn't expect her family to understand why she wanted to try to make it on her own in a cold, smelly, faraway place where she would have to indulge in manual labor. She had something to prove to herself. This venture was the Boston Tea Party and the Alamo and Custer's Last Stand all rolled into one. In the short run she might lose a few battles, but she was determined to win the war.

At last Harry broke the awesome silence that had descended on the dinner table. "Nothing you've said has changed my mind," she told her family. "I'll be leaving at the end of the week."

Nothing her family said the following week, and they'd said quite a lot, had dissuaded Harry from the course she'd set for herself. She'd been delighted to find, when she arrived a week later in Big Timber, the town closest to great-uncle Cyrus's ranch, that at least she hadn't been deceived about the beauty of the mountains in southwestern Montana. The Crazy Mountains provided a striking vista to the north, while the majestic, snow-capped Absarokas greeted her to the south each morning. But they were the only redeeming feature in an otherwise daunting locale.

The Boulder River Valley was a desolate place in late

February. The cottonwoods that lined the Boulder River, which meandered the length of the valley, were stripped bare of leaves. And the grass, what wasn't covered by patches of drifted snow, was a ghastly straw-yellow. All that might have been bearable if only she hadn't found such utter decay when she arrived at great-uncle Cyrus's ranch.

Her first look at the property she'd inherited had been quite a shock. Harry had been tempted to turn tail and run back to Williamsburg. But something—perhaps the beauty of the mountains, but more likely the thought of facing her family if she gave up without even trying—had kept her from giving John Wilkinson the word to sell. She would never go home until she could do so with her head held high, the owner and manager of a prosperous sheep ranch.

Harry had discovered dozens of reasons to question her decision ever since she'd moved to Montana, not the least of which was the meeting today with her nearest neighbor. Nathan Hazard hadn't exactly fulfilled her expectations of the typical Western hero. A more provoking, irritating, exasperating man she had never known! Whether he admitted it or not, it had been a pretty sneaky thing to do, helping her so generously with the difficult lambing when he knew all along he was only softening her up so that he could make an offer on her land.

Thoughts of the difficult birthing reminded her that she still had to dispose of the dead lamb. Harry knew she ought to bury it, but the ground was frozen. She couldn't imagine burning it. And she couldn't bear the thought of taking the poor dead lamb somewhere up into the foothills and leaving it among the juniper and jack pine for nature's scavengers to find. None of the brochures she'd read discussed this particular problem. Harry knew there must be some procedures the local ranchers followed. Surely they also had deaths at lambing time. But she'd dig a hole in the frozen

ground with her fingernails before she asked Nathan Hazard
what to do.

For now Harry decided to move the dead lamb behind
the barn and cover it with a tarp. As long as the weather
stayed cold, the body wouldn't decay. When she could spare
the time, she would take a trip into Big Timber and strike
up a conversation with Slim Harley at the feed store. Somehow she would casually bring up the subject of dead lambs
in the conversation and get the answers she needed. Harry's
lips twisted wryly. Western conversations certainly tended
to have a grittier tone than those in the East.

Harry couldn't put off what had to be done. She slipped
her vest back on, pulled her cap down on her head and
stepped back into her galoshes. A quick search turned up
some leather work gloves in the drawer beside the sink. A
minute later she was headed back out to the sheep pens.

Harry actually shuddered when she picked up the dead
lamb. It had stiffened in death. It was also heavier than she'd
expected, so she had to hold it close to her chest in order
to carry it. Despite everything Harry had read about not
getting emotionally involved, she was unable to keep from
mourning the animal's death. It seemed like such a waste.
Although, if the lamb had lived it would have gone to mar-
ket, where it would eventually have become lamb chops on
some Eastern dinner table.

Maybe she ought to call Nathan Hazard and take him up
on his offer, after all.

Before Harry had a chance to indulge her bout of maudlin
conjecture she heard another sheep baaing in distress.

Not again!

Harry raced for the sheep pens where she had separated
the ewes that were ready to deliver. Instead she discovered
a sheep had already given birth to a lamb. While she
watched, it birthed a twin. Harry had learned from her ex-

tensive reading that her sheep had been genetically bred so they bore twins, thus doubling the lamb crop. But to her it was a unique happening. She stopped and leaned against the pen and smiled with joy at having witnessed such a miraculous event.

Then she realized she had work to do. The cords had to be cut and dipped in iodine. And the ewe and her lambs had to be moved into a jug, a small pen separate from the other sheep, for two or three days until the lambs had bonded with their mothers and gotten a little stronger.

Harry had read that lambing required constant attention from a rancher, but she hadn't understood that to mean she would get no sleep, no respite. For the rest of the night she never had a chance to leave the sheep barn, as the ewes dropped twin lambs that lived or died depending on the whims of fate. The stack under the tarp beside her barn got higher.

If Harry had found a spare second, she would have swallowed her pride and called Nathan Hazard for help. But by the time she got a break near dawn, the worst seemed to be over. Harry had stood midwife to the delivery of forty-seven lambs. Forty-three were still alive.

She dragged herself into the house and only then realized she'd forgotten about the orphan lamb in her kitchen. He was bleating pitifully from hunger. Despite her fatigue, Harry took the time to fix the lamb a bottle. She fell asleep sitting on the wooden-plank floor with her back against the wooden-plank wall, with the hungry lamb in her lap sucking at a nippled Coke bottle full of milk replacer.

That was how Nathan Hazard found her the following morning at dawn.

Nathan had lambing of his own going on, but unlike Harriet Alistair, he had several hired hands to help with the work. When suppertime arrived, he left the sheep barn and came inside to a hot meal that Katoya, the elderly Blackfoot Indian woman who was his housekeeper, had ready and waiting for him.

Katoya had mysteriously arrived on the Hazard doorstep on the day Nathan's mother had died, as though by some prearranged promise, to take her place in the household. Nathan had been sixteen at the time. No explanation had ever been forthcoming as to why the Blackfoot woman had come. And despite Nathan's efforts in later years to ease the older woman's chores, Katoya still worked every day from dawn to dusk with apparent tirelessness, making Nathan's house a home.

As Nathan sat down at the kitchen table, he wondered whether Harriet Alistair had found anything worth eating in her bare cupboards. The fact he should find himself worrying about an Alistair, even if it was a woman, made him frown.

"Were you able to buy the land?" Katoya asked as she poured coffee into his cup.

Nathan had learned better than to try to keep secrets from the old Indian woman. "Harry Alistair wouldn't sell," he admitted brusquely.

The diminutive Blackfoot woman merely nodded. "So the feud will go on." She seated herself in a rocker in the kitchen that was positioned to get the most heat from the old-fashioned woodstove.

Nathan grimaced. "Yeah."

"Is it so important to own the land?"

Nathan turned to face her and saw skin stretched tight with age over high, wide cheekbones and black hair threaded with silver in two braids over her shoulders. He suddenly wondered how old she was. Certainly she had clung to the old Blackfoot ways. "It must be the Indian in you," he said at last, "that doesn't feel the same need as I do to possess land."

Katoya looked back at him with eyes that were a deep black well of wisdom. "The Indian knows what the white man has never learned. You cannot own the land. You can only use it for so long as you walk the earth."

Katoya started the rocker moving, and its creak made a familiar, comforting sound as Nathan ate the hot lamb stew she'd prepared for him.

Nathan had to admit there was a lot to be said for the old woman's argument. Why was he so determined to own that piece of Alistair land? After all, when he was gone, who would know or care? Maybe he could have accepted Katoya's point of view if he hadn't met Harry Alistair first. Now he couldn't leave things the way they stood. That piece of land smack in the middle of his spread had always been a burr under the saddle. He didn't intend to stop bucking until the situation was remedied.

Nathan refilled his own coffee cup to keep the old woman from having to get up again, then settled down into the kitchen chair with his legs stretched out toward the stove. Because he respected Katoya's advice, Nathan found himself explaining the situation. "The Harry Alistair who inherited the land from Cyrus turned out to be a woman, Harry-et Alistair. She's greener than buffalo grass in spring and doesn't know a thing about sheep that hasn't come out of an extension service bulletin. Harry-et Alistair hasn't got a snowball's chance in hell of making a go of Cyrus's place. But I never saw a woman so determined, so stubborn...."

"You admire her," Katoya said.

"I don't... Yes, I do," he admitted with a disbelieving shake of his head. Nathan kept his face averted as he continued, "But I can't imagine why. She's setting herself up for a fall. I just hate to see her have to take it."

"We always have choices. Is there truly nothing that can be done?"

"Are you suggesting I offer to help her out?" Nathan demanded incredulously. "Because I won't. I'm not going to volunteer a shoulder to cry on, let alone one to carry a yoke. I've learned my lessons well," he said bitterly. "I'm not going to let that woman get under my skin."

"Perhaps it is too late. Perhaps you already care for her. Perhaps you will have no choice in the matter."

Nathan's jaw flexed as he ground his teeth. The old woman was more perceptive than was comfortable. How could he explain to her the feeling of possessiveness, of protectiveness that had arisen the moment he'd seen Harry-et Alistair. He didn't understand it himself. Hell, yes, he already cared about Harry-et Alistair. And that worried the dickens out of him. What if he succumbed to her allure? What if he ended up getting involved with her, deeply, emotionally involved with her, and it turned out she needed more than he could give? He knew what it meant to have someone solely dependent upon him, to have someone rely upon him for everything, and to know that no matter how much he did it wouldn't be enough. Nathan couldn't stand the pain of that kind of relationship again.

"You must face the truth," Katoya said. "What will be must be."

The old woman's philosophy was simple but irrefutable. "All right," Nathan said. "I'll go see her again tomorrow morning. But that doesn't mean I'm going to get involved in her life."

Nathan repeated that litany until he fell asleep, where he dreamed of a woman with freckles and braids and bibbed overalls who kissed with a passion that had made his pulse race and his body throb. He woke up hard and hungry. He didn't shave, didn't eat, simply pulled on jeans, boots, shirt, hat and coat and slammed out the door.

When he arrived at the Alistair place, it was deathly quiet. There was no smoke coming from the stone chimney, no sounds from the barn, or from the tiny, dilapidated cabin.

Something's wrong.

Nathan thrust the pickup truck door open and hit the ground running for the cabin. His heart was in his throat, his breath hard to catch because his chest was constricted.

Let her be all right, he prayed. *I promise I'll help if only she's all right.*

The kitchen door not only wasn't locked, it wasn't even closed. Nathan shoved it open and roared at the top of his voice, ''Harry-et! Are you in here? Harry-et!''

That was when he saw her. She was sitting on the floor in the corner with a lamb clutched to her chest, her eyes wide with terror at the sight of him. He was so relieved, and so angry that she'd frightened him for nothing, that he raced over, grabbed her by the shoulders and hauled her to her feet.

''What the hell do you think you're doing, leaving the back door standing wide open? You'll catch your death of cold,'' he yelled, giving her shoulders a shake to make his point. ''Of all the stupid, idiotic, greenhorn—''

And then it dawned on him what he was doing, and he let her go as abruptly as he'd grabbed her. She backed up to the wall and stood there, staring at him.

Harry Alistair had a death grip on the lamb in her arms. There were dark circles under her eyes, which were wide and liquid with tears that hadn't yet spilled. Her whole body was trembling with fatigue and the aftereffects of the shaking Nathan had given her. Her mouth was working but the words weren't coming out in much more than a whisper.

Nathan leaned closer to hear what she was trying to say.

"Get out," she rasped. And then, stronger, "Get out of my house."

Nathan felt his heart miss a thump. "I'm sorry. Look, I only came over—"

Her chin came up. "I don't care why you came. I want you to leave. And don't come back."

Nathan's lips pressed flat. *What will be must be.* It was just as well things had turned out this way. It would have been a mistake to try to help her, anyway. But there was a part of him that died inside at the thought of not seeing her again. He wanted her. More than he'd ever wanted a woman in his life. But she was all wrong for him. She needed the kind of caretaking he'd sworn he was through with forever.

It took every bit of grit he had to turn on his booted heel and walk out of the room. And out of her life.

3

What is accepted dress-for-success garb for country women? *Answer:* Coveralls, scabby work shoes, holey hat and shredded gloves.

I am not a failure. I can do anything I set my mind to do. I will succeed.

Over the next two months there were many times when Harry wanted to give up. Often, it was only the repetition of those three sentences that kept her going. For, no matter how hard she tried, things always went awry. She had been forced to learn some hard lessons and learn them fast.

About a week after the majority of the lambs had been born, most of them got sick. Harry called in the vet, who diagnosed lamb scours and prescribed antibiotics. Despite her efforts, a dozen more lambs died. She stacked them under the tarp beside the barn.

Early on the lambs had to have their tails docked, and the ram lambs, except those valuable enough to be sires, had to be castrated. Several of the older brochures described cutting off the lamb tails with a knife and searing the stump with a hot iron. Castration was described even more graphically. Faced with such onerous chores, Harry had known she would never make it as a sheepman.

At her lowest moment a brochure describing a more modern technique for docking and castration mysteriously arrived in her mailbox. An "elastrator" and rubber bands were placed on the appropriate extremities, which wasted away and dropped off on their own within two to three weeks. She found the process unpleasant, time-consuming work. But with the information provided in the timely brochure, she'd succeeded when she might have given up.

Unfortunately Harry also lost several ewes during delivery and found herself with more orphan lambs, which she had learned were called bums, that had to be fed with milk replacer. Bottle-feeding lambs turned out to be surprisingly expensive, and she had to dip into the meager financial reserves Cyrus had left in the bank. She would have run out of money except Harley's Feed Store had a sale on milk replacer. That had seemed a little odd to Harry, but a blushing Slim had assured her that he'd ordered too much replacer, and if he didn't sell it cheap, it was just going to sit on the shelf for another year. Cyrus's money had gone further than she'd dared to hope.

It was a month of exhausting days and nights before Harry could wean the lambs to a solid feed of pellet rations. But she'd made it. She still had money in the bank, and the lambs had all gotten fed. In fact, Harry was still bottle-feeding some that had been born late in the season. She'd forgotten what it was like to get more than four hours of sleep in a row. When there was work to be done, she'd repeat those three pithy sentences. They kept her awake and functioning despite what felt very much like battle fatigue. But then, wasn't she engaged in the greatest battle of her life?

By now even a novice like Harry had figured out that in its best days, Cyrus's sheep ranch had been a marginal proposition. With all the neglect over the years, it took every bit of time and attention she had simply to keep her head above water. But she was still afloat. And paddling for all she was worth. She hadn't failed. Yet. With a lot of hard work, and more than a little luck, she just might surprise everyone and make a go of Cyrus's ranch.

In the brief moments when Harry wasn't taking care of livestock—she had six laying hens, a rooster, a sow with eight piglets and a milk cow, as well as the sheep to attend—she'd thought over her last meeting with Nathan Hazard.

Perhaps if she hadn't been quite so tired the morning he had come to see her, or if he hadn't woken her quite so abruptly or been quite so upset, she might have been able to listen to what he had to say. If he had offered help, she might have accepted. She would never know for sure. Harry hadn't seen hide nor hair of him since.

Nor had anyone else come to visit. She'd made a number of phone calls to John Wilkinson at the bank for advice and had managed to get a few more tidbits of information from Slim every time she made a trip to Harley's Feed Store. But, quite frankly, Harry was beginning to feel the effects of the extreme isolation in which she'd been living for the past two months.

Which was probably why she hadn't argued more when her mother, father and brother had said they were coming out to Montana to visit her. Unfortunately, with the time it had taken her to finish her chores this morning, she only had about fifteen minutes left to put herself together before she had to meet them at The Grand, the bed-and-breakfast in Big Timber where they were staying.

The varnished wooden booths that lined one wall of the luncheon dining room at The Grand had backs high enough to conceal the occupants and give them privacy. Thus, it wasn't until Nathan heard her exuberant greeting that he realized who was soon to occupy the next booth.

"Mom, Dad, Charlie, it's so good to see you!" Harry said.

"I'm sorry I can't say the same, darling," an uppity-sounding woman replied in a dismayed voice. "You look simply awful. What have you done to yourself? And what on earth is that you have on your head?"

Nathan smiled at the thought of Harry-et in her Harley's Feed Store cap.

A young man joined in with, "For Pete's sake, Harriet. Are you really wearing bibbed overalls?"

Nathan grinned. Very likely she was.

Before Harry had a chance to respond, an older man's bass voice contributed, "I knew I should have put my foot down. I didn't think you could manage on your own in this godforsaken place. And from the look of you, I wasn't wrong. When are you coming home?"

Nathan listened for Harry-et's answer to that last question with bated breath.

There was a long pause before she answered, "I am home. And I have no intention of going back to Williamsburg, if that's what you're asking, Dad."

Nathan took advantage of the stunned silence that followed her pronouncement to take a quick swallow of coffee. He knew he ought not to eavesdrop on the Alistairs, but it wasn't as though he'd come here with that thought in mind. He'd been minding his own business when *they'd* interrupted *him*. He signaled Tillie Mae for a refill of his coffee and settled back to relax for a few minutes after lunch as was his custom. He didn't listen, exactly, but he couldn't help but hear what was being said.

"I've been to see John Wilkinson at the bank," her father began. "And he—"

"Dad! You had no right—"

"I have every right," he interrupted. "I'm your father. I—"

"In case you haven't noticed, I'm not a child anymore," Harry interrupted right back. "I can take care of myself."

"Darling," her mother said soothingly, "take a good, close look at yourself. There are dark circles under your eyes, your fingernails are chipped and broken and those awful clothes you're wearing are filthy. All I can conclude is that you're not taking good care of yourself. Your father and I only want the best for you. It hurts us to think of you suffering like this for nothing when in the end you'll only fail."

"I'm *not* suffering," Harry protested. "And I will *not* fail. In fact, I'm doing just fine." That might have been an overstatement, but it was in a good cause.

"Fine?" her father questioned. "You can't possibly know enough about sheep ranching to succeed on your own. Why, even ranchers who know what they're doing sometimes fail."

"Dad…"

Nathan heard the fatigue and frustration in Harry-et's voice. Her father shouldn't be allowed to browbeat her like that. Nathan ignored the Western code that admonished him not to interfere, in favor of the one that said a woman must always be protected. A moment later he was standing beside the next booth.

Harry was explaining, "I know what I'm doing, Dad. I've been reading all the brochures I can find about sheep ranch-ing—"

"And she's had help from her neighbors whenever she ran into trouble," Nathan finished. A charming smile lit his face as he tipped his hat to Mrs. Alistair and said, "Howdy, ma'am. I'm Nathan Hazard, a neighbor of your daughter's."

Nathan bypassed Harry's stunned expression and turned an assessing gaze to her father and brother. "I couldn't help overhearing you, sir," he said to Harry's father. "And I just want to say that we've all been keeping an eye on Harry-et to make sure—''

''You've been what?''

Nathan turned to Harry, who'd risen from her seat and was staring at him with her eyes wide and her mouth hanging open in horror.

''I was just saying that we've been keeping a neighborly eye on you.'' Before Harry could respond he'd turned back to her father and continued, ''You see, sir, we have a great deal of respect for women out here, and there isn't a soul in the valley who would stand by if he thought Harry-et was in any real trouble.

''Of course, you're right that she probably won't be able to make a go of Cyrus Alistair's place. But then it's doubtful whether anyone could. That's why I've offered to buy the place from her. And I have every hope that once she's gotten over the silly notion that—''

''Don't say another word!'' Harry was so hot she could have melted icicles in January. She hung on to her temper long enough to say, ''Mom, Dad, Charles, I hope you'll excuse us. I have a few words to say to Mr. Hazard. Alone.''

Harry turned and stalked out to the front lobby of The Grand without waiting to see whether Nathan followed her. After tipping his hat once more to Mrs. Alistair, he did.

Just as Harry turned and opened her mouth to speak, Nathan took her by the elbow and started upstairs with her.

''Where do you think you're going?'' Harry snapped, tugging frantically against his hold.

''Upstairs.''

''There are *bedrooms* upstairs!''

''Yep. Sarah keeps all the doors open to show off her fancy antiques. We can use one of the rooms for a little privacy.'' He pulled her into the first open bedroom and shut the door behind them. ''Now what's on your mind?''

"What's on my—?" Harry was so furious she was gasping for air. "How dare you drag me up here—"

"We can go back downstairs and argue. That way everyone in the valley will know your business," he said, reaching for the doorknob.

"Wait!" Harry made the mistake of touching his hand and felt an arc of heat run up her arm. She jerked her hand away and took two steps back from him, only to come up against the edge of the ornate brass bed. She stepped forward, only to find herself toe-to-toe with Nathan.

"Hold on a minute," she said, trying desperately to regain the upper hand. "How dare you insinuate to my family that I haven't been making it on my own! I most certainly have!"

Nathan shook his head.

"Don't try to deny it," she retorted. "I haven't seen a soul except Slim Harley for the past two months. Just who, may I ask, has been helping me?"

"Me."

Harry was so stunned that she took a step back. When the backs of her legs hit the bed, she sat down. Her eyes never left Nathan's face, so she saw the flash of guilt in his blue eyes and the tinge of red growing on his cheeks. "You helped me? How?"

Nathan lifted his hat and shoved his fingers through his hair in agitation, then pulled his hat down over his brow again. "Little ways."

"How?"

He cleared his throat and admitted, "Dropped off a brochure once. Broke the ice on your ponds."

That explained some things she'd wondered about. She'd needed the knowledge the farm brochure had provided, but it wasn't as though he'd come over and helped with the docking and castration of the lambs. And while she'd appreciated having the ice broken on her ponds, she could have done that herself. His interference didn't amount to as much as she'd feared.

"And I talked Slim into putting his milk replacer on sale," he finished.

That was another matter entirely. Without the sale on milk replacer she'd have run out of money for sure. "You're responsible for that?"

"Wasn't a big deal. He really did order too much."

"Did anybody else get their milk replacer on sale?" she asked in a strained voice.

"No."

Harry's chest hurt. She couldn't breathe. "Why did you bother if you were so certain I'd fail in the end?"

"Thought you'd come to your senses sooner than this," he said gruffly. "Figured there was no sense letting all those lambs starve."

Harry turned to stare out a window draped with antique lace curtains. Her hand gripped the brass bedstead so hard her knuckles were white. "Did it ever occur to you that I'd rather not have your help? Did it ever occur to you that whether I was going to fail or succeed I would rather do it all by myself?"

Nathan didn't know how to answer her. He willed her to look up at him, but he could tell how she felt even without seeing her face. Her pulse pounded in her throat and her jaw worked as she ground her teeth.

To tell the honest truth, he didn't know why he'd interfered in her life. If he'd just left well enough alone, she would probably have quit and gone home a long time ago. Maybe that had something to do with it. Maybe he didn't want her to go away. He still felt the same attraction every time he got anywhere near her. And it was impossible to control his protective instincts whenever she was around. Just look what had happened today.

He reached out to touch her on the shoulder, and she jumped like a scalded cat. Only, when she came up off the bed, she ran right flat into him. Instinctively his arms surrounded her.

The only sound in the room was the two of them breathing. Panting, actually, as though they'd just run a footrace. Nathan didn't dare move, for fear she'd bolt. It felt good holding her. He wanted more. Slowly, ever so slowly, he raised a hand and brushed his knuckles across her cheek. It was so smooth!

She looked up at him then, and he saw her pupils were wide, her eyes dark. Her mouth was slightly open, her lips full. Her eyelids closed as he lowered his mouth to touch hers. He felt the tremor run through her as their lips made contact. Soft. So incredibly soft, and moist.

When he ran his tongue along the edge of her mouth, she groaned. And her mouth opened wider to let him in.

He took his time kissing her, letting his lips learn the touch and taste of her. He felt the tension in her body, felt her resistance even as she succumbed to the desire that flared between them.

Nathan felt the same war within himself that he knew she was fighting. Lord, how he wanted her! He knew he shouldn't be kissing her. But there was something about her, something about the touch and taste of her, that drew him despite his resolve not to become involved.

When he broke the kiss at last, she leaned her forehead against his chest, and all the starch seemed to come out of her. "Why did you do that?" she asked in a whisper.

"I can't explain it myself. I don't want…I don't think we're very well suited to each other." He felt her tense in his arms. "I don't mean to hurt your feelings. I'm only telling you the truth as I see it."

Harry dropped her hands, which she discovered were clutching either side of Nathan's waist, and stepped away from him. She raised her eyes to meet his steady gaze. "I can't disagree with you. I don't think we're well suited, either. I can't explain..." A rueful smile tilted her mouth up on one side. "You're quite good at kissing. You must have had a lot of practice."

Harry didn't realize she was fishing for information until the words were out of her mouth. She wanted to know if she was only one of many.

"I...uh...don't have much time for this sort of thing," he admitted. "Kissing women. A relationship with a woman, I mean."

"Oh?"

"Haven't had time for years," he blurted.

Harry was fascinated by the red patches that began at Nathan's throat and worked their way up. But his admission, however much it embarrassed him, gave Harry a reason for their tremendous attraction to each other. "I think I know why this...thing...is so strong between us," Harry said, as though speaking about it could diffuse its power.

This time Nathan said, "Oh?"

"Yes, you see, I haven't had much time for a relationship with a man. That has to be it, don't you think? We have these normal, primitive urges, and we just naturally..."

"Naturally kiss each other every time we meet?" Nathan said with disbelief.

"Have you got a better explanation?" Harry said. Her fists found her hips in a stance that Nathan recognized all too well.

He shrugged. "I can't explain it at all. All I can say is I don't plan to let this happen again."

"Well, that's good to hear," Harry said. "Now that we have that settled, I'm going back downstairs to inform my family that I'm managing fine *on my own*. And you will not contradict me. Is that clear?"

"Perfectly."

"Let's go, Mr. Hazard." She opened the door, waited for him to leave, then followed him toward the stairs.

"Wait!" He turned and she collided with his chest. His arms folded around her. The desire flared between them faster than they could stop it. Nathan swore under his breath as he steadied Harry and took a step back from her.

"I only wanted to say," he said harshly, "that if you plan to stay in the valley, you'd better get your fallow fields planted with some kind of winter forage."

Harry wrapped her arms around herself as though that would protect her from the feelings roiling inside. "Fine. Is that all?"

He opened his mouth to say something about the stack of dead lambs beside her barn and shut it again. She'd already asked Slim Harley what to do about them. He didn't understand why she hadn't buried them yet, but the closed expression on her face didn't encourage any more advice, let alone the offer of help he'd been about to make. "That's all," he said.

Nathan made his way back downstairs to the bar without once looking at Harry again. As he passed her family, he merely tipped his hat, grim-faced, and resumed his seat in the high-backed booth next to theirs.

Harry made quick work of reassuring her family that she was fine and that she wouldn't be leaving Montana. There was no sound from the next booth. But Harry knew Nathan was there. And that he was listening.

"We'd like to see where you're living," her brother said. "What's it like?"

"Rustic," Harry said, her smile reappearing for the first time since she'd entered The Grand.

"It sounds charming," her mother said.

"That it is," Harry said, her sense of humor making her smile broaden. "I'm afraid I can't invite you out to visit. It's a little small. And it doesn't have much in the way of amenities."

She heard Nathan snort in the next booth.

"Well, I feel better knowing your neighbors are keeping an eye on you," her father said. "That Hazard fellow seems a nice enough man."

Harry didn't think that deserved further comment, so she remained silent.

"Are you sure you can handle the financial end of things?" her father asked. "Mr. Wilkinson said you've got a big bill due next month for—"

"I can handle things, Dad," Harry said. "Don't worry."

She watched her father gnaw on his lower lip, then pull at the bushy white mustache that covered his upper lip. "All right, Harriet. If you insist on playing this game out to the bitter end, I suppose we have no choice except to go along— for now. But I think I should warn you that if you aren't showing some kind of profit by the fall, I'll have to insist that you forget this foolishness and come home before winter sets in."

Harry was mortified to think that Nathan was hearing her father's ultimatum. She was tempted to let his words go without contesting them. That was the sort of passive resistance she'd resorted to in the past. But the Harry who'd come to Montana had turned over a new leaf. She felt compelled to say, "You're welcome to come and visit in the fall, Dad. I expect you'll be pleasantly surprised at how well I'm doing by then. But don't expect me to leave if I'm not."

Harry allowed her mother to admonish her to take better

care of herself before she finally said, "I have to be getting back to the ranch. I've got stock that needs tending."

She rose and hugged her mother, father and brother, wishing things could be different, that she hadn't lived her life by pretending to fail. She would prove she could make it on her own if it was the last thing she did. Harry wished her family a pleasant drive from Big Timber to the airport in Billings, and a safe flight home. "I'll be in touch," she promised.

They would never know the effort it took to summon the confident smile with which she left them. "Things should be less hectic for me later in the summer," she said. "I'll look forward to seeing you then."

She could tell from their anxious faces that they didn't want to leave her in Montana alone. She reassured them the best she could with, "I'm all right, really. A little tired from all the hard work. But I love what I'm doing. It's challenging. And rewarding."

Harry smiled and waved as she left the restaurant. She was out the door before she realized Nathan Hazard had been standing behind her left shoulder the whole time she'd been waving goodbye.

"I'll follow you home," he said.

"Why on earth would you want to do that?"

Nathan looked up at a sky that was dark with storm clouds. "Looks like rain. All those potholes in your road, you could get stuck."

"If I do, Mr. Hazard, I'll dig myself out." Harry indignantly stalked away, but had to yank three or four times on the door to Cyrus's battered pickup before she finally got inside. She spent the entire trip home glaring at Nathan Hazard's pickup in her rearview mirror. He followed her all the way up to the tiny cabin door.

Harry hopped out of the pickup and marched back to

Nathan's truck. He had the window down and his elbow stuck out.

"Rain, huh?" Harry said, looking up as the sun peered through the clouds, creating a glare on his windshield.

"Could have."

"Sheep dip," Harry said succinctly. "I've had it with helpful neighbors. From now on I want you to stay off my property. Stay away from me, and don't do me any more favors!"

"All right, Harry-et," he said with a long-suffering sigh. "We'll do it your way. For a while."

"For good!" Harry snapped back.

It was doubtful Nathan heard her, because he'd already turned his pickup around and headed back down the jouncy dirt road.

Harry kicked at a stone and sent it flying across the barren yard. Yes, the work was hard, and yes, she was tired. But she'd loved every minute of the challenge she'd set for herself. Before her talk with Nathan Hazard today she'd indulged fully in the satisfaction of knowing she'd done it all by herself. Damn him! Damn his interference! Damn the man for being such a damn good kisser!

If Nathan Hazard knew what was good for him, he wouldn't show his face around here anytime soon.

4

What do you do when people drop by to visit and they haven't been invited?
Answer: Serve them coffee.

Harry was standing in the pigpen, slopping the hogs and thinking about Nathan, when she spied a pickup bumping down the dirt road that led to her place. At first she feared it was her nemesis and began tensing for another battle with Nathan. But the battered truck wasn't rusted in the right places to be Nathan's. After two months of being left so completely alone, Harry was surprised to have visitors. She couldn't help wondering who had come to see her, and why.

The man who stepped out of the driver's side of the beat-up vehicle was a stranger. Harry stood staring as a beautiful woman dressed in form-fitting jeans and a fleece-lined denim jacket shoved open the passenger door of the truck. The couple exchanged a glance that led Harry to believe they must be married, probably some of her neighbors, finally come to call.

The slight blond woman approached her and said, "Hello, I'm Abigail Dayton. Fish and Wildlife Service."

Harry was dumbfounded. *The woman was a government official!* What on earth was someone from the Fish and Wildlife Service doing here? Her heart caught in her throat, keeping her from responding. Her mind searched furiously for the reason for such a visit. Had she done something wrong? Broken some law? Forgotten to fill out some form?

Had she let too many lambs die? Was there a penalty for that?

Harry recognized the instinct to flee and fought it. She had come west to start over, to confront her problems and deal with them. She would have to face this woman and find out what she wanted. Only first she had to get out of the pigpen, which wasn't as easy as it sounded.

Harry finally resorted to climbing over the top of the pen instead of going through the gate, which was wired shut. She heard a rip when her overalls caught on a stray barb but ignored it as she extended her hand to the Fish and Wildlife agent. When the woman didn't take her hand immediately, Harry realized she was still wearing her work gloves, tore them off and tried again. "I'm Harriet Alistair. People mostly call me Harry."

"It's nice to meet you, Harry," Abigail said. She shook Harry's hand once, then let it go.

Harry turned and looked steadily at the tall, dark-haired, gray-eyed man standing beside Abigail Dayton, until he finally held out a callused hand and said, "I'm Luke Granger, your neighbor to the south. Sorry I haven't been over to see you sooner."

Harry was so glad Luke Granger was just a neighbor and not another government official that she smiled, exposing the tiny space between her teeth, and said, "I've been pretty busy myself. It's good to meet you."

So, one agent, one neighbor. Not related. But still no explanation as to why they'd come.

Harry felt a growing discomfort as she watched Luke and Abigail survey her property. It wasn't that they openly displayed disgust or disbelief at what they saw; in fact, they were both careful to keep their expressions neutral. But a tightening of Luke's jaw and a clenching of Abigail's hand made their feelings plain.

Harry wasn't exactly ashamed of her place. After all, she was hardly responsible for the sad state of repairs. But her stomach turned over when Abigail narrowed her green-eyed gaze on the stack of dead lambs beside the barn that were only partially covered by a black plastic tarp. Harry waited for the official condemnation that was sure to come.

"Have you seen any wolves around here?" Abigail asked.

"Wolves?" That wasn't at all what Harry had been expecting the Fish and Wildlife agent to say. The thought of wolves somewhere on her property was terrifying. "Wolves?" she repeated.

"A renegade timber wolf killed two of Luke's sheep," Abigail continued. "I wondered if you've suffered any wolf depredation on your spread."

"Not that I know of," Harry said. "I didn't even know there were any wolves around here."

"There aren't many," Abigail reassured her. "And there's going to be one less as soon as I can find and capture the renegade that killed Luke's sheep."

Harry watched a strange tension flare between her two visitors at Abigail's pronouncement. Before Harry had time to analyze it further, Abigail asked, "Have you seen any wolf sign at all?"

Harry grimaced and shook her head. "I wouldn't know it if I saw it. But you're welcome to take a look around."

"I think I will if you really don't mind."

Abigail carefully looked the grounds over with Luke by her side. Harry did her best to keep them headed away from the tiny log cabin. She'd already tasted their disapproval once and was reluctant to have them observe the primitive conditions in which she lived. However, before Harry knew it, they were all three standing at her kitchen door. There wasn't much she could do except invite them inside.

Harry felt a flush of embarrassment stain her cheeks when both Luke and Abigail stopped dead just inside the door. The scene that greeted them in the kitchen was pretty much the same one that had greeted Nathan the first time he'd come to visit. Only now there were six lambs sleeping on a blanket wadded in the corner instead of just one. The shambles in Harry's kitchen gave painful evidence of how hard she was struggling to cope with the responsibilities she'd assumed on Cyrus Alistair's death. Harry didn't know what to say. What could she say?

Abigail finally broke the looming silence. "I'd love some coffee. Wouldn't you, Luke?"

Grateful for the simple suggestion, Harry urged her company to seat themselves at the kitchen table. While she made coffee, Harry lectured herself about how it didn't really matter what these people thought. The important thing was that she'd survived the past two months.

Harry poured three cups of coffee and brought them to the table, then seated herself across from Abigail, who was saying something about how wolves weren't really as bad as people thought, and how their reputation had been exaggerated by all those fairy tales featuring a Big Bad Wolf.

Harry wasn't convinced. She took a sip of the hot, bitter coffee and said, "I've been meaning to learn how to use a rifle in case I had trouble with predators, but—"

Abigail leaped up out of her chair in alarm. "You can't *shoot* a timber wolf! They're an endangered species They're protected!"

"I'm sorry," Harry said. "I didn't know." She shook her head in disgust. "There's just so much I don't know."

Abigail sat back down a little sheepishly. "I'm afraid I tend to get on my high horse whenever the discussion turns to wolves."

Harry ran her fingers aimlessly across the pamphlets and

brochures that littered the table, shouting her ignorance of sheep ranching to anyone who cared to notice.

"You really shouldn't leave those dead lambs lying around, though," Abigail said. "They're liable to attract predators."

Harry chewed on her lower lip. "I know I'm supposed to bury them, but I just can't face the thought of doing it."

"I've got some time right now," Luke said. "Why don't you let me help?"

Harry leaned forward to protest. "But I can't pay—"

"Neighbors don't have to pay each other for lending a helping hand," he said brusquely. A moment later he was out the door.

"You know, I bet there's a really nice man behind that stony face he wears," Harry said as she stared after him.

"I wouldn't know," Abigail said. "I only met him this morning."

"Oh, I thought…" Harry didn't finish her thought, discouraged by the shuttered look on Abigail's face. There was something going on between Luke and Abigail, all right. But if they'd just met, the sparks must have been pretty instantaneous. Just like the desire that had flared between her and Nathan. Harry felt an immediate affinity to the other woman. After all, they'd both been attracted to rough-hewn Montana sheepmen.

Abigail rose and took her coffee cup to the sink, and without Harry quite being aware how it happened, Abigail was soon washing the mound of dirty dishes while Harry dried them and put them away. While they worked, they talked, and Harry found herself confiding to Abigail, "Sometimes I wake up in the morning and wonder how long it'll take me to get this place into shape, or if I ever will."

"Why would you want to?" Abigail blurted. "I mean… This place needs a lot of work."

Harry's sense of humor got the better of her, and she grinned. "That's an understatement if I ever heard one. This place is a *wreck*."

"So tell me why you're staying," Abigail urged.

"It's a long story."

"I'd like to hear it."

Harry took a deep breath and let it out. "All right."

It was a tremendous relief to Harry to be able to tell someone—someone who had no reason to be judgmental—how she'd lived her life. Abigail's interested green eyes and sympathetic *oohs* and *aahs* helped Harry relate the various fiascos that littered her past. It wasn't until she started talking about Nathan Hazard that words became really difficult to find.

"At first I was so grateful he was there," Harry said as she explained how Nathan had helped in the birthing of the dead lamb and its twin. "I think that was why I was so angry when it turned out he'd only come because he wanted to buy this place from me.

"I'm determined to manage on my own, but the man keeps popping up when I least expect him. And somehow, every time we've crossed paths, we end up—"

"End up what?"

"Kissing," Harry admitted. "I know that sounds ab surd—"

"Not so absurd as you think," Abigail muttered. "Must be more to these Montana sheepmen then meets the eye," she said with a rueful smile.

"Nathan Hazard is driving me crazy," Harry said. What she didn't add, couldn't find words to explain, was how every time she inevitably ended up in his arms, the fire that rose between them seemed unquenchable. "I wish he'd just leave me alone."

That wasn't precisely true. What she wanted was a different kind of attention from Nathan Hazard than she was getting. Something more personal and less professional. But that was too confusing, and much too complicated, to contemplate.

Harry looked around her and was amazed to discover that while she'd been talking Abigail had continued doing chores around the kitchen. The dishes were washed, the floor was swept, the counters were clear and the brochures on the table had been separated into neat stacks. Several lambs had woken, and Abigail had matter-of-factly joined Harry on the floor to help her bottle-feed the noisy bums.

"Have you thought about getting a hired hand to help with the heavy work?" Abigail asked.

"Can't afford one," Harry admitted. "Although Mr. Wilkinson at the bank said there's a shepherd who'll keep an eye on my flock once I get it moved onto my federal lease in the mountains for the summer. Anyway, I'm determined to make it on my own."

"That's a laudable goal," Abigail said. "But is it realistic?"

"I thought so," Harry mused. "Since I didn't know a thing about sheep ranching when I arrived in Montana, I've made my share of mistakes. But I'm learning fast."

"You don't have to answer if you don't want to," Abigail said, "but why on earth don't you just sell this place—"

"To Nathan Hazard? Don't get me started again. I'll never sell to that man. Nathan Hazard is the meanest, ugliest son of a—"

Harry never got a chance to finish her sentence because Luke arrived at the door and announced, "I've buried those lambs. Anything else you'd like me to do while I'm here?"

"No thanks," Harry said, scrambling to her feet. "We're about finished here." She put the empty nippled Coke bottle on the kitchen counter and said, ''I really appreciate your help, Luke.''

''You're welcome, anytime.''

It took a moment for Harry to realize that although Luke was speaking to her, his attention was totally absorbed by the woman still sitting on the floor feeding the last ounce of milk replacer to a hungry lamb. From the look on Luke's face it appeared he would gladly take the lamb's place. Harry had wondered why Luke had come visiting with the Fish and Wildlife agent. Now she had her answer.

Harry was envious of what she saw in Luke Granger's eyes. No man had ever looked at her with such raw hunger, such need.

Unless you counted Nathan Hazard.

Harry watched as Abigail raised her eyes to Luke, a beatific smile on her face, watched as the smile faded, watched as Abigail's eyes assumed the wary look of an animal at bay.

Luke's gray eyes took on a feral gleam, and his muscles tensed and coiled in readiness.

The hunter. And the hunted. Harry recognized the relationship because she'd felt it herself. With Nathan Hazard.

An instant later Luke reached out a hand and pulled Abigail to her feet. Harry was uncomfortably aware of the frisson of sexual attraction that arced between them as they touched. She observed their cautious movements as Abigail inched past Luke in the tiny kitchen and joined Harry at the sink.

''I suppose Luke and I should get going,'' Abigail said. ''We've got a few more ranchers to ask about wolf sightings before the day's done. I've enjoyed getting to know you, Harry. I wish you luck with your ranch.''

''Thanks,'' Harry said with a smile, as she escorted Abigail and Luke back outside. ''I need all the luck I can get.''

She turned to Luke and said, "I hope you'll come back and visit again soon, neighbor."

"Count on it," he replied, tipping his Stetson.

"And I hope you capture that renegade wolf," Harry said to Abigail.

Harry watched as Abigail gave Luke a determined, almost defiant, look and said, "Count on it."

Abigail had trouble getting the passenger door of the pickup open, and Harry was just about to lend a hand when Luke stepped up and yanked it free. Abigail frowned at him and said, "I could have done that."

He shrugged. "Never said you couldn't." But he waited for her to get inside and closed the door snugly behind her before heading around to the driver's side of the truck.

"So long," Harry shouted after them as they drove away. "Careful on that road. It's a little bumpy!" A perfect farewell, Harry thought with an ironic twist of her mouth, seeing as how this had been a day for understatement.

Harry felt sorry to see them leave. She was probably being unnecessarily stubborn about trying to manage all by herself. Nathan Hazard was convinced she couldn't manage on her own. She should probably take advantage of Luke's offer of help and avoid making any more costly mistakes. But the whole purpose of coming to Montana, of putting herself in this isolated position, was to prove that she could do anything she set her mind to do *on her own*. She wasn't the person she'd led her parents to believe she was.

Harry had realized over the past two months that she wanted to prove that fact to herself even more than she wanted to prove it to them.

It would be too easy to stop resisting Nathan Hazard's interference in her business. Harry reminded herself that Nathan didn't really want her to succeed; he wanted Cyrus's land. And he wanted to take care of her, as one would care for someone incapable of taking care of herself. Letting Nathan Hazard into her life right now would be disastrous. Because Harry didn't want any more people taking care of her. She wanted to prove she could take care of herself.

Harry had another motive for wanting to keep Nathan at a distance. Whenever he was around she succumbed to the attraction she felt for him. At a time when she was trying to take control of her life, the feelings she had for Nathan Hazard were uncontrollable. She wanted to touch him and have him touch her, to kiss him and be kissed back with all the passion she felt whenever he held her in his arms, to share with him and to have him share the feelings she was hard put to name, but couldn't deny. Those powerful emotions left her feeling threatened in a way she couldn't explain. It was far better, Harry decided, to keep the man at a distance.

The next time Nathan Hazard came calling, if there was a next time, he wouldn't be welcome.

Harry woke the next day to the clang of metal on metal. She bolted upright in bed, then sat unmoving while she tried to place the sound. She couldn't, and quickly pulled on a heavy flannel robe and stepped into ice-cold slippers as she headed for the window to look outside. Her jaw dropped at what she saw. Nathan Hazard stood bare-chested, wrench in hand, working on the engine of Cyrus's farm tractor.

Her first thought was, *He must be freezing to death!* Then she looked at the angle of the sun and realized it had to be nearly midday and would be much warmer outside than in the cabin, which held the cold. How had she slept so long? The lambs usually woke her at dawn to be fed. She hurried to the kitchen, and they were all there—sleeping peacefully. A quick glance at the kitchen counter revealed several empty nippled Coke bottles. Nathan Hazard had been inside her house this morning. He'd fed her lambs!

Harry felt outraged at Nathan's presumption. And then she had another, even more disturbing thought. Had he come into her bedroom? Had he seen her sleeping? She blushed at the thought of what she must have looked like. She'd worn only a plain white torn T-shirt to sleep in Cyrus's sleigh bed. Harry was disgusted with herself when she realized that what upset her most was the thought that she couldn't have looked very attractive.

It took three shakes of a lamb's tail for Harry to dress in jeans, blue work shirt and boots. She stomped all the way from her kitchen door to the barn, where the tractor stood. Nathan had to hear her coming, but he never moved from his stance, bent over concentrating on some part of the tractor's innards.

"Good morning," she snarled.

Slowly, as though it were the most ordinary thing in the world for him to be working on her tractor, he straightened. "Good afternoon," he corrected.

Harry caught her breath at the sight of him. She didn't see the whole man, just perceptions of him. A bead of sweat slid slowly down the crease in his muscular chest to dampen the waist of his jeans. Only the waist wasn't at his waist. His jeans had slid down over his hips to reveal a navel and a line of downy blond hair that disappeared from sight under the denim. She didn't see any sign of underwear. The placket over the zipper was worn white with age.

When she realized where she was staring, Harry jerked her head up to look at his face and noticed that a stubble of beard shadowed his jaws and chin. Hanks of white-blond hair were tousled over his forehead. And his shockingly bright blue eyes were focused on her as though she were a lamb chop and he were a starving man.

Harry's mouth went dry. She slicked her tongue over her lips and saw the resulting spark of heat in Nathan's gaze. His nostrils flared, and she felt her body tighten with anticipation.

The hunter. Its prey.

Only Harry had no intention of becoming a sacrificial lamb to this particular wolf.

"Don't you know how to knock?" she demanded.

It might have seemed an odd question, but Nathan knew what she was asking. "I did knock. You didn't answer. I was worried, so I came inside."

"And fed my lambs!" Harry said indignantly.

"Yes. I fed them."

"Why didn't you come wake me up?"

Nathan had learned enough about Harry-et Alistair's pride to know he couldn't tell her the truth. She'd looked tired. More than tired, exhausted. He had figured she could use the sleep. So he'd fed her lambs. Was that so bad? Obviously Harry-et thought so.

But her need for sleep wasn't the only reason he hadn't woken her. When Nathan had entered Harry-et's bedroom, she was lying on her side, with one long, bare, elegantly slender leg curled up outside the blankets. The tiny bikini panties she'd been wearing had revealed a great expanse of hip, as well. Her long brown hair was spread across the pillow in abandon. One breast was pushed up by the arm she was lying on, and he'd seen a dark nipple through the thin cotton T-shirt she was wearing.

Not that he'd looked on purpose. Or very long. In fact, once he'd realized the full extent of her dishevelment, he'd backed out of the room so fast he'd almost tripped over her work boots, which lay where they'd fallen when she'd taken them off the previous night.

He'd wanted to wake her more than she'd ever know.

He'd wanted to take her in his arms and feel her nipples against his bare chest. He'd wanted to wrap those long, luscious legs around himself and... No, she was damn lucky he hadn't woken her. But he could never tell her that. Instead he said, "Anybody offered me another hour or two of sleep, I'd be grateful."

Harry sputtered, unable to think of an appropriate retort. She *was* grateful for the sleep. She just didn't like the way she'd gotten it. "What are you doing to this tractor?"

"Fixing it."

"I didn't know it was broken."

"Neither did I until I tried starting it up."

"Why would you want to start it up?"

Nathan leaned back over and began tinkering again, so he wouldn't have to look her in the eye when he said, "So I could plow your fallow fields."

"So you could..." Harry was flabbergasted. "I thought you were too busy doing your own work to lend me a hand."

Nathan stood and leaned a hip against the tractor while he wiped his hands on his chambray work shirt. "I had a visit yesterday from a good friend of mine, Luke Granger. He was with an agent of the Fish and Wildlife Service, Abigail—"

"They were here yesterday. So?"

"Luke pointed out to me that I haven't been a very good neighbor."

Harry felt her stomach churn. "What else did he have to say?"

"That was enough, don't you think?"

Harry met Nathan's solemn gaze and found it even more unsettling than the heat that had so recently been there.

Nathan never took his eyes off her when he added, "I

think maybe I've been a little pigheaded about helping you out. On the other hand, Harry-et, I can't help thinking—''

The blaring honk of a truck horn interrupted Nathan. A battered pickup was wending its way up the rutted dirt road.

Harry recognized Luke Granger and Abigail Dayton. ''I wonder what they're doing back here today.''

''I invited them.''

Harry whirled to face Nathan. ''You what?''

''I called Luke this morning to see if he could spare a little time to do some repairs around here.'' He took a look around the dilapidated buildings and added, ''There's plenty here for both of us to do.''

''You all got together and figured I needed help, so here you are riding to the rescue like cowboys in white hats,'' Harry said bitterly. ''Damn. Oh, damn, damn, damn.'' Harry fisted her hands and placed them on her hips to keep from hauling off and hitting Nathan. She clamped her teeth tight to keep her chin from quivering. She wanted to scream and rant and rave. And she was more than a little afraid she was going to cry.

Nathan couldn't understand what all the fuss was about. In all the years he'd been offering help to others, the usual response had been a quick and ready acceptance of his assistance. This woman was totally different. She seemed to resent his support. He found her reaction bewildering. And not a little frustrating.

He should have been glad she didn't need his help. He should have been glad she didn't need any caretaking. But he found himself wanting to help, needing to help. Her rejection hurt in ways he wasn't willing to acknowledge.

He turned and began working on the tractor again, keeping his hands busy to keep from grabbing Harry and kissing some sense into her.

"Hello, there," Luke said as he and Abigail approached the other couple.

"Hello," Harry muttered through clenched teeth. Her angry eyes remained on Nathan.

Nathan never looked up. "I ran into a little problem, Luke. The tractor needs some work before I can do anything about those fallow fields."

"Anything I can do?" Luke asked Nathan.

Harry whirled on him and said, "You can turn that truck around and drive right back out of here."

"We just want to help," Abigail said quietly.

"I don't need your charity," Harry cried in an anguished voice. "I don't need—"

Nathan suddenly dropped his wrench on the engine with a clatter and grabbed Harry by the arms, forcing her to face him. "That'll be enough of that!"

"Just who do you think you are?" Harry rasped. "I didn't ask you to come here. I didn't ask you to—"

"I'm doing what a good neighbor should do."

"Right! Where was all this neighborliness when I had lambs dying because I didn't know how to deliver them? Where was all this friendly help when I really needed it?"

"You need it right now," Nathan retorted, his grip tightening. "And I intend to give it to you."

"Over my dead body!" Harry shouted.

"Be reasonable," Nathan said in a voice that was losing its calm. "You need help."

"I don't need it from you," Harry replied stubbornly.

"Maybe you'd let us help," Abigail said, stepping forward to place a comforting hand on Harry's arm.

Harry's shoulders suddenly slumped, all the fight gone out of her. Maybe she should just take their help. Maybe her parents had been right all along. She bit her quivering lower lip and closed her eyes to hold back the threatening tears.

But some spark inside Harry refused to be quenched by the dose of reality she'd just suffered. She could give up and give in, as she had in the past. Or she could fight.

Her shoulders came up again, and when her eyes opened, they focused on Nathan Hazard, flashing with defiance. "I want you off my property, Nathan Hazard. Now. I..." Her voice caught in an angry sob, but her jaw stiffened. "I have things to do inside. I expect you can see yourself off my land."

Harry turned and marched toward the tiny log house without a single look back to see if he had obeyed her command.

5

What do you say when asked, "How's it going?"
Answer: "Oh, could be worse. Could be better."

Nathan spent the rest of the afternoon working outside with Luke, while Abigail worked in and around the barn with a still-seething Harry. Luke and Abigail left just before sundown, knowing Harry's fallow fields were plowed and planted and that the pigpen gate, among other things, had been repaired. Nathan worked another quarter hour before admitting there wasn't enough light to continue. He pulled on the chambray shirt he'd been using for an oil rag and headed toward the only light on in Cyrus's log cabin.

He knocked at Harry's kitchen door, but didn't wait for an answer before he pushed the screen door open and stepped inside. Harry was standing at the sink rinsing out Coke bottles. She turned when she saw him, grabbed a towel from the counter and wiped her hands dry. She stood backed up against the sink, waiting, wary.

"I'm sorry." Nathan hadn't said those two words very often in his lifetime, and they stuck in his craw.

It didn't help when Harry retorted, "You should be!"

"Now look here, Harry-et—"

"No, *you* look here, Nathan," she interrupted. "I thought I'd made it plain to you that I didn't want your help. At least not the way you're offering it. I wouldn't mind so much if you wanted to teach me how to run this place. But you seem bound and determined to treat me like the worst sort of tenderfoot, which I am—a tenderfoot, I mean. But not the worst sort. Oh, this isn't making any sense!''

Harry was so upset that she gulped air, and she trembled as though she had the ague. Nathan took a step toward her, wanting to comfort her, but stopped when she stuck out a flat palm.

"Wait. I'm not finished talking. I don't know how to make it any plainer. I don't want the sort of help you're offering, Nathan."

Nathan opened his mouth to offer her the kind of help she was asking for and snapped it shut. Even if he taught her what she wanted to know, she would be hard-pressed to make a go of this place by herself. And if, by some miracle, she did succeed, he would only be stuck with another Alistair planted square in the middle of Hazard land.

"All right, Harry-et," he said, "I'll stop trying to help."

Her shoulders sagged, and he wasn't sure if she was relieved or disappointed. Neither reaction pleased him. So he said, "I think maybe what we ought to do is call a truce."

"A truce?"

"Yeah. You know, raise the white flag. Stop fighting. Call a halt to hostilities." He tried a smile of encouragement. It wasn't his best, but apparently it was good enough, because she smiled back.

"All right," she agreed. "Shall we shake on it?"

She stuck her hand out and, like a fool, he took it. And suffered the consequences. Touching her was like shooting off fireworks on the Fourth of July. He liked what he felt. Too much. So he dropped her hand and turned to leave.

Before he even got to the door he had turned back—he didn't have the faintest idea why—and caught her looking bereft. The words were out of his mouth before he could stop them. "What would you say to a dinner to celebrate

our truce?'' She looked doubtfully around her kitchen, and
he quickly added, ''I meant dinner out.''

''A date?''

''Not a date,'' he quickly reassured her. ''Just a dinner
between two neighbors who've agreed to make peace.''

''All right.''

It was the most reluctant acceptance he'd ever heard. Nathan figured he'd better get the plans finalized and get out
of here before she changed her mind. ''I'll pick you up at
eight. Dress up fancy.''

''Fancy?''

''Sure. Something soft and ladylike. You have a dress like
that, don't you?'' He hadn't realized how much he wanted
to see her in a dress, so he could admire those long legs of
hers again.

''Where is this dinner going to be?'' she asked suspiciously.

''Have you ever been to the hot springs at Chico?''

''No. Where is that?''

''About an hour south. Best lamb chops in two counties.''
He saw her moue of distress and added, ''Or you can have
beef prime ribs if you'd rather.''

She smiled, and he felt his heart beat faster at the shy
pleasure revealed in the slight curl of her lips.

''All right. I'll be ready,'' she said.

Nathan left in a hurry before he did something really stupid, like take her in his arms and kiss that wide, soft mouth
of hers and run his hands all over her body. He had it bad,
all right. The worst. The woman was under his skin and
there was no denying it.

Nathan drove home so fast that his head hit the top of
the pickup twice on his way down Harry-et's road. He show-
ered and shaved and daubed some manly-smelling, female-
alluring scent on himself in record time. He donned a sandy-

colored, tailored Western suit that hugged him across the shoulders like a second skin and added snakeskin boots and a buff felt cowboy hat.

Nathan wasn't conscious of how carefully he'd dressed until Katoya stopped him at the bottom of the stairs and said, "You are going hunting."

"I'm not exactly dressed for bear."

"Not for bear. For dear. One dear," the old woman clarified with a cackle of glee.

Nathan grimaced. "Is it that obvious?"

"Noticeable, yes. As a wolf among sheep."

He started back up the stairs again. "I'll change."

"It will do no good."

Nathan walked back down to her. "Why not?"

"Even if you change the outer trappings, she will know what you feel."

"How?" he demanded.

"She will see it in your eyes. They shine with excitement. And with hunger."

Nathan looked down at his fisted hands so that his lids would veil what the old woman had seen. "I want her," he said. He looked up, and there was a plea in his eyes he didn't know was there. "I know I'm asking for trouble. She's all wrong for me. But I can't seem to stop myself."

"Maybe you shouldn't try," Katoya said softly. "Maybe it is time you let go of the past."

"Wish I could," he said. "It isn't easy."

"We do the best we can," the Blackfoot woman said. "Go. Enjoy yourself. What must be will be."

He grabbed the tiny woman and hugged her hard. "You're a wise old woman. I'll do my best to take your advice."

He let her go and hurried out the door, anxious to be on his way. He didn't see the sadness in her eyes as he left or the pain in her step as she headed for the window to watch him drive away in a classic black sports car that spent most of its time in his garage.

For the entire trip to Cyrus's ranch Nathan imagined how wonderful Harry-et would look dressed up. But the reality still exceeded his expectation.

"I can't believe it's you," he said in an awestruck voice when Harry opened the front door to the cabin. She stepped out, rather than inviting him in, and having seen the broken-down couch and chairs from the 1950s that served as living room furniture, Nathan understood why. But he wouldn't let Harry into his car until he'd taken a good look at her.

"Wait. Turn around."

"Do you like it?" she asked anxiously.

How could he describe how beautiful she looked to him? He didn't think he could find the words. "I love it," he managed.

The dress was a vibrant red and made of material that looked soft to the touch. The skirt was full, so it floated around her. The bodice was fitted, crisscrossing in a V over her breasts, so for the first time he could see just how lovely she was. The chiffonlike material fell off her shoulders, leaving them completely bare, but enticed with a hint of cleavage. She'd taken her hair out of the tomboyish braids, and a mass of rich brown curls draped her bare shoulders, begging to be taken up in his hands. She was wearing high heels that lengthened her already-long legs and brought her eyes almost even with his.

He could see how easy it would be to push the material down from her shoulders, leaving her breasts free to touch and taste. How easy it would be to slip his hands under the full skirt and capture her thighs, pulling her close. That thought pushed him over the edge. He felt himself responding to the wanton images that besieged him while she stood there looking lovely and desirable.

"Get in the car," he said in a voice harsh with the need he was struggling to control.

He hates the dress, Harry thought as she obeyed Nathan's curt order. She'd known the red dress was all wrong for her when she'd bought it two years ago. Too bright. Too sexy. Too sensual. Not at all like the Harriet Alistair of Williamsburg, Virginia. But tonight, when she'd looked into her closet, there it was. And it had seemed exactly right for the bold and daring woman who'd moved to Big Timber, Montana. The one who was attracted to Nathan Hazard.

Apparently Nathan didn't agree.

On the other hand, Harry thought Nathan looked wonderful. His Western suit fit him to perfection. The tailoring showed off his broad shoulders and narrow hips, his flat stomach and long legs. Of course, she had never found any fault with the way Nathan looked. Indeed, she'd wanted to touch the rippled chest and belly she'd seen this morning. Would Nathan's skin be soft? Or as hard as the muscles that corded his flesh? Harry had even fantasized what Nathan would look like without a stitch on. But she'd never seen a naked man, and the only images she could conjure were the marble statues of Greek gods she'd seen. And a leaf had always covered the pertinent parts.

Tonight there was a barely leashed power in the way Nathan moved that made Harry want to test the limits of his control. She wanted to touch. She wanted to taste. And she wanted to tempt Nathan to do the same.

Their personal relationship had nothing to do with the land, Harry told herself. It was separate and apart from that. She could desire Nathan without compromising her stand, because they were in the midst of a truce. So when she sat down in Nathan's sports car, she let her skirt slip halfway up her thighs before pulling it back down and leaned toward Nathan so that her breast brushed against his arm.

He inhaled sharply.

Harry looked at him, stunned by the flood of desire in his eyes. And began to reevaluate Nathan's reaction to her red dress.

Nathan didn't leave her in doubt another moment. He leaned over slowly but surely until their mouths were nearly touching and said, "Don't do that again unless you mean it."

Harry shivered and made a little noise in her throat.

Nathan groaned as his lips covered hers and sipped the nectar there. Her mouth was soft and oh, so sweet, and his body tightened like a bowstring with need. His tongue found the edge of her lips and followed it until she opened her mouth and his tongue slipped inside. He mimed the stroke of their two bodies joined and heard her moan. He reached up a hand to cup her breast and felt the weight of it in his hand. His thumb stroked across the tip, and he realized it had already tightened into a tiny nub. His hand followed the shape of her, from her ribs to her waist and down her thigh to the hem of her skirt, where Harry caught his wrist and stopped him.

Abruptly Nathan lifted his mouth from hers. Damn if she didn't have him as hot and bothered as a high school kid! And she'd stopped him as if she were some teenage virgin who'd never done it before. On the other hand, though he felt like a kid, he wasn't one. The small car was damn close for comfort. He could wait. Before the night was through he'd know what it was like to hold her in his arms and feel himself inside her. She wanted it. And so did he.

"All right, Ms. Alistair," he said through gritted teeth. "We'll do this your way."

Nathan started the car, made a spinning turn and, in deference to his delicate suspension, headed at a slow crawl back down the bumpy dirt road toward the main highway and Chico.

Harry was stunned. How had one kiss turned into so much so fast? She hadn't wanted to stop Nathan. But things were moving too quickly. She didn't want their first time to be in the front seat of a car. They both deserved more than that.

Nathan was on the verge of suggesting they forget dinner and go back to his place. But from the nervous fidgeting Harry was doing, that probably wasn't a good idea. He figured he'd better say something quick before he said what was really on his mind. So he cleared his throat of the last remnants of passion and asked, "What was your life like before you came to Montana?"

"Overprotected."

Nathan glanced briefly at Harry-et to see if she was kidding. She wasn't. "I guess I saw a little of that when your parents were here. They sure don't think you can make a go of Cyrus's ranch, do they?"

"That isn't their fault," Harry said, coming to their defense. "I wasn't exactly what you'd call a roaring success when I lived in Williamsburg."

"What were you, exactly?"

Harry paused for a moment before she admitted, "I had several occupations, but I wasn't interested in any of them. I managed to do poorly at them, so I could get fired."

"Why did you take the jobs in the first place if you weren't interested in them?"

"Because I couldn't say no to my father."

Nathan snorted. "You haven't had any trouble saying no to me."

"I turned over a new leaf when I came to Montana," Harry said with an impish smile. "I made up my mind to do what I wanted to do, my way." Her expression became earnest. "That's why I was so upset by your interference. Don't you see? I wanted to prove to my family, and to myself, that I could succeed at something on my own."

"I'm sorry I butted in," Nathan said curtly.

Harry put a hand on Nathan's arm and felt him tense beneath her fingertips. "How could you know? Now that we've called this truce, things will be better, I'm sure. What about you? Did you always want to be a sheep rancher?"

"No. Actually, I had plans to be an architect once upon a time."

"What happened?"

Nathan glanced at Harry and was surprised by the concerned look on her face. He hardened himself against the growing emotional attachment he felt to her. "Things got in the way."

"What kind of things?"

"Parents."

"You weren't overprotected, too, were you?"

"Not hardly. I was the one who did the protecting in my household."

Harry was stunned by the bitterness in his voice. "I don't understand. Are you saying you took care of your parents? Were they hurt or something?"

"Yes, and yes."

But he didn't say any more. Harry wasn't sure whether to press him for details. His lips had flattened into a grim line, and the memories obviously weren't happy ones. But her curiosity got the better of her and she asked, "Will you tell me about it?"

At first she thought he wasn't going to speak. Then the words started coming, and the bitterness and anger and regret and sadness poured out along with them.

"My mother was an alcoholic," he said. "I didn't know her very well. But I took care of her the best I could.

Dumped the bottles when I found them. Cleaned up when I could. Made meals for me and my dad. She didn't eat much. The alcohol finally killed her when I was sixteen.

"It was a relief," he said in a voice that grated with pain. "I was glad she was gone. She was an embarrassment. She was a lush. I hated her." Harry watched him swallow hard and add in a soft voice, "And I loved her so much I would have died in her place."

Harry felt a lump in her own throat and tears burning her eyes. What a heavy burden for a child.

"My father and I missed her when she was gone. Dad wanted me to stay on the ranch—Hazards had been sheep ranchers for a hundred years—but I wanted to be an architect. So I went away to college despite his wishes and learned to design buildings to celebrate the spirit of life.

"The month I graduated my father had an accident. A tractor turned over on him and crippled him. I came home to take over for him. And to take care of him. That was fifteen years ago. He died two years ago an old man. He was fifty-eight."

"Did you ever have the opportunity to design anything?"

"I designed and built the house I live in now. I haven't had time to do more than that."

She could hear the pride in his voice. And the disappointment. "I'm sorry."

"Don't pity me. I've had a good life. Better than most."

"But it wasn't the life you had planned for yourself. What about a wife? Didn't you ever want to marry and have children?"

"I was too busy until two years ago to think about anything but making ends meet," Nathan said. "Since then I've been looking. But I haven't found the right woman yet."

Harry heard Nathan's "yet" loud and clear. Nathan knew her, therefore he must have excluded her from consideration.

Which hurt more than she'd expected. "What kind of woman are you looking for?"

Nathan didn't pull any punches. "One who can stand on her own. One who can carry her half of the burden. Ranching's a hard life. I can't afford to marry a woman who can't contribute her share to making things work."

Harry threaded her hands together in her lap. Well, that settled that. She obviously wasn't the kind of woman who could stand on her own two feet. In fact, Nathan had been holding her up for the past two months.

How he must have hated that, Harry thought. He had taken care of her with concern and consideration, but he'd done it because she was someone who was helpless to help herself. Not as though she were an equal. Not as though she were someone who could one day be his partner. How Harry wanted the chance to show Nathan she could manage on her own! Maybe with this truce it would happen. She would continue to learn and grow. As success followed success, he would see her with new eyes. Maybe then...

Harry suddenly realized the implications of what she was thinking. She was thinking of a future that included Nathan Hazard. She pictured little Nathans and Harrys—blue-eyed blondes and brown-eyed brunettes with freckles. Oh, what a lovely picture it was!

However, a look at Nathan's stern visage wasn't encouraging. He was obviously not picturing the same idyllic scene.

In fact, Nathan was picturing something very similar. And calling himself ten times a fool for doing so. How could he even consider a life with Harry-et Alistair. The woman was a disaster waiting for a place to happen. She didn't know the first thing about ranching. She was a tenderfoot. A city girl. She would never be the kind of partner who could pull her own weight.

Fortunately they'd reached the turnoff to the restaurant at Chico. The lag in the conversation wasn't as noticeable because Nathan took the opportunity to fill Harry-et in on the history of Chico. The hotel and restaurant were located at the site of a natural hot spring that now fed into a swimming pool that could be seen from the bar. It had become a hangout for all the movie stars who regularly escaped the bright lights and big city for what was still Montana wilderness. The pool was warm enough that it could be used even when the night was cool, as it was this evening.

Nathan and Harry were a little early for their dinner reservations, so Nathan escorted her into the bar where they could watch the swimmers.

"Would you like to take a dip in the pool?" Nathan asked. "They have suits—"

"Not this time," Harry said. "I don't think—" Harry stopped in midsentence, staring, unable to believe her eyes. She pointed toward the sliding glass doors. "Doesn't that man in the pool look a lot like—"

"Luke," Nathan finished for her. "I think you're right. He seems to be with someone. Maybe they'd like to join us for a drink. I'll go see."

Nathan had grasped at the presence of his friend as though it were a lifeline. He'd realized, suddenly and certainly, that it wasn't a good idea to be alone with Harry-et Alistair. The more time he spent with her, the lower his resistance to her. If he wasn't careful, he'd end up letting his heart tell his head what to do. He could use his friend's presence to help him keep his sense of perspective.

Of course, knowing Luke, and seeing how cozy he was with the lady, he knew his friend wasn't going to appreciate the interruption. But, hell, what were friends for?

Thus, a moment later he was standing next to Luke and

the woman who had her face hidden against his chest. "Hey, Luke, I thought it was you. Who's that with you?"

After a brief pause, Luke answered, "It's Abby."

Nathan searched his memory for any woman he knew by that name. "Abby?"

"Abigail Dayton," Luke bit out.

"From Fish and Wildlife?" Nathan asked, astonished.

Abigail turned at last to face him. "Luke and I are just relaxing a few tired muscles."

Nathan grinned. "Yeah. Sure."

A female voice from the doorway called, "Nathan?"

The light behind Harry-et made her face nearly invisible in the shadows. At the same time it silhouetted a fantastic figure and a dynamite pair of legs. It irked Nathan that Luke couldn't seem to take his eyes off the woman in the doorway.

"Who's that with you?" Luke asked Nathan.

"Uh..."

"Nathan, is it Luke?" Harry asked. "Oh, hello. It is you. Nathan thought he recognized you."

This time it was Luke who stared, astonished. "Harry? That's Harry?"

Harry grinned. "Sure is. Nathan tried to convince me to take a swim, but I was too chicken. How's the water?" she asked Abigail.

"Marvelous."

"What are you two doing here together?" Luke asked his friend sardonically. "I thought you hated each other's guts."

Nathan stuck a hand in the trouser pocket of his Western suit pants to keep from clapping it over his friend's mouth. "We called a truce. Why don't you two dry off and join us for a drink?" he invited.

Nathan could see Luke wasn't too hot on the idea. But

he gave his friend his most beseeching look, and at last Luke said, "Fine."

Luke gave Nathan a penetrating stare, but made no move to leave the pool. Obviously Luke wanted a few more minutes alone with the Fish and Wildlife agent. Nathan turned to Harry-et and suggested, "Why don't we go inside and wait for Luke and Abby."

He took Harry's arm and led her back inside. "You really look beautiful tonight, Harry-et," he said as he seated her at their table.

"Thank you, Nathan." Ever since she'd come outside Nathan had been looking at her a little differently. She'd seen the admiration in Luke's eyes and watched Nathan stiffen. Really, men could be so funny sometimes. There was no reason for Nathan to be jealous. She didn't find Luke's dark, forbidding looks nearly so attractive as she found Nathan's sharp-boned Nordic features.

She was almost amused when Nathan took her hand possessively once he was seated across from her. He held it palm up in his while his fingertips traced her work-roughened palm and the callused pads of her fingertips.

Harry felt goose bumps rise on her arm. She was all set for a romantic pronouncement when Nathan said, "It's a shame you have to work so hard. A lady like you shouldn't have calluses on her hands."

Harry jerked her hand from his grasp. "I have to work hard."

"No, you don't. Look at you, Harry-et. You spend so much time in the sun your face is as freckled as a six-year-old's."

"Are you finished insulting me?" Harry asked, confused and annoyed by Nathan's behavior.

"I think you ought to sell your place to me and get back to being the beautiful woman—"

Harry's hand came up without her really being aware it had. She slapped Nathan with the full force of the anger and betrayal she was feeling. The noise was lost in the celebration of the busy bar, but it was the only sound Harry heard above the pounding of her heart. "You never wanted a truce at all, did you, Nathan? You just wanted a chance to soften me up and make another plea to buy my land. I can't think of anything lower in this life than a lying, sneaky snake-in-the-grass Hazard!"

"Now just a minute, Harry-et. I—"

She grabbed his keys from the table where he'd set them and stood up. "I'm taking your car. You can pick it up at my place tomorrow. But I don't want to see your sorry face when you do it."

"Be reasonable, Harry-et. How am I supposed to get home?"

"You can ask your friend, Luke, to give you a ride, but I'd be pleased as punch if you have to walk."

"Harry-et—"

"Shut up and listen! You're going to have an Alistair ranching smack in the middle of your land for the rest of your life, Nathan. And you can like or lump it. I don't really care!"

Harry marched out of the bar with her head held high, but she couldn't see a blamed thing through the haze of tears in her eyes. How could she have believed that handsome devil's lies? And worse, oh, far worse, how could she still want a man who only wanted her land?

Nathan stood up to follow her and then sat back down. That woman was so prickly, so short-tempered, and so stubborn—how on earth could he want her the way he did? It was his own fault for provoking her. But he'd been frightened by his possessive feelings when Luke had admired Harry-et. So, perversely, he'd enumerated to her all the reasons why he couldn't possibly be attracted to her and managed to drive her away.

He had to find a way to make peace with the woman. This Hazard-Alistair feud had gone on long enough. There had to be a happy medium somewhere, some middle ground, neither his nor hers, on which they could meet.

Nathan made up his mind to find it.

6

How should you behave in a Woolly West bar?
Answer: You don't have to behave in a Woolly West bar.

Over the next three weeks Nathan thought about all the ways he could end the Hazard-Alistair feud. And kept coming back to the same one: *He could marry Harry-et Alistair.* Of course, that solution raised its own set of problems. Not the least of which was how he was going to convince Harry-et Alistair to marry him.

The way Nathan had it figured, marrying Harry-et would have all kinds of benefits. First of all, once they were married, there wouldn't be any more Alistair land; it would all be Hazard land. Second, the feud would necessarily come to an end, since all future Hazards would also be Alistairs. And third—and Nathan found this argument for marriage both the most and the least compelling—he would have Harry-et Alistair for his wife.

Although Nathan was undeniably attracted to Harry-et, he wasn't convinced she was the right woman for him. Except every time he thought of a lifetime spent without her, it seemed a bleak existence, indeed. So maybe he was going to have to take care of her more than he would have liked. It wasn't something he hadn't done in the past. He could handle it. He'd finally admitted to himself that he was willing to pull ten times the normal load in order to spend his life with Harry-et Alistair.

Only the last time he'd driven onto her place she'd met

him at the end of her road with a Winchester. He'd had no choice except to leave. He hadn't figured out a way yet to get past that rifle.

Nathan was sitting at his regular booth at The Grand, aimlessly stirring his chicken noodle soup, when Slim Harley came running in looking for him.

"She's done it now!" Slim said, skidding to a stop at Nathan's booth.

"Done what?"

"Lost Cyrus's ranch for sure," Slim said.

Nathan grabbed Slim by his shirt at the throat. "Lost it how? You didn't call in her bill, did you? I told you I was good for it if you needed the cash."

"Weren't me," Slim said, trying to free Nathan's hold without success. "It's John Wilkinson at the bank. Says he can't loan her any money to pay the lease on her government land. Says she ain't a good credit risk."

"Where is she now?"

"At the bank. I just—" Slim found himself talking to thin air as Nathan shoved past him and took off out the door of The Grand, heading for the bank across the street.

When Nathan entered the bank, he saw Harry-et sitting in front of John Wilkinson's desk. He casually walked over to one of the tellers nearby and started filling out a deposit slip.

"But I've told you I have a trust I can access when I'm thirty," Harry was saying.

"That's still four years off."

Nathan folded the deposit slip in half and stuck it in his back pocket. He meandered over toward John's desk and said, "I couldn't help overhearing. Is there anything I can do to help, Harry-et?"

She glared at him and stared down at her hands, which were threaded tightly together in the lap of her overalls.

"So, John, what's the problem?" Nathan asked, setting a hip on the corner of the banker's oversize desk.

"Don't expect it's any secret," John said. "Mizz Alistair here doesn't have the cash to renew her government lease. And I don't think I can risk the bank's money making her a loan."

"What if I cosign the note?" Nathan asked.

"No!" Harry said, shooting to her feet to confront Nathan. "I don't want to get the money that way. I'd rather lose the ranch first!"

The banker stroked his whiskered chin with a bony hand. "Well, now, sounds like maybe we could work something out here, Mizz Alistair."

"I meant what I said," Harry declared, her chin tilting up mulishly. "I don't want your money if Nathan Hazard has to cosign the note. I'll go to a bank in Billings or Bozeman. I'll—"

"Now hold on a minute. There's no call to take your business elsewhere." John Wilkinson hadn't become president of the Big Timber First National Bank without being a good judge of human nature. What he had here was a man-woman problem, sure as wolves ate sheep. Only both the man and the woman were powerful prideful. The man wanted to help; the woman wanted to do it on her own.

"I might be willing to make that loan to you, Mizz Alistair, if Nathan here would agree to advise you on ranch management till your lamb crop got sold in the fall."

Nathan frowned. Teaching ranch management to Harry-et Alistair was a whole other can of worms from cosigning her note.

"Done," Harry said. She ignored Nathan and stuck out her hand to the banker, who shook it vigorously.

"Now wait a minute," Nathan objected. "I never said—"

"Some problem, Nathan?" the banker asked.

Nathan saw the glow of hope in Harry's eyes, and didn't have the heart to put it out. "Aw, hell, I'll do it."

"I'll expect you over later today," Harry said, throwing a quick grin in Nathan's direction. "I have a problem that needs solving right away." She turned to the banker and added, "I'll pick up that check on Monday, John."

Nathan stood with his mouth hanging open as Harry marched by him and out the door.

"That's quite a woman," the banker said as he stared after her.

"You can say that again," Nathan muttered. "She's Trouble with a capital T."

"Never saw trouble you couldn't handle," the banker said with a confident smile. "Anything else you need, Nathan?"

"No thanks, John. I think you've done quite enough for me today."

"We aim to please, Nathan. We aim to please."

Nathan was still half stunned as he walked out of the bank door and headed back to The Grand. He found Slim sitting at his booth, finishing off his chicken noodle soup.

"Didn't know you was coming back, Nathan," Slim said. "I'll have Tillie Mae ladle you up another bowl."

"I'm not hungry."

"What happened?" Slim asked. "Mizz Alistair get her loan?"

"She got it," Nathan snapped. "But it's going to cost me plenty."

"You loan her the money?" Slim asked, confused.

"I loaned her *me*." Nathan sat down and dropped his head into his hands. "I'm the new manager for Cyrus's ranch."

Word spread fast in the Boulder River Valley, and by

suppertime it was generally believed that Nathan Hazard must have lost his mind...or his heart. Nathan was sure it was both.

Of course, on the good side, he had Harry-et Alistair exactly where he wanted her. She would have to see him, whether she wanted to or not. He would have a chance to woo her, to convince her they ought to become man and wife. Unfortunately, he still had a job to do—making her ranch profitable—which he took seriously. And Harry-et didn't strike him as the sort of woman who was going to take well to the kind of orders he would necessarily have to give.

Meanwhile, Harry was in hog heaven. She had what she'd always wanted—not someone to do it for her, but someone to teach her how to do it herself. Of course, having Nathan Hazard for her ranch manager wasn't a perfect solution. She still had to put up with the man. But once she'd learned what she needed to know, she wouldn't let him set foot on her place again.

Harry was especially glad that she'd secured Nathan's expertise today, because now that she had the funds to pay the lease on her mountain grazing land, she had another problem that needed to be resolved. So when Nathan arrived shortly after dark, Harry greeted him at her kitchen door with a smile of genuine welcome.

"Come in," she said, gesturing Nathan to a seat at the kitchen table. "I've got some coffee and I just baked a batch of cookies for you."

"They smell great," Nathan said, finding himself suddenly sitting at the table with a cup of coffee and a plateful of chocolate chip cookies in front of him.

Harry fussed over him like a mother hen with one chick until he had no choice except to take a sip of coffee. He'd just taken his first bite of cookie, and was feeling pretty good about the way this was turning out, when Harry said, "Now, to get down to business."

With a mouthful of cookie it was difficult to protest.

"The way I see it," Harry began, "I haven't been doing all that badly on my own. All I really need, what I expect from you, is someone I can turn to when I hit a snag."

"Wait a minute," Nathan said through a mouthful of cookie he was trying desperately to swallow. "I think you're underestimating what it takes to run a marginal spread like this in the black."

"I don't think I am," Harry countered. "I'll admit I've made some mistakes, like the one I wanted to see you about tonight." Harry paused and caught her lower lip in her teeth. "I just never thought he'd do such a thing."

"*Who* would do *what* thing?" Nathan demanded.

"My shepherd. I never thought he'd take his wages and go get drunk."

"You paid your shepherd his wages? Before the summer's even begun? Whatever possessed you to do such a thing?"

"He said he needed money for food and supplies," Harry said. "How was I supposed to know—"

"Any idiot could figure out—"

"Maybe an idiot could, but I'm quite intelligent myself. So it never occurred to me!" Harry finished.

"Aw, hell." Nathan slumped back into the chair he hadn't been aware he'd jumped out of.

Harry remained standing across from him, not relaxing an inch.

"So what do you want me to do?" Nathan asked when he thought he could speak without shouting.

"I want you to go down to Whitey's Bar in Big Timber and get him out, then sober him up so he can go to work for me."

"I don't think this is what John Wilkinson had in mind when he suggested I manage your ranch," Nathan said, rubbing a hand across his forehead.

"I would have gone and done it myself if I'd known you were going to make such a big deal out of it," Harry muttered.

Suddenly Nathan was on his feet again. "You stay out of Whitey's. That's no place for a woman."

"I'm not just a woman. I'm a rancher. And I'll go where I have to go."

"Not to Whitey's, you won't."

"Oh, yeah?" she said. "Who's going to stop me?"

"I am."

Harry found herself in Nathan's grasp so quickly that she didn't have a chance to escape. She stared up into his blue eyes and saw he'd made up his mind she wasn't going anywhere. She hadn't intended to force a confrontation, yet that was exactly what she'd done. She didn't want Nathan doing things *for* her; she wanted him doing things *with* her. So she made herself relax in his hold, and even put her hands on his upper arms and let them rest there.

"All right," she said. "I won't go there alone. But I ought to be perfectly safe if I go there with you."

"Harry-et—"

"Please, Nathan." Nathan's hands had relaxed their hold on her shoulders, and when Harry stepped closer, they curved around her into an embrace. Her hands slid up to his shoulders and behind his neck. He seemed a little unsure of what she intended. Which was understandable, since Harry wasn't sure what she intended herself—other than persuading Nathan to make her a partner rather than a mere petitioner. "I really want to help," she said, her big brown eyes locked on Nathan's.

"But you—"

She put her fingertips on his lips to quiet him, then rested one hand against his chest, so she could feel the heavy beat of his heart, while she let the other drift up to play with the hair at his nape. "This is important to me, Nathan. Let me help."

Harry felt Nathan's body tense beneath her touch, and thought for sure he was going to say no. A second later she was sure he was going to kiss her.

She was wrong on both counts.

Nathan determinedly put his hands back on her shoulders and separated them by a good foot. Then he looked her right in the eye. "Just stay behind me and let me do the talking."

"You've got a deal. When are we going?"

A long-suffering sigh slipped through Nathan's lips. "I suppose there's no time like the present. If we can get your shepherd dried out, we can move those sheep up into the mountains over the weekend."

Whitey's Bar in Big Timber was about what you would expect a Western bar to be: rough, tough and no holds barred. It was a relic from the past, with everything from bat-wing doors to a twenty-foot-long bar with a brass rail at the foot, sawdust on the floor and a well-used spittoon in the corner. The room was thick with cigarette smoke—no filter tips to be found here—and raucous with the wail of fiddles from a country tune playing on the old jukebox in the corner.

Some serious whiskey-drinking hombres sat at the small wooden tables scattered around the room. Harry was amazed that both cowboys and sheepmen caroused in the same bar, but Nathan explained that they relished the opportunity to argue the merits of their particular calling, with the inevitable brawl allowing them all an opportunity to vent the violence that civilization forced them to keep under control the rest of the time.

"Is there a fight every night?" Harry asked as they edged along the wall of the bar, hunting for her shepherd.

"Every night I've been here," he answered.

Harry gave him a sideways look, wondering how often that was. But her attention was distracted by what was happening on the stairs. Two men were arguing over a woman. Nathan hadn't exactly been honest when he'd said no women ever went to Whitey's. There were women here, all right, but they were working in an age-old profession. Twice in the few minutes they'd been in the bar, Harry had seen a woman head upstairs with a man.

The argument over the female at the foot of the stairs was escalating, and Harry noticed for the first time that one man appeared to be a cowboy, the other a sheepman.

Then she spotted her shepherd. "There he is," she said to Nathan, pointing at a white-bearded old man slumped at a table not too far from the stairs.

Nathan swore under his breath. In order to get to the shepherd, he had to get past the two men at the foot of the stairs. He turned to Harry-et. "Wait for me outside."

Harry started to object, but the fierce look in Nathan's eyes brooked no refusal. Reluctantly she turned and edged back along the wall toward the door. She never made it.

"Why, hello there, little lady. What brings you here to-night?"

The cowboy had put one hand, which held a beer bottle, up along the wall to stop her. When she turned to face him, he braced his palm on the other side of her, effectively trapping her.

"I was just leaving," Harry said, trying to duck under his arm.

He grabbed her sleeve, and she heard a seam rip as he pushed her back against the wall. "Not so fast, darlin'."

Harry's eyes darted toward Nathan. He had just slipped

his hands under the drunken shepherd's arms and was lifting him out of his chair. She couldn't bear the thought of shouting for help, drawing the attention of everyone in the bar. So she tried again to handle the cowboy by herself. "Look," she said, "I just came here to find someone—"

"Hell, little lady, you found me. Here I am."

Before Harry realized what he was going to do, the cowboy had pressed the full length of his body against her to hold her to the wall and sought her mouth with his.

She jerked her face from side to side to avoid his slobbering kisses. "Stop! Don't! I—"

An instant later the cowboy was decorating the floor and Nathan was standing beside her, eyes dark, nostrils flared, a vision of outrage. "The lady doesn't care for your attentions," he said to the burly cowboy. "I suggest you find someone who does."

The cowboy dragged himself up off the ground, still holding the neck of the beer bottle, which had broken off when he'd fallen. He recognized Nathan for a sheepman, which magnified the insult to his dignity. With all eyes on him there was no way he could back down. "Find your own woman," he blustered. "I saw her first."

"Nathan, please, don't start anything," Harry begged.

Nathan took his eyes off the other man for a second to glance at Harry, and the cowboy charged.

"Nathan!" Harry screamed.

Nathan's hand came up to stop the downward arc of the hand holding the broken bottle, while his fist found the cowboy's gut. The cowboy bent over double, and Nathan straightened him with a fist to the chin. The man crumpled to the floor, out cold.

Nathan looked up to find that pandemonium had broken out in the bar. He grabbed Harry's wrist. "Let's get out of here."

"Not without my shepherd."

"Are you crazy, woman? There's a fight going on."

"I'm not leaving without my shepherd!"

Nathan dodged a flying chair to reach the drunken man he'd left sitting against the wall. He picked the man up, threw him over his shoulder fireman-style and marched back through the melee to Harry. "Are you satisfied?"

Harry grinned. "Now I am."

Nathan grabbed her wrist with his free hand, and glaring at anyone foolish enough to get in his way, was soon standing outside in front of Whitey's. He dumped the shepherd none too gently into the back of his pickup and ordered Harry to get in.

She hurried to obey him.

Nathan took out his fury at Harry-et on the truck, gunning the engine, only to have to slam on the brakes when he caught the red light at the corner. He raced the engine several times and made the tires squeal when he took off as the light turned green.

"Did that bastard hurt you?" he demanded through tight lips.

"I'm all right," Harry said soothingly. "I'm fine, Nathan. Nothing happened."

"You had no business being there in the first place. You should have stayed home where you belong."

"I had as much right to be there as you. More right," she argued. "It was my shepherd we went after."

"You and your damned shepherd. The greenest greenhorn would know not to pay the man in advance. This whole business tonight was your fault."

"I didn't do anything," Harry protested.

"You were there. That was enough. If I hadn't been there—"

"But you were," Harry said. "And you were wonder-ful."

That shut him up. How could you complain when a woman was calling you wonderful? But if anything had happened to her... Nathan had known his feelings toward Harry-et were possessive, but he hadn't known until tonight that she was *his woman*. Woe be unto the man who harmed the tiniest hair on her head.

Nathan shook his head in disbelief. He hadn't been involved in one of Whitey's barroom brawls since he'd been a very brash young man. If this evening was any indication of what he had in store as the manager of Cyrus's ranch, he had a long, hot summer ahead of him.

As they pulled up in front of Cyrus's cabin, Harry said, "If you'll leave my shepherd in the sheep barn, I'll do what I can to sober him up."

"I'll take him home with me," Nathan countered. "I'm sure my housekeeper has some Blackfoot remedy that'll do the trick. We'll be back here bright and early tomorrow morning. Think you can stay in a Western saddle long enough to help us drive your sheep into the mountains?"

"I rode hunters and jumpers in Virginia."

Nathan shook his head in disgust. "I should have known. All right. I'll be here at dawn. Be ready."

Harry stepped down out of the truck and started toward the house. An instant later she ran back around the truck and gestured for Nathan to open his window.

"I just wanted to thank you again." She leaned over and kissed him flush on the mouth. "You were really wonder-ful." Then she turned and ran into the cabin.

Nathan waited until he saw the lights go on before he gunned the engine and took off down the rutted road. Before he'd gone very far he reached up to touch his lips where she'd kissed him. There was still a bit of dampness there, and he touched it with his tongue. And tasted her. His lips turned up in a smile.

He felt as if he could move mountains.

He felt as if he could soar in the sky.

He felt like a damn fool in love.

He felt really wonderful.

7

When Wade or Clyde or Harley comes a-courtin', how will you, the greenhorn female person, recognize a compliment? *Answer:* He'll compare your hair to the mane on his sorrel horse.

Harry had aches where she'd forgotten she had muscles. She knew how to ride, but that didn't mean she'd done much riding lately. Her back, thighs and buttocks could attest to that. But she'd accomplished what she'd set out that morning to do. Her flock of sheep had been moved up into the leased mountain pastures, and the wiry old shepherd had been settled in his gypsy wagon with a stern warning to keep a sharp eye out for wolves.

Harry was doing the same thing herself. Actually, she was keeping a sharp eye out for one particular wolf. Nathan Hazard had been acting strangely all day. Silent. Predatory. He hadn't done anything overtly aggressive. In fact, he seemed to be playing some sort of game, stalking her, waiting for the moment when he could make his move. Her nerves were beginning to fray.

After the fracas of the previous evening, Harry hadn't expected Nathan to be enthusiastic about joining her on this mountain pilgrimage. Nor was he. But at least he hadn't said a word about what had happened in Whitey's Bar. Of course, he hadn't said much of anything. Harry had been determined not to provoke him in any way, so she'd kept her aches and pains to herself. Was it any wonder she'd leaped at Nathan's suggestion that they halt their trek half-way down the mountain and take a rest? She had to bite her lip to keep from groaning aloud when she dismounted, but she was so stiff and sore that her knees nearly buckled when she put her weight on them.

Nathan heard Harry-et's gasp and turned to watch her grab the horn of the saddle and hang on for a few moments until her legs were firmly under her. He had to hand it to the woman. She was determined. He couldn't help admiring her gumption. Nathan had suspected for some time that Harry-et was feeling the effects of the long ride. That had suited him just fine. He'd had plans of his own that depended on getting her off that horse while they were still in the mountains. They had reached Nyla's Meadow. The time had come.

He spread a family heirloom quilt in the cool shade of some jack pines and straightened the edges over the layer of rich grass that graced the mountain meadow. At the last moment he rescued a handful of flowers that were about to be crushed, bringing them to Harry-et.

"Here. Thought you might like these."

Harry smiled and reached out a hand for the delicate blossoms. She brought them to her nose and was surprised at the pungent sweetness of the colorful bouquet. "They smell wonderful."

"Thought you also might like to lie down for a while here on Nyla's Meadow," Nathan said nonchalantly, gesturing toward the inviting square of material.

Harry wasted no time sagging down onto the quilt. She groaned again, but it was a sound of satisfaction as she stretched out flat on her back. "You have no idea how good this feels."

He settled himself Indian-style on a corner of the quilt

near her head. "Don't guess I do. But if you moan any louder some moose is going to come courting."

Harry laughed. "I'll try to keep it down." She turned on her side and braced her head on her elbow, surveying the grassy, flower-laden clearing among the pines and junipers. "Nyla's Meadow. That sounds so beautiful. Almost poetical. How did this place get its name?"

Nathan's lips twisted wryly. "It's a pretty far-fetched story, but if you'd like to hear it—"

"Yes, I would." Harry tried sitting up, but groaned and lay back down. "Guess I've stiffened up a little." She massaged the nape of her neck. "Make that a lot."

"I'd be glad to give your shoulders a rubdown."

That sounded awfully good to Harry. "Would you?"

"Sure. Turn over on your stomach."

A moment later Nathan was straddling her at the waist and his powerful hands had found the knots in her shoulders and were working magic. "You have no idea how good that feels," she said with another groan of pleasure.

Nathan's lips curled into a satisfied smile. Oh, yes, he did. He longed for the time when there would be nothing between his fingertips and her skin. It seemed like he'd been waiting his whole life for this woman. He didn't plan to wait much longer.

Harry felt the strength in Nathan's hands, yet his touch was a caress. A frisson of excitement ran the length of her spine. She imagined her naked body molded to Nathan's. Joined to Nathan's. Harry closed her eyes against the vivid picture she'd painted. She had no business thinking such thoughts. The sheepman only wanted her land. He'd as much as told her she wasn't the woman for him. Last night certainly couldn't have convinced him she'd be the kind of wife he had in mind. No, the minute she'd learned all she could from him, she intended to bid him a fast farewell.

So why was her body coming alive to his touch? Why did she yearn for his hands to slip around and cup her breasts, to mold her waist and stroke the taut and achy places that had nothing to do with the long ride of the morning? Harry tensed against the unwelcome, uncontrollable sensations deep inside.

"Relax," Nathan murmured as his hands slipped down from her shoulders to the small of her back and began to massage the soreness away.

"Tell me about Nyla's Meadow," Harry said breathlessly.

Nathan's thumbs slowly worked their way up her spine, easing, soothing, relaxing. "Nyla was an Egyptian princess."

Harry lifted herself on her hands and turned to eye Nathan over her shoulder. "What?"

Nathan shoved her back down. "Actually, the princess's name was N-I-L-A, after the Nile River, but somewhere over the years the spelling got changed."

"How did a Montana meadow get named after an Egyptian princess?" Harry asked suspiciously.

"Be quiet and listen and I'll tell you. Long before the first settlers came to the Boulder River Valley, a mountain man named Joshua Simmons arrived here. He'd traveled the world over just for the pleasure of seeing a new horizon, or so the story goes. He'd been to Egypt and China and the South Sea islands. But when he reached Montana, he knew he'd found God's country—limitless blue skies, snowcapped mountains and grassy prairies as far as the eye could see."

"You're making this up, aren't you?" Harry said with a grin.

"Shut up and listen," Nathan insisted. His hands moved down Harry's back to her waist and around to her ribs, where they skimmed the fullness of her breasts at the sides before moving back to her spine.

Harry shivered. She would have asked Nathen to stop what he was doing, but his hands were there and gone before she could speak. The sensations remained. And the ache grew.

"When Joshua reached this meadow, he encountered an Indian maiden," Nathan continued. "She appeared as exotic to him, as foreign and mystical, as an Egyptian princess."

"The Princess Nila," Harry murmured sardonically.

"Right. They fell in love at first sight. And made love that same day here on the meadow. When he awoke, the Indian maiden—though she was a maiden no more—was gone. Joshua never learned her name and he never saw her again. But he never forgot her. He named this place Nyla's Meadow after the Egyptian princess she had reminded him of."

Harry shifted abruptly so her buttocks rocked against Nathan. He felt his loins tighten and rose slightly to put some space between the heat of their two bodies.

Oblivious to Nathan's difficulties, Harry rolled over between his legs and scooted far enough away to sit up facing him. He was still straddling her at thigh level.

She pulled the band off one braid and began to unravel it, seemingly unconscious of the effect her action would have on Nathan. "So Nyla's Meadow is a place for falling in love? A place where lovers meet?"

Nathan swallowed hard. "Yes. A place for lovers." He couldn't take his eyes off Harry-et. Her gaze was lambent, her pupils dilated, her lids lowered. She was clearly aroused, yet her mood seemed almost playful, as though she didn't realize the powerful need she'd unleashed within him.

When Harry started to free her other braid, Nathan reached out a hand. "I'll do it."

Her hands dropped onto his thighs. And slid upward.

Nathan hissed in a breath and put his hands over hers to keep them from moving any farther. There was no need for her to actually touch him. The mere thought of her hands on him excited him. He slid her hands back down his thighs, away from the part of him that desperately wanted her touch. When he was relatively sure he'd made his position clear, he let her hands go and reached for the other braid.

Her hair was soft and rippled where the tight braids had left their mark. When both braids were unraveled, he thrust his hands into her rich brown hair and spread the silky mass around her head and shoulders like a nimbus. "You are so beautiful, Harry-et."

Harry hadn't meant to let the game go so far. She hadn't realized just how aroused Nathan was. She hadn't realized how the sight of his desire would increase her own. She wanted to see what would happen next. She wanted to feel what she had always imagined she would feel in a lover's embrace. Her hands once again followed the corded muscles along Nathan's thighs until she reached the part of him that strained against the worn denim. She molded the shape of him with her hands, awed by the heat and hardness of him.

Nathan closed his eyes and bit the inside of his mouth to keep from groaning aloud. The sweetness of it. The agony and the ecstasy of it. "Harry-et," he gasped. "Do you know what you're doing?"

"No," she replied. "But I'm learning fast."

Choked laughter erupted from Nathan's throat. At the same time he grabbed her by her wrists and lowered her to the ground, pinning her hands above either side of her head. He stretched out over the length of her, placing his hips in the cradle of her thighs. "That's what you're doing, lady," he said in a guttural voice, thrusting once with his hips. "I want you, Harry-et."

Harry heard the slight hesitation between the two syllables as he spoke her name that made the word an endearment. He wanted her, but he hadn't spoken of needing, or caring. Maybe that was as it should be. Alistairs and Hazards were never meant to love. History was against it. She wanted him, too. Wasn't that enough?

The decision was made for her when Nathan captured both her wrists in one hand and reached down between the two of them to caress the heart of her with the other. She felt herself arching toward him, toward the new and unbelievable sensations of pleasure.

Nathan caught her cries of ecstasy with his mouth. His kisses were urgent, needful. He let go of her wrists because he needed his hand to touch her, to caress her. When he did, Harry's fingers thrust into Nathan's hair and tugged to keep him close, so she could kiss him back. Her hands slipped down to caress his chest through his shirt, but the cotton was in her way. She yanked on his shirt and the snaps came free. She quickly helped him peel the shirt down off his shoulders. Just as quickly he freed the buttons of her shirt and stripped it off, along with her bra.

An instant later they paused and stared at each other.

Harry had seen Nathan's muscular chest once before and wanted to touch. Now she indulged that need. Her fingertips traced the crease down the center of his chest to his washboard belly.

Nathan had imagined her naked a dozen, dozen times, but still had failed to see her as beautiful as she was. Her breasts were full and the nipples a rose color that drew his eye, his callused fingers and finally his mouth.

Harry's fingernails drew crescents on Nathan's shoulders as his mouth and tongue suckled her breast. She arched toward him, urging him to take more of her into his mouth. He cupped her breast with his hand and let his mouth surround her, while his teeth and tongue turned her nipple into a hard bud.

Harry moaned. Her body arched into his, her softness seeking his hardness.

"Please." She didn't know what came next. She'd always stopped in the past before she got this far. Only this time she didn't want to stop. She wanted to know how it ended.

"It's all right, sweetheart," he murmured in her ear. "Soon. Soon."

"Now, Nathan. Now."

He sat up and pulled off her boots, then began pulling off his own. They both rid themselves of their jeans in record time. Nathan threw his jeans aside, then went searching for them a moment later. He ransacked the pockets, cursing as he went.

"Did you forget something?" Harry asked.

Nathan grinned as his fisted hand withdrew from his jeans pocket. "Nope."

Suddenly Harry was aware of her nakedness. And Nathan's. He looked awfully big. Not that she had anything to compare him with, but surely that thing was too large to fit...

"What's the matter, Harry-et?" Nathan said as he lay down beside her and pulled her into his embrace.

"Nothing," she mumbled against his chest.

"Having second thoughts?" Nathan held his breath, wondering why he was giving her a chance to back away when he wanted her so much that he was hurting.

Harry had opened her mouth to suggest maybe this wasn't such a good idea when Nathan's lips closed over hers. His tongue traced the edges of her mouth and then slipped inside, warm and wet. Seducing. Entrancing. Changing her mind all over again.

"Hold this for me," he said. "I need both hands free."

"What is it?" she asked through a haze of euphoria.

He quickly removed the foil packet and dropped a condom into her palm.

"Oh. Dear." Harry was unable to keep from blurting something she'd read in a magazine article. "It's Mr. Prophylactic. The guy with the cute little button nose."

Nathan burst out laughing.

Harry blushed a fiery red. Thank goodness Nathan still had his sense of humor. Maybe this wasn't going to be so impossible, after all. Her relief was premature.

"Would you like to put it on me?" he asked.

"I've never done it before," she admitted. "I wouldn't know how. I might do it wrong."

A frown arose between Nathan's brows. He couldn't believe she'd be so irresponsible as not to use some kind of protection in this day and age. As Harry-et's eyes fell, the truth dawned on Nathan. *She hadn't used protection because she hadn't needed it.*

"How long?" he demanded, grasping her hair and angling her face up toward him.

"What?"

"How long since you've been with a man."

"I haven't ever...that is...this is the first time."

Nathan watched as she lowered her eyes to avoid his gaze, as if she'd committed some kind of crime. Didn't she know what a precious gift she was giving him? Didn't she know how special she'd made him feel? He pulled her into his arms and held her tightly. He had never felt so protective of a woman in his life. Both awed and terrified by the responsibility she'd placed in his hands.

"The first time for a woman...sometimes there's pain," he said, his mouth close to her temple. "I don't want to hurt you, sweetheart."

"You won't," Harry reassured him.

"Darling, sweetheart, I wouldn't mean to, but I'm afraid—"

Harry pushed him far enough away that she could see his face. "You? Afraid? Of what?"

He looked her in the eye. "That it won't be everything you expect. That it won't be perfect."

Harry smiled a beatific smile. "If I'm with you, Nathan, it will be perfect. Trust me."

He eased her back down on the quilt and lowered himself beside her, giving her a quick, hard hug.

Harry noticed something different about the embrace. Something missing. She chanced a brief glance down at him. "Oh, no," she said, dismayed.

"What's the matter, Harry-et?"

"You're not...well, you're not...anymore," she said, pointing at a no-longer-aroused Nathan.

Nathan chuckled. "You're precious, Harry-et," he said with a quick grin. "One of a kind."

Harry took a swipe at his shoulder with her fist—the same fist that was still holding the condom he'd handed to her. "I don't like being laughed at, Nathan."

He laughed. "I'm not laughing at you." He rolled over onto his back and let his arms flop free, a silly grin on his face.

Harry tackled him.

An instant later she was under him, his body mantling hers. His mouth found hers, and he kissed her with all the passion he felt for her. His hands found her breasts and teased the nipples to a peak. He felt the blood thrumming through the veins in her throat with his mouth. By the time his hand finally slipped between their bodies, she was wet.

And he was hard.

"Oh. It's back," she said.

Nathan grinned. "So it is. Where is Mr. Prophylactic?"

Harry grinned and opened her hand to reveal a slightly squashed condom. "Will it still work?"

"Not unless you put it on."

Her chin slipped down to her chest. She glanced up at him shyly. "Will you help me?"

Nathan helped her place the condom and roll it on until he was fully covered. The way she handled him so carefully, as though he would break, made him feel treasured and very, very special.

"Is that all there is to it?" she asked.

"Pretty simple, huh?"

She caressed him through the sheath. "Can you still feel that?"

Nathan jerked. "Uh-huh."

"Really?" She let her fingers trace the shape of him, encircle him, run down the length of him from base to tip. "You can feel that?"

Nathan inhaled sharply. Slowly he inserted a finger inside her. "Can you feel that?"

Harry gasped. "Uh-huh."

He inserted another finger. "And that?"

Harry tightened her thighs around his hand, reminding Nathan this was new to her. He slowly worked his fingers inside her, stretching her, feeling the tightness and the wetness. He had to be patient. And gentle. And exercise rigid control over a body that ached with wanting her.

"Harry-et," he breathed against her throat. "Touch me."

Harry had been too caught up in her own sensations to think about Nathan's. Until he'd spoken she hadn't been aware that her hands each grasped a handful of quilt. She brought her hands up to grasp his waist instead. Slowly her fingers slipped around to his belly and down to the crease where hip met thigh.

Nathan grunted. The feel of her fingertips on his skin, on

his belly, in those other places he hadn't known were so sensitive, was exquisite.

Harry relaxed her thighs, allowing Nathan greater freedom of movement. His mouth found a breast and teased it, then moved down her ribs to her belly, and then lower, where it replaced his hands at the portal she'd guarded against invasion for so many years.

Her hands clutched his hair as she arched up toward the sensations of his mouth on her flesh. "Nathan, please," she cried. She had no idea what it was she needed, but she was desperate.

Nathan's eyes glittered with passion as he rose over her. She expected one quick thrust and was prepared for the pain. Instead she felt the tip of him pushing against her. Just when she started to feel the pain, he distracted her by nipping her breast. Then his mouth found hers and his tongue mimed the action below. Thrusting and withdrawing. Pushing farther each time. Teasing and tempting. A guttural sound rose in her throat as she surged toward him, urging him inside.

Nathan thrust once more with tongue and hips and filled her full.

Harry tensed with the extraordinary feeling of being joined to Nathan. Her legs captured his hips and held him in thrall. As he withdrew and thrust again, she met his rhythm, feeling the tension build within. His hand came between them to touch her and intensify the need for relief. For release. For something.

Harry was gasping for air, her heart pounding, her pulse racing. "Nathan," she cried. "Please. I ache. Make it stop."

God, he loved her! He wanted to say the words. Here. Now. But once said, they couldn't be taken back. He had no idea how she felt about him. She trusted him, that much was clear. But did her feelings for him run as deep as his for her? She hadn't offered those three words, and there was no way he could ask for them. He could only show her how he felt and trust that it would be enough.

"Come with me, sweetheart. Let yourself fly. It's all right. I'll take care of you."

Harry took him at his word and let herself soar. Nathan joined her in her aerie, two souls surpassing the physical, seeking a world somewhere beyond Nyla's Meadow.

It was long moments later before either of them touched ground again. Their bodies were slick with sweat, despite the shade in which they lay. Nathan was stretched out beside her with an arm and a leg thrown possessively over her. He couldn't see Harry-et's face, so he wasn't able to judge what she was thinking. But there was a tension in her body that was at odds with the release he'd felt within her just moments before.

"Harry-et? What's wrong?" He must have hurt her. He hadn't meant to, but he had.

She sighed. A huge, deafening sound. Those last few words Nathan had spoken before she'd found ecstasy resounded in her ears: "I'll take care of you." Those words reminded her of why it would be foolish to give her heart to Nathan Hazard. She wanted to stand on her own two feet. He was liable to sweep her off them. She freed herself from his embrace and sat up, pulling her knees to her chest and hugging them with her arms. "This can't happen again, Nathan."

"I'm sorry if I hurt you I—"

"You didn't hurt me, Nathan. I just don't want to do it...this...with you again."

"It sounds to me like you're sorry it happened the first time," he said angrily, sitting up to face her. "You were willing. Don't try to deny it."

"I'm not denying it. I wanted this as much as you," she admitted. "I'm only saying that it can't happen again."

"Give me one good reason why not," he demanded.

Because I'm in danger of falling in love with you.

Because I'm in danger of losing myself to you.

Because I find you irresistible, even though I know we have no business being together like this.

That was three reasons. None of which she had any intention of mentioning to him. Harry turned away from him and slipped on her bra and panties. She could hear the rustle of clothing behind her as he dressed. The metal rasp of the zipper on his jeans was loud in the silence. She stood and pulled up the zipper on her own jeans before reaching for her boots.

He grabbed the boot out of her hand and shook it, then handed it back to her. "Snakes," he said. "And spiders."

Harry shivered and made sure she dumped the other boot as well before she slipped it on. His warning had been an abrupt reminder that she was a very sore tenderfoot. Harry couldn't very well avoid Nathan until she learned everything from him that she needed to know. She would just have to learn to control the need to touch, and be touched, that arose every time she got near him.

Nathan had no idea what he'd done that was so wrong, but after the most profound lovemaking he'd ever experienced, Harry-et was avoiding him as if he had the measles. She wasn't going to get away with it.

"Harry-et."

"Yes, Nathan?"

"Come here."

"No." Harry turned and marched over to the tree where her horse was tied. She tried to mount, but couldn't raise her leg high enough to reach the stirrup. She laid her face against the saddle and let her shoulders slump.

An instant later Nathan grabbed her by the waist and

hoisted her into the saddle. "Move your leg out of the way, tenderfoot," he ordered.

Harry gritted her teeth and did as he ordered, painfully sliding her leg up out of his way as he worked on the saddle.

"Good thing you couldn't reach the stirrup," he snarled. "Damn cinch wasn't tightened. Saddle would have slid around and dumped you flat."

"Stop treating me like I'm helpless," she said. "I can take care of myself."

"I'll believe it when I see it," he retorted.

"I pulled my own weight today. Don't tell me I didn't."

Nathan neither confirmed nor denied her assertion. He tightened the cinch on his own saddle and mounted, then reined his horse to face her. "That story I told you about Nyla's Meadow?"

"Yes?"

"I made it all up."

Harry struggled to keep the disappointment out of her voice. "All of it?"

"Every last word. No one knows how the meadow got its name."

He'd invented a place for falling in love. A place where lovers met. Then brought her here. And made love to her. Now he wanted her to believe it had all been a lie.

"We made love in Nyla's Meadow, Nathan. That was real."

Nathan met her imploring gaze with stony eyes. "We had sex. Damn good sex. But that's all it was." And if she believed that, he had a bog he'd like to sell her for grazing land.

He was waiting for the retort he was sure was on her lips. But she didn't argue, just kicked her horse and loped away from him toward the trail back down the mountain.

"Damn you, Harry-et," he muttered. "Damn you for stealing my heart and leaving *me* feeling helpless."

He kicked his horse and loped down the mountain after her. As he followed her down the mountain, he thought back on the day he'd spent working with Harry-et. Not once had she asked for his help. Not once had she complained. In fact, she'd done extraordinarily well for a tenderfoot. Was it possible that someday Harry-et Alistair could actually stand on her own two feet? He found the idea fascinating, if far-fetched. He stared at the way she rode stiff-backed in the saddle. She had grit, that woman. It sure couldn't hurt to hang around long enough to find out.

Harry's thoughts weren't nearly so sanguine. All day she'd been careful not to let Nathan do too much. If she was going to feel like a success, she had to make it on her own. She had left her family to get away from people ordering her around.

But Nathan had never ordered her to do anything. He'd made suggestions and left the decisions up to her. So maybe she could endure his company a little longer. Maybe she could forget what had happened between them today in Nyla's Meadow and simply take advantage of his expertise.

But it was clear she was going to have to be careful. Give Nathan an inch and he might take an acre. And the man had made no secret of the fact that he wanted the whole damn spread.

8

In a small town out West what do you do if you become ill?

Answer: Put on a big pot of coffee, because an hour after you get your prescription from the drugstore, five people will phone with sympathy and two will fetch you a hot dish.

Harry didn't see Nathan for a week, but he called her every day with instructions for some job or other that she had to complete: repairing the henhouse, planting a vegetable garden, spreading manure, harrowing the fields and cleaning the sheep shed. She took great pride in the fact that she managed to accomplish every task alone. Successfully. She knew Nathan had expected her to cave in and ask for help long before now. So when he phoned one evening and told her to clean out all the clogged irrigation channels on her property in preparation for starting the irrigation water through the main ditch, she headed out bright and early the next morning, expecting to get the job done. And failed abysmally.

All Harry could figure was that Nathan had left something out of his instructions. She tried calling him for more directions, but he was out working in his fields and couldn't be reached until noon. She left a message with Nathan's housekeeper for him to call her as soon as he got in.

Nathan did better than that. Shortly after noon he arrived on her kitchen doorstep. "Harry-et, are you in there? Are you all right?"

He didn't wait for her to answer, just shoved the screen door open and stepped inside. When Nathan saw her sitting at the table with a sandwich in her hand, his relief was palpable. His heart had been in his throat ever since he'd read the message Katoya had left him. He'd had visions of Harry-et wounded and bleeding from some farm accident. He was irritated that he cared enough about her to feel so relieved that she wasn't hurt. He forced the emotion he was feeling from his voice and asked, "What was the big emergency?"

"No emergency," Harry answered through a mouthful of peanut butter and jelly. "I just couldn't get the irrigation system to work with the directions you gave me."

"What was wrong with my directions?"

"If I knew that, I wouldn't have called you."

"I'll go take a look."

"I'll come with you." She threw her sandwich down and headed toward him.

Nathan felt his groin tighten at the sight of Harry-et sucking a drop of grape jelly off her finger. "Don't bother. I can do it quicker on my own."

Harry hurried to block his exit from the kitchen. "But if I don't come along, I won't know what I did wrong the next time I have to do it by myself," she pointed out in a deceptively calm voice.

Nathan stared at the jutting chin of the woman standing before him. Stubborn. As a mule. And sexy. Even in bibbed overalls. "All right," he muttered. "But don't get in my way."

When Nathan crossed behind the barn, he saw the backhoe sitting in the middle of her field by the main irrigation ditch. "I didn't know you could manage a backhoe." Handling the heavy farm machinery was how he'd feared she'd hurt herself.

"It wasn't so hard to figure out. I used it to widen the main ditch and clear the larger debris from the irrigation channels. But I still didn't get any water."

She was a remarkable woman, all right. It wasn't the first time he'd had that thought, but Nathan didn't understand why it irritated him so much to admit it now. Could it be that he *wanted* her to need him? *Needed* her to need him? What if she turned out to be really self-sufficient? Where did that leave him? *With an Alistair smack in the middle of his property.* Nathan pursed his lips. The thought didn't irk him near as much as it ought to.

When they arrived at the main ditch, Nathan examined her work. He could find no fault with it. "Did you follow the main ditch all the way across your property?"

"As far as that stand of cottonwoods over there along the river." She didn't add that the thought of snakes hiding in the thick vegetation around the cottonwoods had scared her off.

"Let's go take a look."

Harry was happy to follow him. The way Nathan was stomping around it wasn't likely any snake was going to hang around long enough to take him on.

Harry stayed close behind Nathan and actually bumped into him when he stopped dead and said, "There's your problem."

She leaned around him to see where he was pointing. "That bunch of sticks?"

"Beaver dam. Has to come out of there. It's blocking the flow of water along the main ditch."

"How do I get rid of it?"

Nathan grinned ruefully. "Stick by stick. You'd better head back to the house and get your thigh-high rubber boots."

"Rubber boots? Thigh-high?"

"I take it you don't have any rubber boots," Nathan said flatly.

"Just my galoshes."

He sighed. "They're better than nothing. Go put them on. Get a pair of gloves, too."

"All right. But don't start without me," she warned.

"Wouldn't think of it."

Harry ran all the way to the cabin, stepped into her galoshes and galomphed all the way back to the beaver dam. True to his word, Nathan was sitting on a log that stuck out from the dam, doing nothing more strenuous than chewing on a blade of sweetgrass. But he hadn't been idle in her absence. He was leaning on two shovels, wore thigh-high rubber boots and had a pair of leather gloves stuck in his belt.

"All ready?" he asked.

"Ready."

The beaver dam was several feet long and equally wide and thick, and Harry felt as if she were playing a game of Pick-up Sticks. She never knew whether the twig she pulled would release another twig or tumble a log. Leaves and moss also had to be shoveled away from the elaborate dam. The work was tedious and backbreaking. Toward the end of the afternoon it looked as if they might be able to clear the ditch before the sun went down, if they kept working without a break.

Harry was determined not to quit before Nathan. Sweat soaked her shirt and dripped from her nose and chin. Her face was daubed with mud. Her hands were raw beneath the soaked leather gloves. There were blisters on her heels where the galoshes rubbed as she mucked her way through the mud and slime. It was little consolation to her that Nathan didn't look much better.

He had taken off his shirt, and his skin glistened with

sweat. He kept a red scarf in the back pocket of his jeans, and every so often he pulled it out and swiped at his face and neck and chest. Sometimes he missed a spot, and she had the urge to take the kerchief from his hand and do the job for him. But it was as plain as peach pie cooling on a windowsill that Nathan was a heap better at dishing out help than he was at taking it. And though they worked side by side all day, he kept his distance.

Touching might be off-limits, but that didn't mean she couldn't look. Harry was mesmerized by the play of corded muscles under Nathan's skin as he hefted logs and shoveled mud. She turned abruptly when he caught her watching and was thankful for the mud that hid her flush of chagrin.

Nathan hadn't been as unaware of Harry-et as he'd wanted her to think. The outline of her hips appeared in those baggy overalls every time she stretched to reach another part of the dam. He'd even caught a glimpse of her breasts once when she'd bent over to help him free a log. There was nothing the least bit attractive about what she had on. He didn't understand why he couldn't take his eyes off her.

Suddenly, as though they'd opened a lever, the water began to rush past them into the main irrigation ditch and outward along each of the ragged channels that crisscrossed Harry's fields.

"It's clear! We did it," Harry shouted, exuberantly throwing her arms into the air and leaping up and down.

Nathan saw the moment she started to fall. One of her galoshes was stuck in the mud, and when Harry-et started to jump, one foot was held firmly to the ground while the other left it.

Nathan was never quite sure later how it all happened. He made a leap over some debris in an attempt to catch Harry-et before she fell, but tripped as he took off. Thus, when he caught her, they were both on their way down. He twisted his body to take the brunt of the fall, only his boot was caught on something and his ankle twisted instead of coming free. They both hit the ground with a resounding "Ooomph!"

Neither moved for several seconds.

Then Harry untangled herself from the pile of arms and legs and came up on her knees beside Nathan, who still hadn't moved. "Nathan? Are you all right? Say something."

Nathan said a four-letter word.

"Are you hurt?"

Nathan said another four-letter word.

"You *are* hurt," Harry deduced. "Don't move. Let me see if anything's broken."

"My shoulder landed on a rock," he said between clenched teeth as he tried to rise. "Probably just bruised. And my ankle got twisted."

"Don't move," Harry ordered. "Let me check."

"Harry-et, I—" He sucked in a breath of air as he sat up. His right shoulder was more than bruised. Something was broken. "Help me up."

"I don't think—"

"Help...me...up," he said through gritted teeth.

Harry reached an arm around him and tried lifting his right arm to her shoulder. He grunted.

"Try the other side," he told her.

She slipped his other arm over her shoulder and used the strength in her legs to maneuver them both upright.

Nathan tried putting weight on his left leg. It crumpled under him. "Help me get to that boulder over there."

Harry supported Nathan as best she could, and with a sort of hopping, hobbling movement that left him gasping, they made it. She settled Nathan on the knee-high stone and stood back, facing him with her hands on her hips. "I'll go get the pickup. You need a doctor."

"I'll be fine. Just give me a minute to rest." A moment later he tried to stand on his own. The pain forced him back down.

"Are you going to admit you need some help? Or do I have to leave you sitting here for the next few weeks until somebody notices you're missing?"

"Go get the pickup," he snarled.

"Why thank you, Mr. Hazard, for that most brilliant suggestion. I wish I'd thought of it myself." She sashayed away, hips swaying. Her attempt at nonchalance was a sham. As soon as she was out of sight, she started running and sprinted all the way to her cabin. She tore through the kitchen, hunting for the truck keys, then remembered she'd left them in the ignition. She headed the pickup straight back across the fields, skidding the last ten feet to a stop in front of Nathan.

"You just took out half a field of hay," Nathan said.

"I'm afraid I was in too much of a hurry to notice," she retorted. She forced herself to slow down and be gentle with Nathan as she helped him into the truck, but even so, the tightness of his jaw and his silence attested to his pain.

"Where's the closest hospital?" she demanded as she scooted behind the wheel.

"Take me home."

"Nathan, you need—"

"Take me home. Or let me out and I'll walk there myself."

"You need a doctor."

"I'll call Doc Witley when I get home."

It didn't occur to her to ask whether Doc Witley practiced on humans. It shouldn't have surprised her that he turned out to be the local vet.

Several hired hands came running when Harry drove into Nathan's yard, honking her horn like crazy. They helped her get Nathan upstairs to the loft bedroom of his A-frame home. Harry's mouth kept dropping open as she took in her surroundings. She had never suspected Nathan's home would be so beautiful.

The pine logs of which the house was constructed had been left as natural as the day they were cut. The spacious living room was decorated in pale earth tones, accented with navy. A tan corduroy couch and chair faced a central copper-hooded fireplace. Nearby stood an ancient wooden rocker. The living room had a cathedral ceiling, with large windows all around, so that no matter where you looked there was a breathtaking view: the sparkling Boulder River bounded by cottonwoods to the east; the Crazy Mountains to the north; the snowcapped Absarokas to the south; and to the east, pastureland dotted with ewes and their twin lambs.

If this was an example of how Nathan Hazard designed homes, the world had truly lost someone special when he'd given up his dream.

If she'd had any doubt at all about his eye for beauty, the art and artifacts on display in his home laid them fully to rest. Bronze sculptures and oil and watercolor paintings by famous Western artists graced his living room. Harry indulged her curiosity by carefully examining each and every one during the time Doc Witley spent with Nathan.

When the vet finally came downstairs, he found Harry waiting for him.

"How is he?"

"Nothing's broke."

"Thank God."

"Dislocated his shoulder, though. Put that to rights. Couldn't do much with his ankle. Bad sprain. May have cracked the bone. Can't tell without an X ray and don't think he'll hold still for one. Best medicine for that boy is rest. Keep him off his feet and don't let him use that shoulder for a few weeks. I'll be going now. Have a prize heifer calving over at the Truman place. You mind my words now. Keep that boy down.'' He gave her a bottle of pills. ''Give him a couple of these every four hours if he's in pain.''

Harry looked down to find the vet had handed her a bottle of aspirin. She showed him out the door and turned to stare up toward the loft bedroom that could be seen from the living room. Nathan must have heard what the doctor had said. It shouldn't be too hard to get him to cooperate.

Harry looked around and realized Nathan's housekeeper hadn't made an appearance. Maybe Katoya was out shopping. If so, Harry would have to stick around until she got back. Nathan was in no shape to be left alone.

Nathan's bedroom was done in darker colors—rust, burnt sienna and black. The four-poster bed was huge and flanked by a tall, equally old-fashioned piece of furniture that Harry assumed must hold his clothes. The other side of the room was taken up by a rolltop desk. The oak floor was mantled with a bearskin rug. Of course there were windows, wide, clear windows that brought the sky and the mountains inside.

Nathan had pillows piled behind his shoulders and an equally large number under his left foot.

She took a step into his bedroom. ''Is there anything I can do for you?''

''Just leave me alone. I'll manage fine.''

''Your home is lovely. You show a lot of promise as an architect,'' she said with a halting smile.

''It turned out all right,'' he said. ''As soon as it was built, I thought of a dozen things I could have done better.''

She didn't feel comfortable encroaching farther into his

bedroom, so she leaned back against the doorway. "You'll make all those improvements next time."

"A sheepman doesn't have the leisure time to be designing houses," he said brusquely.

"Actually, you're going to have quite a bit of free time over the next couple of weeks," she replied. "The vet gave orders for you to stay in bed. By the way, I haven't seen your housekeeper. Do you expect her back soon?"

"In about a month," Nathan said. "She left right after I got home to visit her granddaughter, Sage Littlewolf, on the Blackfoot reservation up near Great Falls."

"Do you suppose she'd come back if she knew—"

"Yes, she would. Which is why I have no intention of contacting her. There's some problem with her granddaughter that needs settling. She's gone there to settle it. I'll manage."

Harry marched over to stand at Nathan's bedside. "How do you intend to get along without any help?"

"It's not your problem."

"I'm making it my problem."

"Look, Harry-et, I don't need your help—"

"You need help," she interrupted. "You can't walk."

"I'll use crutches."

"With your right arm in a sling?"

"I'll hop."

"What if you fall?"

"I won't."

"But if you do—"

"I'll get back up. I don't need you here, Harry-et. I don't want you here. I don't think I can say it any plainer than that."

"I'm staying. Put that in your pipe and smoke it, Mr. Hazard." Harry turned and headed for the door.

"Harry-et, come back here! Harry-et!"

She kept on marching all the way downstairs until she stood in his immaculate, perfectly antiquated kitchen, trying to decide what she should make for his supper.

Nathan spent the first few minutes after Harry left the room, proving he could get to the bathroom on his own. With his father's cane in his left hand he was able to hobble a little. But it was an awkward and painful trip, to say the least. He couldn't imagine trying to get up and down the stairs to feed himself. Of course, he could sleep downstairs on the couch, but that would put the closest bathroom too far away for comfort.

By the time Harry showed up with a bowl of chicken noodle soup on a wicker lap tray, Nathan was willing to concede that he needed someone to bring his meals. But only for a day or so until he could get up and and down stairs more easily.

"All right, Harry-et," he said, "you win. I'll send a man to take care of your place for the next couple of days so you can play nursemaid."

"Thank you for admitting you need help. I, on the other hand, can manage just fine on my own."

"Look, Harry-et, be reasonable. There's no sense exhausting yourself trying to handle two things at once."

"I *like* exhausting myself," Harry said contrarily. "I feel like I've accomplished something. And I'm quite good at managing three or four things at once, if you want to know the truth."

"Stop being stubborn and let me help."

"That's the pot calling the kettle black," she retorted.

"Have it your way, then," he said sullenly.

"Thank you. I will. I'll be back in a little while to collect your soup bowl. Be sure it's empty." She stopped on her way out the door and added, "I'll be sleeping on the couch downstairs. That way you can call if you need me during the night.''

Nathan was lying back with his eyes closed when Harry returned for the dinner tray he'd set aside. She sat down carefully beside him on the bed, so as not to wake him. He was breathing evenly, and since she believed him to be asleep, she risked checking his forehead to see if he had a fever. Just as she was brushing a lock of blond hair out of the way, his eyes blinked open. She saw the pain before he thought to hide it from her.

She finished her motion, letting it be the caress it had started out as when she'd thought he was asleep. ''I was checking to see if you have a fever.''

''I don't.''

''You do.''

He didn't argue. Which was all the proof she needed that he wasn't a hundred percent. ''Doc Witley left some aspirin. He said you might need it for the pain. Do you?''

''No.''

She sighed. ''I'll leave two on the bedside table with a glass of water, just in case.''

He grabbed her wrist as she was rising from the bed to keep her from leaving. ''Harry-et.''

''What is it, Nathan?''

The words stuck in his throat, but at last he got them out. ''Thank you.''

''You're welcome, Nathan. I—''

Harry was interrupted by a commotion downstairs. ''What on earth—'' Someone was coming up, taking the stairs two at a time.

''Hey, Nathan,'' a masculine voice shouted, ''heard you slipped and landed flat on your ass—'' Luke stopped abruptly when he saw Harry Alistair standing beside Nathan.

"Sorry about the language, ma'am." He tipped his hat in apology. "Didn't know there was a lady present."

"How on earth did you find out what happened?" Harry asked. "I swear I haven't been near a phone—"

"No phone is as fast as gossip in the West," Luke said with a grin. "I'm here to see if there's anything I can do to help out."

Nathan opened his mouth to respond and then closed it again, staring pointedly at Harry.

"I was just taking this downstairs," she said, grabbing Nathan's dinner tray. "I'll leave you two alone." She hurried from Nathan's bedroom, closing the door behind her.

Luke turned back to Nathan and waggled his eyebrows. "Should have known you wouldn't spend your time in bed all alone."

"Watch what you say, Luke," Nathan warned. "You're talking about a lady."

"So that's the way the wind blows."

"Harry-et is only here as a nurse."

"One of the hired hands could nurse you," Luke pointed out.

"She refuses to leave, so she might as well do some good while she's here," Nathan said defensively.

"Who's going to take care of her place while she's taking care of you?"

Nathan grimaced. "I offered to have one of my hands help her out. She insists on doing everything herself. Look, Luke, I'd appreciate it if you'd look in on her over the next couple of days. Make sure she doesn't overdo it."

"Sure, Nathan. I'd be glad to."

"I'd really appreciate it. You see, Harry-et just doesn't know when to quit."

"Sounds a lot like my Abby."

"Your Abby?"

"Abigail Dayton and I got engaged yesterday."

"I thought you hadn't seen her since she caught that renegade wolf and headed back home to Helena."

"Well, I hadn't. Until yesterday. I figured life is too short to live it without the woman you love. I was already headed over here to give you the big news when I heard about your accident."

Nathan reached out and grasped Luke's hand. "I really envy you. When's the wedding?"

Luke grinned wryly. "As soon as my best man is back on his feet again. You'd better make it quick, because Abby's pregnant."

Harry heard Nathan's whoop at the same time she heard the front door knocker. She didn't know which one to check out first. Since the door was closer, she hurried to open it.

"Hi! I'm Hattie Mumford. You must be Harry Alistair. I'm pleased to meet you. I brought one of my apple spice cakes for Nathan. Thought it might cheer him up. Can I see him?"

The door knocker rattled again.

"Oh, you get the door, dear," Hattie said. "I know the way upstairs."

Harry just barely resisted the urge to race up ahead of Hattie to warn Nathan what was coming. The knocker rapped again. She waited to answer it because Luke was skipping down the stairs.

"Is he all right?" Harry asked anxiously. "I heard him holler."

Luke grinned. "Nathan was just celebrating the news of my engagement and forthcoming marriage to Abigail Dayton."

"You and Abigail?" Harry smiled. "How wonderful. Congratulations!"

"You'd better get that door," Luke said. "I'll just let myself out the back way."

Harry opened the door to a middle-aged couple.

"I'm Babs Sinclair and this is my husband, Harve. We just heard the bad news about Nathan. Thought he might enjoy my macaroni-and-cheese casserole. I'll just take this into the kitchen. Harve, why don't you go up and check on Nathan."

For want of something better to do, Harry followed Babs Sinclair into the kitchen. The woman slipped the casserole into the oven and turned on the heat. Harry didn't have the heart to tell her Nathan had already eaten his supper.

"You better get some coffee on the stove, young'un," Babs said. "If I know my Harve, he'll—"

"Babs," a voice shouted down from the loft, "send some coffee up here, will you?"

The door knocker rapped.

"You better get that, young'un. I'll take care of making the coffee."

For the next three hours neighbors dropped by to leave tokens of their concern for Nathan Hazard. Besides the apple spice cake and the macaroni-and-cheese casserole, Nathan had been gifted with a loaf of homemade bread and a crock of newly made butter, magazines, and a deck of cards. The game of checkers was only on loan and had to be returned once Nathan was well. Harry met more people that evening than in the nearly four months since she'd moved to the Boulder River Valley.

What she hadn't realized until Hattie Mumford mentioned it was that her neighbors had been waiting for her to indicate that she was ready for company. They would never have thought to intrude on her solitude without an invitation. Now that Harry was acquainted with her neighbors, Hattie assured her they would all make it a point to come calling.

Over the next few weeks as she nursed Nathan, Harry was blessed with innumerable visits from the sheepmen of Sweet Grass County and their wives. They always turned up when she was busy with chores and managed to stay long enough to see them finished. She found herself the recipient of one of Hattie's apple spice cakes. And she thoroughly enjoyed Babs Sinclair's macaroni-and-cheese casserole.

It never occurred to her, not once in all the propitious visits when she'd been exhausted and a neighbor had arrived to provide succor, that while she'd been acting as Nathan's hostess in the kitchen, he'd been upstairs entreating, encouraging and exhorting his friends and neighbors to keep an eye out for her while he was confined to his bed.

So when Harry overheard Hattie and Babs talking about how she was a lucky woman to have Nathan Hazard *taking care of her,* she began asking a few questions.

When Nathan woke up the next morning and stretched with the sunrise, he yelped in surprise at the sight that greeted him at the foot of his bed.

9

How do you know when a handsome Woolly Westerner is really becoming dead serious about you?
Answer: He invites you to his ranch and shows you a basket overflowing with three hundred unmated socks. You realize your own heart is lost when you begin pairing them.

Nathan wasn't a good patient. He simply had no experience in the role. He was used to being the caretaker. He didn't know how to let somebody take care of him. Harry bore the brunt of his irascibility. Well, that wasn't exactly true. Nathan had more than once provoked an argument and found himself shouting at thin air. Over the three weeks he'd spent recuperating, he'd learned that Harry picked her fights.

So when he woke up to find her standing at the foot of his bed, fists on hips, brown eyes flashing, jaw clamped tight to still a quivering chin, he knew he was in trouble.

"I have tried to be understanding," she said hoarsely. "But this time you've gone too far."

"I haven't left this bed for three weeks," he protested.

"You know what I mean. I found out what you did, Nathan. There's no sense trying to pretend you didn't do it."

Nathan stared at her, completely nonplussed. "If I had the vaguest idea what you're talking about, Harry-et—"

"I'm talking about what you said to Hattie Mumford and Babs and Harve Sinclair and Luke Granger and all the other neighbors who've been showing up at my place over the past three weeks to *help* me. How could you?'' she cried. ''How could you?''

Harry turned her back on him and walked over to the window to look out at the mountains. ''I thought you understood how important it was to me to manage on my own,'' she said in an agonized voice.

She swiped the tears away, then turned back to face him. ''Do you know how many times over the past three weeks I've let you do something for yourself, knowing it was more than you could handle? Sometimes you surprised me and managed on your own. More often you needed my help. But I never offered it until you asked, Nathan. I respected your right to decide for yourself just how much you could handle.

''That's all I ever wanted, Nathan. The same respect I was willing to give to you.'' Her lips curled as she spit out, ''Equal partners. You have no concept of what that means. Until you do, you're going to have a hard time finding a woman to *share* your life.''

As she whirled and fled the room, Nathan shouted, ''Harry-et! Wait!'' He shoved the covers out of the way and hit the floor with both feet.

Harry was halfway down the stairs when she heard him fall. She paused, waiting for the muttered curse that would mean he was all right. When it didn't come, she turned and ran back up the stairs as fast as she could. He was lying facedown on the bearskin rug, his right arm hugged tightly to his body. She fell onto her knees beside him, her hands racing over him, checking the pulse at his throat. ''Nathan. Oh, God. Please be all right. I—''

An instant later he grasped her wrist and pulled her down beside him. A moment after that he had her under him and was using the weight of his body to hold her down. ''Stop bucking like that,'' he rasped. ''You're liable to throw my shoulder out again.''

"You'll be lucky if that's all the damage I do," she snapped back. She shoved at his chest with both hands and knew she'd hurt him when his lips drew back over his teeth.

"That's it." He caught both of her hands in one of his and clamped them to the floor above her head. With his other hand he captured her chin and made her look at him. "Are you going to listen to me, or not?"

"I don't know anything you could say—"

"Shut up and let me talk!"

She pressed her lips into a flat, uncompromising line and glared at him.

"I want another chance," he began. She opened her mouth, and he silenced her with a hard kiss. "Uh-uh," he said. "Don't interrupt, or I'll have to kiss you again."

She narrowed her eyes but said nothing.

"I've listened to every word you've ever said to me since I met you, but I never really heard what you were saying. Until just now. I'm sorry, Harry-et. You'll never know how sorry. I guess the truth is, I didn't want you to be able to manage on your own."

"Why not?" she cried.

He swallowed hard as he released her hands. "I wanted you to need me." He paused. "I wanted you to love me."

"Oh, Nathan. I do. I—"

He kissed her hard to shut her up so that he could finish, but somehow her lips softened under his. Her tongue found the seam of his lips and slipped inside and searched so gently, so sweetly, that he groaned and returned the favor. It was a long time before he came to his senses.

"So, will you give me another chance?" he asked.

She smiled. "Will you call off your neighbors?"

"Done. I have one more question to ask."

"I'm listening."

"Will you marry me?"

The smile faded from her lips and worry lines furrowed her brow. "I do love you, Nathan, but…"

"But you won't marry me," he finished tersely.

"Not right now. Not yet."

"When?"

"When I've proved I can manage on my own," she said simply. "And when I'm sure you've learned what it means to be an equal partner."

"But—"

She put her fingertips on his lips to silence him. "Let's not talk any more right now, Nathan. There are other things I'd rather be doing with you." She suited deed to word and let her fingers wander over his face in wonder. To the tiny crow's-feet at the corners of his eyes. To the deep slashes on either side of his mouth. To the bristled cheeks that needed shaving.

"Smile for me, Harry-et."

It was harder than she'd thought it would be. She had just turned down a proposal of marriage from a man she loved. Harry told herself she'd done the right thing. If she'd said yes, she would never have known how much she could accomplish by herself. When she sold her lambs in the fall and paid off the bank, then she'd know for sure. Then, if Nathan held to his promise to treat her as an equal, she could marry him. That was certainly something she could smile about.

Nathan watched the smile begin at the corners of her mouth. Then her lower lip rounded and her upper lip curved, revealing the space between her two front teeth that he found so enchanting. He captured her mouth and searched for that enticing space with his tongue, tracing it, and then the roof of her mouth, and the soft underskin of her upper lip. Then his teeth closed gently over her lower lip and nibbled before his tongue sought the honeyed recesses of her mouth once more.

Harry groaned with pleasure. She wasn't an anxious virgin now. She knew what was coming. Her body responded to the memories of Nathan's lovemaking that had never been far from her mind over the past month since they'd made love. But she saw the flash of pain when Nathan tried to raise himself on his arms. And that took away all the pleasure for her.

"Nathan. Stop. I think we should wait until your shoulder's better before—"

He rolled over onto his back and positioned her on his belly, with her legs on either side of him. "There. Now my shoulder will be fine."

"But how..."

His hands cupped her breasts through her shirt, his thumbs teasing the nipples into hard buds. "Use your imagination, sweetheart. Do whatever feels right to you."

Harry smiled. Nathan wasn't wearing a shirt. She took both of his hands and laid them beside him on the bearskin rug. "Don't move. Until I say you can."

Then she leaned over and circled his nipple with her tongue. His gasp widened her grin of delight. Her fingertips traced the faint traces of bruise that were the only remaining signs that he'd dislocated his shoulder. Her lips soothed where her fingers had been. She traced the length of his neck with kisses and nipped the lobe of his ear. Then her tongue traced the rim of his ear, and she whispered two words she'd never thought she'd say out loud to a man. She saw his pulse jump, felt his breath halt. The guttural sound in his throat was raw, filled with need.

His hands clutched her waist and pulled her hard against him, but she sat up abruptly. "You're not playing by the rules, Nathan," she chastised, placing his hands palm down on the floor. "No touching." She smiled a wanton, delicious smile and added, "Yet."

She felt his hardness growing beneath her and rubbed herself against him through his jeans.

"Harry-et," he groaned. "You're killing me. Whatever you do, just don't stop," he rasped.

Harry laughed at his nonsensical request. She reached down and cupped him with her hand, and felt his whole body tighten like a bowstring. Her exploration was gentle but thorough. By the time she was done, Nathan was arched off the floor, his lower lip clenched in his teeth.

"Have I ever told you what a gorgeous man you are, Nathan?"

"No," he gasped.

"You are. These high cheekbones." She kissed each one tenderly. "This stubborn chin." She nipped it with her teeth. "Those blue, blue eyes of yours." She closed them with her fingertips and anointed them with kisses. She moved down his body, her fingertips tracing the ridges and curves of his masculine form, her mouth following to praise without words.

With every caress Harry gave Nathan she felt herself blossom as a woman. She wanted a chance to return the pleasure he'd given her on Nyla's Meadow. She unsnapped his jeans and slowly pulled the zipper down. She started to pull his jeans off, then paused. Her hand slipped into his pockets one by one. Right front. Left front. Right rear. In the left rear pocket she found what she was looking for. "My, my," she said, holding out what she'd found. "Mr. Prophylactic."

"I don't know how that got there," Nathan protested.

"Just thank goodness it was and shut up," Harry said with a laugh. She dropped the condom onto the bearskin nearby and finished dragging Nathan's jeans down, pulling off his briefs along with them, leaving him naked. And aroused.

She couldn't take her eyes off him. She certainly couldn't keep her hands off him. She opened the condom and sheathed him with it, taking her time, arousing him, teasing him, taunting him.

Nathan had reached his limit. He grasped Harry-et's shirt and ripped the buttons free. Her jeans didn't fare much better. He had her naked in under nine seconds and impaled her in ten. She was slick and wet and tight. "You feel so good, Harry-et. Let me love you, sweetheart."

Harry felt languorous. Her body surged against Nathan's. He put a hand between them, increasing the tension she felt as he sought out the source of her desire. When she leaned over, he captured her breast in his mouth and suckled her. Sensations assaulted her: pleasure, desire, and her body's pulsing demand for release.

"Nathan," she gasped.

His mouth found hers as his hands captured her hips. They moved together, man and woman, part and counterpart, equal to equal.

Harry clutched Nathan's waist, arching toward the precipice, reaching for the satisfaction that was just beyond her reach.

Nathan felt her tensing, felt her fight against release. "Let go, sweetheart. It's all right. Soar. Back to Nyla's Meadow, darling. We can go there together."

Then it was too late for words. She was rushing toward satisfaction. Nathan stayed with her, his face taut with the passion raging within him. She cried out, and he thrust again. A harsh sound rose from deep in his throat as he released his seed.

Harry felt the tears coming and was helpless to stop them.

They stung her cheeks, hot and wet. Nathan felt them against his face and raised his head in disbelief.

"Harry-et?"

She reached a hand up to brush the golden locks from his brow. "It's all right, Nathan. I just felt so...overwhelmed for a moment."

He pulled her into his arms and held her tightly. "You have to marry me Harry-et. I love you. I want to keep you safe."

Harry buried her face in his shoulder. "I love you, Nathan, but it scares me."

"How so?"

"It's taken me a long time to get the courage to strike out on my own. I've hardly had a chance to try my wings."

"We'll learn to fly together, Harry-et."

What she couldn't explain, what she hardly understood herself, was her fear of surrendering her newfound control over her life. Nathan needed to be needed. She loved him enough to do anything she could to make him happy. That gave him a great deal of power. She simply had to find a way to accept his gestures of loving concern...and still keep the independence she was fighting so hard to achieve.

A knock on the door sent them both scrambling for their clothes.

"That'll be Luke," Nathan said as he yanked on his jeans. "I told him I wanted to talk over the plans for his bachelor party."

"Abigail's likely to be with him," Harry said as she tied her buttonless shirt in a knot. "I wanted to make sure it's all right with her to plan a combination bridal/baby shower."

They finished dressing at almost the same time, then stood grinning at each other.

"Shall we go greet our guests?" Nathan asked.

"I'm ready."

Harry fitted herself against Nathan as he slipped his arm around her shoulder for support. It took them a while to get downstairs, but Nathan had already shouted at Luke to let himself in and make himself at home. Sure enough, when they reached the living room, they found that Abigail was with him. After exchanging greetings, Nathan and Luke settled down in the living room while Harry and Abigail headed for the kitchen.

Luke waited only long enough for the two women to disappear before he asked, "Did you ask her?"

"Yep."

"So?"

"She said she'd think about it."

"For how long?"

Nathan thrust a hand through his hair in frustration. "She didn't give me a definite timetable. But at least until she sells her lambs in the fall."

"Guess that shoots the double wedding," Luke muttered.

"There's no reason why we can't go ahead and plan your wedding to Abby," Nathan said.

"We've got a few months yet before the baby comes. I'm willing to wait a while." He grinned. "I've gotten sort of attached to the idea of having a double wedding with my best friend."

Nathan smiled. "What's Abigail going to say about the delay?"

"You won't believe this, but I'm the one in a rush to get married. Abby says she won't love me any less if we never have a ceremony and get a legal piece of paper that proclaims us man and wife."

At that moment Harry was hearing approximately the same speech from Abigail's lips.

"I'm willing to wait to have a ceremony until you and

Nathan can stand at the altar with us," Abigail said. "Really, Harry, I can't believe you turned him down!"

"I had no idea you and Luke were thinking about a double wedding with the two of us," Harry said as she measured the coffee into the pot.

"Well, now that you know, why not change your mind and say yes to Nathan?" Abigail said with an impish grin.

Harry pursed her lips. "I'm sorry to throw a screw in the works, but I have some very good reasons for wanting to wait."

"Fear. Fear. And fear," Abigail said.

"Do I hear the voice of experience talking?"

Abigail bowed in recognition of the dubious honor. "But of course. You're speaking to a woman who was afraid to fall in love again. Everyone I had ever cared about had died. I didn't want to face the pain of losing someone else I loved."

"But Luke is perfectly healthy!" Harry exclaimed.

"Reason has very little to do with fear. What is it you're afraid of, Harry?"

Harry poured a cup of coffee and stared into the blackness. "That I'll be swallowed up by marriage to Nathan." She turned and searched out Abigail's green eyes, looking for understanding. "I'm just learning to make demands. With Nathan it's too tempting to simply acquiesce. Does that make any sense?"

"Like I said, there's nothing rational about our fears. I know mine was very real. You just have to figure out a way to overcome it."

"I thought I was taking a big step just coming to Montana," Harry said. "Nathan's proposal strikes me as a pretty big leap into a pretty big pond."

"Come on in," Abigail said with a smile. "The water's fine."

Harry couldn't help smiling back at Abigail. She had come to Montana knowing there were battles to be fought and won. At stake now was a lifetime of happiness with Nathan. All she had to do was find the courage to deal with whatever the future brought.

There was yet another war to be fought, but on an entirely different field. Harry wanted to convince Nathan it wasn't too late to pursue the dreams he'd given up so long ago. She had already put her battle plan in motion.

While searching for some extra sheets in a linen closet, Harry had discovered Nathan's drafting table. It was in pieces, and she'd spent the past few weeks finding the right place to locate it. She had finally set it up in front of the window that overlooked the majestic, snowcapped Absarokas. Surely such a view would provide the inspiration an aspiring architect needed.

She'd seen Nathan eye the table when they'd come downstairs to greet Luke and Abigail. She knew that as soon as the couple left, she would have some fast talking to do. As Nathan waved a final goodbye to Luke and Abigail, Harry walked into the living room and settled herself in the rocker that Nathan usually claimed.

The instant he closed the front door, Nathan turned to Harry and demanded, "What's that doing in here?"

"I would think that's obvious. It's there so you can use it."

"I've already told you I don't have time for drawing," he said harshly.

"Not drawing, designing," she corrected. Harry watched him limp over to the table. Watched as his hand smoothed lovingly over the wooden surface. *He misses it.* That revelation was enough to convince Harry she should keep pushing. "I couldn't help thinking that all those movie stars moving into Montana are going to be needing spacious, beautiful homes. Someone has to design their mountain sanctuaries. Why not you?''

''I'm a sheep rancher, that's why.'' He settled into the ladder-back stool she'd found in the tack room in the barn, and shifted the T square up and down along the edge of the drafting table. ''Besides, when would I have time to draw?''

''Montana is blessed with a lot of long winter nights,'' she quipped.

He rose from the table and limped over to stand in front of her. ''There are other things I'd rather be doing on a long winter night.'' He took her hands and pulled her out of the rocker and into his embrace. ''Like holding my woman,'' he murmured in her ear. ''Loving her good and hard.''

''Sounds marvelous,'' she said. ''Designing beautiful houses. Designing beautiful babies.''

''You make it sound simple.''

''It can be. Won't you give it a try?''

He hugged her hard. ''Don't start me dreaming again, Harry-et. I've spent a long time learning to accept the hand fate has dealt me.''

''Maybe it's time to ask for some new cards.''

Nathan shook his head. ''You never give up, do you? All right, Harry-et. I'll give it a try.''

She gave him a quick kiss. ''I'm glad.''

Nathan had no explanation for why he felt so good. He'd given up all hope of designing significant buildings a long time ago. But mountain sanctuaries for movie stars? It was just whimsical enough to work. He would make sure that the structures fitted in with the environment, that they utilized the shapes and materials appropriate to the wide open Montana spaces. Maybe it wasn't such a crazy idea, after all.

He looked down into Harry-et's glowing brown eyes.

He'd never loved anyone as much as he loved her. "Come back upstairs with me," he urged.

"I can't. It's time for me to go home."

"Stay."

"I can't. I'll be in touch, Nathan. Goodbye."

Harry kept her chin up and her shoulders back as she walked out the door. It made no sense to be walking away from the man she loved. Maybe over the next few weeks she could get everything straightened out in her mind. Maybe she could convince herself that nothing mattered as much as loving Nathan. Not even the independence she'd come to Montana to find.

10

Where is a Western small-town wedding reception held?
Answer: The church basement if large enough, otherwise the Moose Hall.

Harry found it hard living in her dilapidated cabin again. Of course, her place was tiny and primitive and utterly unlivable in comparison to Nathan's. But she'd coped with those things for months and never minded. Now she couldn't wait to leave Cyrus's cabin each morning. Because it felt empty without Nathan in it.

Harry had spent a lot of time lately thinking about what was important to her. Nathan headed the list. Independence wasn't even running a close second. Harry was having trouble justifying her continued refusal of the sheepman's wedding proposal. These days Harry was so self-sufficient that it was hard to remember a time when she hadn't taken care of herself. She was starting to feel foolish for insisting that Nathan wait for an answer until she sold her lambs and paid off her loan at the bank.

Everything was clarified rather quickly when she received a call from her father.

"Your mother and I will be coming for a visit in two weeks, Harriet, to check on your progress. While we're there we'd really like to see where you're living."

"My place is too small for company, Dad. I'll meet you at The Grand in Big Timber," Harry countered.

"By the way, how are you, darling?" her mother asked.

"Just fine, Mom. I've had a proposal of marriage," Harry mentioned casually. "From a rancher here."

"Oh, dear. Don't rush into anything, darling," her mother said. "Promise me you won't do anything rash before we get there."

"What did you have in mind, Mom?"

"Just don't get married, dear. Not until your father and I have a chance to look the young man over."

"Your mother is right, Harriet. Marriage is much too important a step to take without careful consideration."

"I'll keep that in mind, Dad. I've got to go now." She couldn't help adding, "I've got to feed the chickens and slop the hogs."

Harry felt a twinge of conscience when she heard her mother's gasp of dismay. But her father's snort of disgust stiffened her resolve. She was proud of what she'd accomplished since coming to the valley. If her parents couldn't appreciate all she'd done, that was their loss. She wasn't going to apologize for what she'd become. And she sure wasn't going to apologize for the man she'd just decided to marry.

As soon as her parents clicked off, she dialed Nathan's ranch. She heard his phone ring once and quickly hung up. This was too important an announcement to make over the phone. Besides, she hadn't seen Nathan for ten long, lonely days. She wanted to be there to see Nathan's face and share her excitement with him. The pigs and the chickens would have to wait.

Halfway to Nathan's house, Harry realized he would probably be working somewhere on the ranch, out of communication with the house. To her surprise, when she knocked on the door, he answered it.

"What are you doing home?" she asked as he ushered

her inside. "You're supposed to be out somewhere counting sheep."

"I'm drawing," he said with a smug smile. "I've been hired to design a house for a celebrity who's moving to Big Timber. Very high muckety-muck. Cost is no object."

She heard the eagerness in his voice. And the pride and satisfaction. "Then I guess I'd better say yes before you get too famous to have anything to do with us small-time sheep ranchers. So, Nathan, the answer is yes."

"What did you say?"

"Yes, I'll marry you."

"Don't play games with me, Harry-et."

"I'm not playing games, Nathan. I said I'll marry you, and I meant it."

A moment later Harry knew why she'd come in person. Nathan dragged her into his arms and hugged her so tightly that she had to beg for air. Then his mouth found hers, and they headed for Nyla's Meadow. When she came to her senses, she was lying under Nathan on the couch and her shirt was unbuttoned all the way to her waist. That didn't do him as much good as it might have, since she was wearing bibbed overalls that got in his way.

Nathan's mouth was nuzzling its way up her neck to her ear when he stopped abruptly. "I don't mean to look a gift horse in the mouth, Harry-et, but what changed your mind?"

"I had a call from my parents. They're coming to visit again."

"And?"

"They wanted to look you over. Like a side of beef. To make sure you were Grade A Prime. I thought that sort of behavior particularly inappropriate for a sheepman. So I've decided to make this decision without them."

"And in spite of them?" Nathan asked somberly. He sat up, pushing Harry-et off him, putting the distance of the couch between them. "I don't want you to marry me to prove a point to your parents. Or to yourself."

"My parents have nothing to do with my decision," Harry protested. "I thought you'd be happy."

"I was. I am. I just don't want you to have regrets later. Once we tie the knot, I expect it to be forever. No backing out. No second thoughts. I want you to be sure you're choosing to be a sheepman's wife—my wife—of your own free will."

Harry felt tears burning behind her eyes and a lump growing in her throat at Nathan's sudden hesitance. "Are you sure you haven't changed your mind?" she accused.

"I was never the one in doubt, Harry-et. I love you. I want to spend my life with you. You're the one who said you didn't want to give up your independence. Do you wonder that I question your sudden about-face?"

"What can I do to prove to you that I'm sincere?"

Nathan took a deep breath. "Introduce me to your parents as your fiancé. Let them get to know me without stuffing me down their throats. Give yourself a chance to react to their reactions. See if you still feel the same way after they've gone. If you want to marry me then, Harry-et, I'll have you at the altar so fast it'll make your head spin."

"It's a deal."

Harry-et held out her hand to seal the bargain and, like a fool, he took it. His reaction was the same today as it had been yesterday, as it would be tomorrow. A bolt of electricity shot up his arm, his heart hammered, his pulse quickened. But instead of letting her go he pulled her into his embrace, holding her close, breathing the scent of her—something stronger than My Sin...more like...Her Sheep. It was the smell of a sheepman's woman. And he loved her for it.

* * *

Harry suffered several bouts of ambivalence in the days before her parents were due to arrive.

Maybe she should have pressed Nathan to get married.

Maybe she should have left well enough alone.

Maybe she should have sold her lambs early.

Maybe she should have sold out and gone home long ago.

Harry didn't know why confronting her parents with her decision to marry Nathan should be so difficult. She only knew it was.

She arrived at The Grand on the appointed day with Nathan in tow. "I'll make the introductions," Harry said. "Just let me do the talking."

"It's all right, Harry-et. Relax. Your parents love you."

"I'll try to remember that." And then they were there and she was hugging her mother and then her father and Nathan was shaking their hands. "Where's Charlie?" she asked.

"Your mother and I decided to come alone."

That sounded ominous. "Mom, Dad, this is Nathan Hazard. Nathan, my mother and father."

"It's nice to see you again Mr. and Mrs. Alistair. Why don't we all go find a booth inside?" Nathan suggested.

Harry let him lead her to a booth and shove her in on one side. He slid in after her while her parents arranged themselves on the other side.

"So, Mr. Hazard—"

"Nathan, please."

"So, Nathan, what's this we hear about you wanting to marry our girl?" Harry's father demanded.

Harry groaned. She felt Nathan's hand grasp her thigh beneath the table. She took heart from his reassurance. Only his hand didn't stay where he'd put it. It crept up her thigh under the skirt she'd worn in hopes of putting her best foot forward with her parents. She grabbed his hand to keep it where it was and tried to pay attention to what Nathan was saying to her father.

"And you'd be amazed at what Harry's done with the place."

"What about that federal lease for grazing land, Harriet? Your banker told me the last time I was here that there wasn't much chance he could make you a loan to cover it."

"We worked it out, Dad," Harry said. "I'll be selling my lambs in a couple of weeks. Barring some sort of catastrophe, I'll make enough money to pay off the bank and have some working capital left over for next year."

"Well. That's a welcome relief, I imagine," Harry's mother said. "Now about this wedding—"

"My mind is made up, Mom. You can't change it. I'm marrying Nathan. I love him. I want to spend my life with him."

"I don't think I've ever heard you speak so forcefully, my dear," her mother said.

"It does appear you're determined to go through with this," her father said.

Harry's hand fisted around her fork. "I am," Harry said. "And I'm staying in Montana. I'm where I belong."

"Well, then, I guess there's nothing left to do except welcome you to the family, young man." Harry's father held out his hand to Nathan, who grinned and let go of Harry's thigh long enough to shake her father's hand.

Harry was stunned at her parents' acquiescence. Was that all it took? Was that all she'd ever needed to do? Had she only needed to speak up for what she wanted all these years to live her life as she'd wanted and not as they'd planned? Maybe it was that simple. But until she'd come to Montana, until she had met and fallen in love with Nathan, Harry hadn't cared enough about anything to fight for it.

She sat up straighter in her seat and slipped her hand

under the table to search out interesting parts of Nathan she could surreptitiously caress. His thigh was rock-hard under her hand. So were other parts of him. The smile never left her face during the entire dinner with her parents.

When the meal was over, Harry's mother and father rose to leave. Nathan stayed seated, excusing himself and Harry. "We have a few more things to discuss before we go our separate ways, if you don't mind."

"Not at all," Harry's father said.

Her mother leaned over and whispered in her ear, "Your young man has lovely manners, dear. You must bring him to Williamsburg for a visit sometime soon. And let me know as soon as you set a date for the wedding."

Harry stood and hugged her mother across the table. "To tell you the truth, we'd really like to get married while you're here, so you can come to the wedding. It isn't going to be a large gathering. Just a simple ceremony with me and Nathan...and another bride and groom."

"A double wedding! My goodness. Who's the other happy couple? Have we met them?"

"You will. They're friends of mine and Nathan's," Harry said.

"At least let me help with the reception," her mother said.

"I don't know, Mom. You don't know anyone in town. How can you possibly—"

"Trust me, dear. Just say you'd like my help."

Harry grinned. "All right, Mom. I'll leave the reception in your hands."

Nathan waited only long enough for Harry's parents to leave before he grabbed her by the hand and hauled her out of the booth. "You've got some nerve, young lady," he said as he dragged her up the stairs and closed one of The Grand's bedroom doors behind them.

"What do you mean, Nathan?"

He caught her by the shoulders and inserted his thigh between her legs, pulling her forward so that she was riding him.

Harry gasped.

His mouth came down on hers with all the passion she'd aroused in him when he'd been unable to take her in his arms. "That'll teach you to play games under the table."

"I've learned my lesson, Nathan," she said with a sigh of contentment. "Teach me more."

Nathan reached over and turned the lock on the door. "Your wish is my command."

"Nathan?"

"Yes, Harry-et."

"I love you."

"I love you, too."

They didn't say anything for long moments because their mouths were otherwise pleasantly occupied.

"Nathan?" Harry murmured.

"Yes, Harry-et."

"Where do you suppose my mother will end up having the reception?"

"The Moose Hall," he said as he nuzzled her throat.

Harry laughed. "You're kidding."

"Nope. It's the only place available except for the church basement, and that's too small."

"Too small? How many people are you inviting?"

Nathan smiled and kissed her nose. "You really are a tenderfoot, Harry-et. Everyone in Sweet Grass County, of course."

Harry's eyes widened. "Will they all show up?"

"Enough of them to make your mother's reception a success. Now, if you're through asking questions, I'd like to kiss that mouth of yours."

"Your wish is my command," Harry replied.

Nathan laughed. "Don't overdo it, Harry-et. A simple 'Yes, dear' will do."

"Yes, dear," she answered with an impudent grin.

"You're mine now, Harry-et. Forever and ever."

"Yes, dear."

"We'll live happily ever after. There'll be no more feuding Hazards and Alistairs. Your land is mine, and my land is yours. It's all *ours*."

"Yes, dear."

"And there'll be lots of little Hazard-Alistairs to carry on after us."

Harry's eyes softened and she surrendered to Nathan's encompassing embrace. "Oh, yes, dear."

*   *   *   *   *